TOUCH OF FONDNESS

Stay in Touch

JOY PENNY

Crimson Fox
PUBLISHING

CHAPTER ONE

If there was one thing Brielle wasn't going to miss about college, it was the soggy, tepid tater tots the cafeteria in Bryant Hall offered students on Breakfast-for-Lunch-and-Dinner Saturdays.

Oh, who am I kidding? I'm going to miss everything, even these undercooked globs of potato.

"Are you crying? Bri, are you actually *crying?*" Lilac laughed like she was the only one in on the joke. Pembroke hastily scooped her compact out of her clutch and dabbed some more foundation on her cheeks to cover her own trail of tears and Gavin blew his nose on his scratchy cafeteria napkin.

Brielle smiled despite the miniature Niagara Falls taking up residence on her face and chomped on another tater, savoring its terribleness for good measure. "Just because some of us are made of stone doesn't mean the rest of us aren't going to miss this place."

Lilac lightly touched the tips of her fingers to her collarbone with one hand and held the other hand above her like a Shakespearean actor. "A college is but four walls and a roof, my dear." She grinned. "Albeit four *very expensive* walls and a roof, but walls and a roof nonetheless. No graduation is going to take away what this place meant to you." She tapped her left breast. "You'll always find it here."

Gavin cocked his head and flashed his best come-hither grin. "In your ginormous boob?"

"Har har." Lilac slapped him on the shoulder and picked up her fork again, pushing her tater tots to the side of her tray. They crumbled into an unappealing mess in the corner of one of the squares. "I don't know," she said, staring at her food instead of eating it. "I think it's about time we move on. Crappy French toast and tater tots served on a divided tray? What are we, middle schoolers or soon-to-be-independent adults?"

Brielle took a sip of her orange juice. "Says the soon-to-be elementary school teacher." She tapped her tray. "Get used to these."

Lilac shrugged. "Maybe someday. Maybe not. I don't have to anytime soon."

"What do you mean?" asked Pembroke. She'd been especially quiet today, not that being quiet was especially odd for Pembroke. "Aren't you going to be teaching at Jacobson Primary this fall?"

"Nope." Lilac popped a mouthful of egg into her mouth.

"*Shut up*," said Gavin. He nudged her. "Are you serious?"

"Would I joke about something like that?" Lilac smiled sweetly, then laughed. "Don't answer that."

"When were you going to tell us?" Brielle was somehow both surprised and not surprised at all at this piece of information. Lilac always did things in the most dramatic way possible. Why not make the last meal they shared before their parents arrived all about her?

She took a deep breath. This was not how she wanted to remember today. Sometimes she wondered if Lilac was her enemy or one of her best friends. But that was just part of the territory that came with being friends with Lilac. And besides, it wasn't like they were going to be able to see each other much after graduation anyway. Or so Brielle had thought. Last she knew, Lilac was moving to a suburb outside of Minneapolis and putting her early education degree to good use. Honestly, what on earth was the point of all of that hard work Lilac had put into getting licensed in another state if she wasn't going to go through with it? She even had her apartment picked out, was interviewing prospective roommates, had made the deposit... No, no. Brielle cradled her forehead. She wasn't going to do this. Not today.

"Don't have a conniption over it." Lilac obviously saw something in Brielle's countenance that made her train of thought more apparent than she'd intended. Lilac shrugged. "Something better came along."

"Better than a firm job offer?" Gavin asked. "A *paying* firm job offer, I might add?" Poor Gavin got to work at the place of his dreams... as an unpaid intern. After graduation. With only a tiny chance of getting offered a paid position by the end of the summer. Brielle had no idea how Gavin could summon the courage to move to Chicago on the hope that he'd be working for this marketing firm as a paid employee by summer's end, even if he was just crashing on a couple of friends' couch until then.

Not that he had much to take with him other than the clothes in his closet and that winning smile of his. His parents were assholes who'd disowned him and thrown out all his stuff last summer after he'd come out to them. His grandma was the only one in his entire family who even spoke to him anymore—other than his little sister, who tried to text him in secret. But, to quote the man himself, there was "no way I'm moving into my grandmother's basement in the middle of bumfuck nowhere and trying for a job at the local hardware-slash-convenience-slash-crafting store that's the only place for miles. Assuming they don't drive me out of town before I step foot into it. Do they even want gay people selling their cakes they don't want sold to gay people?"

Lilac cleared her throat and drummed her fingers on the table. "I repeat: Something better."

Pembroke gasped. "Did you... get a job offer abroad?"

It was no secret how much Lilac had loved spending a semester in Spain her junior year. Just as it was no secret that Pembroke had so badly wanted to spend the year in Japan but had chickened out at the last minute. And how fixated on Lilac's changed-her-life experience Pembroke seemed to be as a result.

Lilac snorted. "I *wish*. About the only thing that would guarantee me that is a job teaching English, and I don't think a change in venue would make enough of a difference when I really wanted a... change in job."

Brielle couldn't keep biting her tongue. "You're not going to be an elementary school teacher? After all the hard work you put into becoming one?"

Lilac raised her eyebrows. "Maybe I wished I'd taken a cue from you," she said, and although her tone seemed cheerful, there was something a little darker under her words, "and had studied something more useless so I didn't have to spend so much time in training and studying for my license."

"*Lilac.*" Gavin shook his head.

Brielle didn't really have a comeback. She knew her philosophy and history dual majors were utterly pointless—she had no ambitions to be a professor or teacher, and that narrowed her already-narrow list of possible ways to put her degree to use—even if she really, really loved studying the subjects. But even her own mom didn't seem happy with her plan of moving back home to work for her mom's cleaning service, just like she had every summer as a teenager and every summer since. No matter how much Brielle tried to convince everyone it wasn't her "forever, ever" plan, that she'd continue to look for something resembling a post-college career between scrubbing mildew out of grout and vacuuming up Mrs. Tanaka's odious cats' scattered kitty litter, no one seemed to believe her that come this time next year, her life would be so much different.

Brielle wasn't sure she believed that, either.

"I'm serious," countered Lilac. "All that wasted time just showed me... I'm not cut out to be a teacher."

"That's not true!" Pembroke frowned. It *was* sometimes hard for Brielle as well to associate unpredictable, party hardy Lilac with reliable daytime guardian of rambunctious seven-year-olds, but she was a different person around kids. She was *really good* with kids.

"That's nice of you to say, sweet pea," said Lilac, almost inevitably going into "teacher mode" around too-quiet Pembroke, "but wait until you hear what I'm going to be doing instead." She pushed her tray to the side slightly so she could lean forward and place both hands on the table for emphasis. "I'm. Going. To. Tildy World."

"Wait, what?" This was not at all what Brielle had expected Lilac to say. Sure, she had a soft spot for Tildy Tapir—she'd practically grown up on Tildy Tapir cartoons and defended them as being better than Mickey Mouse's; it was practically the only outwardly childish thing about her—but she'd been to Tildy World a dozen times throughout her life already. And she still dubiously claimed that the park was better than the nearby Disney World. She'd yet to find anyone who agreed with her, even though, to be fair, the park seemed to give Disney a run for its money.

"Doesn't your aunt live in Orlando?" asked Gavin. How he kept track of insignificant details like that, Brielle would never understand.

"She does! And Mom and Daddy only *approved* of this venture because I'm going to move in with her, at least for the first few months. Not that I need their approval exactly."

"But... are you going to be on vacation for *that* long?" Pembroke couldn't keep the confusion out of her voice. Ah, poor, dear Pembroke. Brielle sometimes herself forgot the petite blue-streaked blonde wasn't a little girl.

Lilac blew an audible breath out. "It's not a vacation." She shrugged. "Well, not that I won't ever just hang out at the park or head to the beach. Kind of the whole point of relocating to Florida instead of even-worse-winters-than-here-like-that's-somehow-possible Minnesota."

Brielle knew that was definitely one thing that Lilac hadn't been happy about when she'd accepted that job offer. But rejecting it now—after she'd already committed to so much of her life there

—would probably hurt her resume. Not that *Lilac* needed to worry about that, apparently.

"Aunt Frankie knows someone who works at one of the resorts as a manager. She knew he was looking for an assistant manager and voila." She gestured at herself. "I became available for the job in an instant."

"They hired you as *an assistant manager?*" said Brielle. "Right out of college? With a degree that has nothing to do with running a hotel at all?"

Lilac smiled. "What can I say? I'm a charming interviewee, even over Skype." Brielle's eyes flitted to Lilac's chest, which even when covered was hard not to notice, and she instantly felt guilty. But she did say "*he*" had been looking for an assistant manager. Lilac's voice interrupted the guilty nature of Brielle's thoughts. "And I'm just in training to start. Earl was especially keen to hear about my experience with elementary school children, since running interference between the resort's childcare center and the management office would be a big part of my duties."

Gavin wrinkled his nose. "You're working for a guy named Earl. *Earl.*"

Lilac waved a hand. "He could be named Billy Bob Jimbo for all I care if he got me a job in Florida."

"I don't know," said Gavin. "There's just something ominous about a guy named Earl."

Lilac punched his shoulder. "I'll behave. It's a thin-haired, chubby-faced man old enough to be my father named Earl. And I'm sure there's a Mrs. Earl."

"Hasn't stopped the type before." Gavin sent Brielle a look. Lilac's ability to attract all the wrong kinds of attention—with or without her intention to do so—was about the number one thing the two friends had to discuss on the rare occasions they were left alone.

"Stop being such a drama queen," said Lilac. "So *anyway*, enough about me. Pem, what about you? I know Brielle's got a plan for the summer until she finds that *amazing job* that awaits her"—

Brielle didn't fail to notice the sarcasm dripping in her words—"but you've never let us know what you have planned. Did you ever find anything?"

Pembroke stared at her lunch tray and the food that was only half-eaten. "No. Not really."

"What?" said Gavin, trying as usual to coax Pembroke out of her shell. "A catch like you with honors in biology? There wasn't any lab or something that would take you?"

Pembroke shrugged. "Nothing local, anyway." Given how much time Pembroke spent on campus, it was easy to forget she was a commuter who'd lived in the area her whole life. Not that Brielle had fared much better, since she was from a suburb only about an hour away and she technically still lived at home, even if she lived in a dorm when school was in session. Lilac had been her roommate the first couple of years—it was how they'd met and how Brielle had become friends with Lilac's instant bestie Gavin—but Lilac's parents had more money than they knew what to do with and had paid for an apartment for Lilac and Gavin to live in off-campus after Lilac had come back from Spain. Just as well, since Brielle had finally gotten into one of those tiny-but-peaceful solo dorm rooms in Lilac's absence.

"And you can't move because...?" Lilac really never had any tact.

Brielle knew better than to pry. Pembroke had family issues, or she was just too shy to break out of her shell entirely, or maybe she was just happy where she was. From what little hints Pembroke dropped of her private life, Brielle imagined it was perhaps a mixture of all three that led the girl to be so unadventurous. It really wasn't Brielle's business anyway.

"I didn't even apply to any jobs outside the area," said Pembroke, as if that answered the question. But no one pried further.

"Well, maybe you can think about med school or nursing school," suggested Gavin. "They need medical professionals everywhere."

Pembroke nodded, but her eyes drifted elsewhere. It wasn't the first time Gavin had tried to be helpful by tossing out career advice Pembroke would likely never bother to take. Gavin certainly wasn't rolling in it, even before his parents had cut him off, but Brielle suspected finances would prove a huge obstacle to Pembroke pursuing any further degrees. If she was even interested in the medical field at all. Brielle realized she wasn't really sure. She didn't talk much to Pembroke outside of social media, and those conversations were usually reserved for gushing about the latest *The Walking Dead* or superhero movie with her.

"Well, good luck with whatever you decide," said Lilac, and Brielle was certain Lilac really couldn't care less about Pembroke's situation. Her eyes were glossing over and her expression was faraway, like she could smell the ocean air and feel the sand beneath her toes already.

Brielle shook her head. Lilac doing an about-face at this point in time was shocking, but it was *so Lilac*.

"Uh-oh, trouble at 3:00," said Gavin. "Bri, isn't it about time you see if your mom's made it here yet?"

"Is it 3:00 already?" asked Lilac dreamily. "I thought all our parents weren't coming until after dinner anyway."

Brielle turned to look in the direction Gavin indicated. *Oh. That kind of 3:00. That kind of trouble.* Brielle bolted upright and gathered her utensils and napkins hastily atop her tray. "Right. Thanks for the heads-up. See you guys tomorrow!" She turned around, ready to put her blinders on, but Daniel managed to meet her halfway to the dishwashing station, where she attempted to deposit her tray.

"Hey! Elle! Congrats."

It was hard to act like a bitch to someone when they were dripping with pleasantness.

A chill coursed through Brielle's body and she settled for dropping the tray on the counter a little too loudly. "Thanks," she mumbled, turning around and staring at Daniel's faded Hershey's Chocolate T-shirt. "And it's 'Brielle' or 'Bri,' not 'Elle.'"

"You'll always be 'Elle' to me." Daniel did this annoying thing where he clutched both hands together over his heart and his voice took on an exaggeratedly dramatic tone, like it was all a big joke. Everything was a big joke with him. "Elle, my *belle*, my sweet little spicy pepper."

Brielle groaned and pushed past him, still not giving him the decency of looking at his face. Ever since the genius had figured out her father—the father who hadn't been a part of her life since she was eight—was Puerto Rican, he hadn't let go of the gross, insensitive jokes. How Brielle could have been stupid enough to date him not once—but *twice*—over the course of these past several years, she would never know. That was a total of four or five months, give or take, she'd never be able to get back. The only year she'd been entirely free of him was freshman year, and that was just because he was a year younger than her and hadn't started school yet.

"Hey," said Daniel, trailing after Brielle as she made her way to the cafeteria doors. "You didn't seem to mind the name when we were dating."

Brielle spun around, looking up at Daniel despite herself. He wasn't even that good-looking, not *really*, not when you couldn't *not* associate his skeevy smile with all the skeevy things he'd done. She would never forgive herself for being so stupid. "Which name? 'Elle' or 'spicy pepper'?"

Daniel grinned, invisible slime practically oozing from the corners of his mouth. "Either one? There were a few lovely evenings in my dorm room betwixt the sheets that I even christened you my 'hot mama.'"

"Grow up." Brielle turned around so Daniel wouldn't mistake the flush on her cheeks for embarrassment because she found him charming. It was rage, pure and simple, but he'd be too simple-minded to figure that out.

Daniel followed her down the stairs. "I'm going to graduation tomorrow!"

"That's nice," clipped Brielle.

"Don't you want to know why?" At the bottom of the stairs,

Daniel grabbed her arm and tugged her back toward him. She slammed against a passing student and mumbled her apologies.

"No," said Brielle, ripping her arm free of his grip. "But I figured if you didn't have a reason, you'd be gone by now. Most underclassmen don't stick around for graduation weekend. Or did you miss the fact that classes ended because you never attend them anyway?"

"Ouch." Daniel gripped his heart mockingly again. "Spicy pepper strikes again."

"Shut up," said Brielle. She poked a finger at his chest. "No, seriously, just *shut up*. I don't care why you're still here or that you're going to tomorrow's ceremony. I'm just glad that you're not going to be in my life at all after tomorrow." Brielle hated the words as soon as they tumbled from her mouth. Daniel had this habit of getting under her skin, of causing her to explode and making it seem like he was constantly on her mind when he *wasn't*. Not at all. He just burrowed into her mind when he wouldn't get out of her way and kept pushing and pushing her until...

"My fiancée is graduating." Daniel's gaze roved over her face. He was probably looking for some sort of reaction.

He didn't get one. "Good for her."

"Aren't you wondering how I got a fiancée since we just broke up three months ago?"

"Nope." "Broke up" was generous. The second time was more like a fling. An ill-advised, stupid, stupid fling.

"Seriously?" Daniel scoffed, loudly enough to catch several passersby's attention. "You know, you're one coldhearted bitch."

Brielle laughed. "You're the bigoted asshole, but I'm the coldhearted bitch?"

"Bigoted?" Daniel shook his head. "If I were bigoted, would I have even dated you?"

Brielle imagined herself wringing his neck and then took a deep breath. "Fine." Brielle waved a hand in the air and turned around. "Whatever."

"Case in point!" said Daniel tauntingly.

But thanks to the energy from the anger coursing through her veins, Brielle summoned her super speed and managed to ditch him before he was compelled to follow and torment her any further.

Too bad she couldn't stop thinking about the asshole the entire rest of the day.

CHAPTER TWO

Daniel was like a case of food poisoning whenever he wormed his way into her mind. He, too, shall pass, after a half a day's torment —anger more at herself than at him. Not that he didn't deserve it. But he wasn't worth it. No matter how much he drove her crazy.

Brielle took a deep breath and closed her eyes, feeling the soft faux leather beneath her fingertips. It was better to remember the great time she'd had the day before at graduation. The pictures she'd taken with Lilac, Gavin, and Pembroke. The hugs her mom and little sister had shared with her. The way even her casual college acquaintances had screamed and hollered when the announcer had called her name and she'd walked across the stage to grab the diploma she now held in her hands. No Daniel around. No fiancée. He'd had at least that much sense—to leave her alone on that day. (Assuming it wasn't just because he'd had so much to do with *his fiancée*. Good luck to her.) It had been the perfect day.

She opened her eyes and sighed. She'd cleared a little space for the diploma on the top of her bookshelf, next to a Funko Pop of Loki (still in box) and a dreamcatcher she'd made in eighth grade at summer camp (one of her last free summers before she'd been doomed to scrub floors for the rest of those sunny days). She stepped back and tried to get the whole picture of her childhood bedroom, but it was cluttered—boxes taken from her dorm room left only the smallest path from her bed to the door, stuffed animals gathered dust atop her shelves, and her closet was full of clothes she hadn't touched since the last time she'd received a diploma. She'd have to make a trip to Goodwill one of these days to free up space in her bedroom closet for the clothes she'd had at the dorm.

May as well swap the clothes to keep with the clothes to go and then unload the boxes in the garage for the next time I'm near the thrift store. Brielle kneeled on her bedroom floor and took a scissors to the tape on the nearest box of clothes and slid her closet door open, grabbing the first thing within reach. *Oh. My Scrubbing Cherubs uniform.* Black pants, a navy blue half-apron, and the pièce de résistance: a bright blue, long-sleeved T-shirt with her mom's business logo on the front over the breast and about five hundred times the size on the back. Brielle's shoulders sagged just looking at it. She held the shirt up to her front and winced, her guess likely proven true. She'd gained a little weight this past year—just a tad, just enough to give her some more defined curves in her opinion—and this uniform was unlikely to still fit.

It's okay, she told herself. *It's just for the summer. Probably. Maybe even less. Who knows when I'll find a job?*

"I hope you're not unpacking *everything*." Brielle looked up where she sat on her shaggy brown carpet to find her mom standing in the doorway, her arms crossed. "It'll just make moving out more of a pain for you—and you won't have a lot of free time as long as you're working for me."

Brielle rolled her eyes. "Surely you could let me skip the whole 'two weeks' notice' thing once I find a job." She tossed the uniform on her bed and reached back into the closet. "I can use that time to pack and figure out what I want to take. I'm just making some room now and starting a pile for Goodwill."

Her mom looked from the open box to the overstuffed closet and back again. "Okay, good idea. I don't know if I can afford to let you stop too suddenly," she said, disappointment creeping into her voice. "I'd need to find a replacement for you. We don't vary our shifts anymore, not without good reason, and I'm not sure I'd be able to scramble to reorganize the other women's time to cover your clients."

"You don't vary shifts anymore?" Brielle raised her eyebrows as she grabbed a crumpled-up bundle from the back of the closet that turned out to be a lacy, see-through black shirt. The kind her mom didn't use to let her wear even if she'd never been stupid enough not to wear it without a tank underneath.

"Too many clients complained about 'differences in cleaning styles.' Once we're sure the client is satisfied, we stick to it." She didn't comment on the top, but she watched it warily as Brielle tossed it on the floor beside her. If she wore it these days, she'd be afraid of being thought of as a Goth. Nothing wrong with Goth style, but it didn't feel appropriate for a college grad.

Great. So I'm probably going to be stuck with Mrs. Tanaka every other day. Most normal clients only requested a cleanup once a week. But not Mrs. Tanaka. If it were within the woman's means, Brielle was certain Mrs. Tanaka would just have a full-time maid move into her guestroom.

"You've got Mrs. Tanaka again this summer," said Brielle's mom, almost reading her mind. "Tracy was so happy you could take her off her hands for a while, and Mrs. Tanaka was always satisfied with your work in the past."

If that was 'satisfied,' I'd hate to see how she acts when she's unsatisfied.

Her mom didn't have anything more to say on the matter. She hated when anyone bashed her clients, even if they were nowhere within earshot. "We started a new client just last week, and I'm giving you him as well." She hesitated. "He's... a bit of a handful."

A handful? That had to be the harshest thing Brielle had ever heard her mom say about one of her paying customers.

"What do you mean?" Brielle wrung the frilly white blouse she'd grabbed.

"Nothing," said her mom, straightening up and throwing back

her shoulders. "Deena and him just haven't clicked yet is all, so I'm shifting things around and giving you the job."

"How can they not have 'clicked'? If he just started last week, she couldn't have been there more than once already. How badly could things have gone?"

"He's a daily client."

"What?" Brielle didn't know if her mom had ever had any daily clients. Mrs. Tanaka certainly would have been, but even she seemed to know that things could only get so dirty in one day's time and that it was worth hanging on to some of your social security and pension dollars.

Her mom shrugged. "Every day except Sunday. I guess his mother makes a point of visiting him on Sundays and she does the cleaning then."

There were so many things wrong with that statement, Brielle didn't even know where to begin. How old was this guy that his mommy still came to clean for him? How filthy was he that he needed someone to *clean every single day*? And wait, so was Brielle going to get *any* days off, other than Sundays? Apparently not?

"Please tell me I at least have Sundays entirely off."

Her mom sighed. "You have Sundays entirely off." Beneath her words was the unspoken "but I don't take any days off, so I don't know why you need even a single day off" that Brielle was sure not to mistake. "And Saturdays, it's just him. I gave you a really easy load this summer. I wanted you to have extra time to job search."

Sure. One and a half days off per week. Plenty of time to go on interviews and scroll through job listings.

She sighed and her mom pinched her lips. "You told me this would just be until you find something better."

"It is! It will be." Brielle waved her hands around her mess of a room. "You'll have your guestroom or sewing room or whatever soon enough."

"Like I have time to sew." Her mom grunted. "Brielle, I don't want you to end up like me."

"...The owner of a successful business?"

"The owner of a *just barely making it business*, sure, but that's not what I mean." Brielle's mom ran a hand up and down one arm, like she had a sudden chill. "I like what I do, don't get me wrong. But it's not what I *wanted*. It's not at all what I had in mind."

Brielle reached up behind her and grabbed her Scrubbing Cherubs shirt, staring at the pudgy little half-naked winged baby holding a mop instead of a bow. "But then you had me and oh, well, there went all your hopes and dreams."

Brielle's mom took in a sharp breath and she stepped over some clothes on the floor with her long gait to sit at the foot of Brielle's bed. "That's not what I meant. I don't regret having you girls." She patted Brielle's shoulder.

Brielle couldn't help herself. "Even though you don't fail to mention how you regret meeting my dad on a near-daily basis."

Her mom's hand clutched her shoulder hard. "Brielle, this isn't what I'm talking about at all. I don't even care whether or not you date or get married or have kids—I don't even care if you do it all this summer and are moved into the house with a white picket fence by September."

"*Mom.*" Brielle shook her head. She'd have to be a gold digger for that to happen, and even if it did, she wasn't going to pop out a baby by summer's end. She was already six months late with that plan. She shuddered. *Kids are for years from now. Even marriage. I mean, I don't even know anyone to date.*

"I just mean that... Whatever you do, I need you to focus first and foremost on what *you* need to do. On what will make *you* happy. And I know for a fact working for me as a house cleaner for the rest of your life is not at all what you have in mind. Even if that might be all your majors prove good for."

Brielle rubbed her fingers over her forehead. "Mom, I just graduated yesterday. Cut me some slack, maybe?"

Her mom held her hands together over her lap and shrugged. "Didn't your friend Lilac have a job offer before she graduated?"

"Yeah, and she totally blew it all on a whim and is off to Florida instead of Minnesota. Something I didn't even know until two days ago, by the way." Brielle thought of the text she'd gotten from Lilac that morning, which had included a photo of her dressed in her Bohemian, flowy, flowery finest with sunglasses perched atop her head, even though she was clearly inside the O'Hare airport with cloudy skies apparent through the window behind her. *So nervous but sooooo excited!* read the text. Lilac hadn't looked nervous at all. *And really, moving* the day *after graduation?*

"So she had *two* job offers. And your gay friend, too?"

"His name is *Gavin*, Mom." She shook her head. She didn't think her mom was bigoted, but little slipups like that drove her crazy.

"Gavin, yes. You told me he got a job at a marketing company in Chicago."

"He got an *unpaid internship*, but yes."

"And internships are far more likely to lead to careers than cleaning houses for your mom. Unless you're studying for the position of becoming a full-time maid."

Brielle knew Mrs. Tanaka would hire her in a heartbeat if she charged less than minimum wage for the pleasure of cleaning full-time after Spark and Tigger, her two snobby cats. The thought sent shivers down her spine.

"That's what I thought." Her mom stood to go. "I'll email you your weekly itinerary with directions to the clients who are new to you."

"Oh, Mom." Brielle held her shirt up. "I think I'm going to need a size up." She could go buy a new pair of pants, but she wasn't going to find this gaudy design on any other piece of clothing even if she spent the rest of her life combing thrift stores and garbage dumps.

"We don't have any Larges right now." She frowned. "I haven't hired anyone in a while, so we only have the Smalls and Extra Smalls in the garage."

Brielle grimaced. That would make things worse. She'd rather have a baggy XL if no Larges were available, but if even those were out of stock, then she'd be stuck with her too-small Medium. "Never mind."

"I'd order you another one, but by the time it arrives, you might have a new job."

"Got it." Brielle also got the underlying "threat" there. How long did it take to have a shirt printed and shipped? Four weeks, if that? Her mom had to be crazy if she thought she'd have a new job by then.

"Okay... Can you have dinner on the table for your sister by five?"

Brielle cocked her head. "But you're home." She didn't say the other words. The "for once." To be fair, it'd been almost a year since she'd seen her mom's daily routine at work. But graduation had taken place over a holiday weekend and the Scrubbing Cherubs actually didn't disperse to dirty homes on national holidays, barring some emergencies.

Her mom cradled her forehead. "Bri, if you knew how much paperwork I have backlogged..."

"All right, all right. Dinner at five." Brielle so wanted to go online for a pizza takeout menu, but this wasn't school anymore, and she knew how her mom felt about eating out or paying someone to make your food for you. Every penny counted, and after you finished eating, you had nothing to show for those extra pennies spent.

Nothing to show except satisfaction and time better spent.

"I'll eat the leftovers later, when I'm done. And make something... healthy." She gave Brielle a onceover before stepping outside.

Brielle pinched the little bit of fat seeping out from her stomach as she slouched on the floor of her bedroom. She sighed. *Maybe I ordered one too many pizzas at school anyway.*

CHAPTER THREE

"You know, it's *possible* to steam vegetables without them turning into rubber." Nora pinched a limp broccoli stalk between her fingers and held it up to the light for a better look.

"Very funny." Brielle let out an exasperated sigh and slid into the chair next to her little sister's. Only she wasn't so "little" anymore. One more year of high school and she'd be off to college, too. Of course, she still had to finish out her junior year. Brielle never understood why colleges let out practically a month earlier than grade schools.

Nora dropped the broccoli back on the plate beside her half-eaten chicken breast and three remaining grains of rice and pushed the plate forward. Brielle glanced at her as she picked up her fork, annoyed that Nora had "finished" before she'd even completed grilling her own chicken breast on the stovetop in the one—very small—frying pan her mom had that was easy to find. Brielle looked around at the state of the kitchen—dishes stacked in the sink, open boxes of cereal on the counters, condiments left out instead of put back in the fridge. If any of the Scrubbing Cherubs clients actually *saw* the house of the company's owner, they'd very much doubt her ability to do the job.

Brielle knew better than to ever say that, though. She knew her mom could clean—she just thought cleaning her own house was a waste of time.

"Why don't you clean up around here?" Brielle asked her sister.

Nora crossed her arms tight over her chest. "You're kidding, right?"

Brielle blinked hard to make sure the mess that was their kitchen was not a mirage. "Uh, no. I've seen boys' dorm rooms that were in better shape than this house."

"Well, why don't you ask *Mom* to do it? She's the supposed expert."

"Nora, Mom's busy, you know that."

"Yeah, sure, busy." Nora fished into her pocket to pull out her phone. Brielle fought the instinct to tell her to put it away at the table. She actually wanted to check her own phone—she'd heard it buzz while she was flipping a chicken breast—but she hadn't spent much time with her sister in ages. But she didn't know what else to say. Nora had still been so cute and little when Brielle had left for college—at least in Brielle's eyes. She'd still *cared* about spending time with her big sister. Brielle wasn't sure when Nora had started pulling away. Mom had kept them both too busy whenever Brielle had been home for the summer.

"Can you, like, ask Mom to lay off me this summer?"

Brielle paused with her fork halfway to her mouth. "What do you mean?"

Nora rolled her eyes. "I *mean* I don't want to be her merry little maid this summer."

"Mom's not going to let you just hang out with your friends..."

Nora groaned and put her phone down on the table. "Heaven forbid I do that. But no, I have plans."

"You have... plans? Does Mom know?"

"Not yet." Nora tossed her long, brown hair back over her shoulder and clasped her hands together. "Summer camp. Well, more like an immersion camp. A good thing for my college resume."

"Immersion in what?" Brielle popped the piece of chicken into her mouth.

"*Spanish!*" Nora spoke as if Brielle were stupid for not reading her mind. "*Some of us* are actually interested in our heritage..."

Brielle stopped chewing. Even the chicken was rubbery. She grabbed a napkin and spit the piece back out. "You don't even remember Dad."

"I do too remember him! And it's not just *about him*, god!"

"Okay," said Brielle, distracted as her phone buzzed again from the kitchen counter. She stood up. "I'll back you up. But you have to tell Mom about it."

Something clanged from the table behind Brielle as she went to check her phone. "She'll just ask me how I plan to afford it," said Nora.

"Well, how do you?" Brielle tapped the screen. There was the email from her mom about her work schedule and a group text that Gavin had sent in reply to Lilac and copied to Pembroke and Brielle.

Nora growled like an angry cat. "God, do I have to think of everything?"

Brielle tapped on the message. "Well, *I* don't have money to send you to camp."

"I wasn't *asking you*! Although since you're working for Mom this summer with no plans to do anything else with your life, I don't see why you couldn't afford to spare a few thousand."

"A few thousand?" Brielle scoffed. "Yeah. Right. Plus, I'm saving for when I do move, and I have student loans that are going to start going into repayment..." Gavin's text included a picture of an immaculate, if incredibly small, loft living room. Brielle could see Lake Michigan in the background. *Stunning view*, wrote Gavin. Another text followed with an image showing the hardwood floor of the apartment, a bunch of clothing crumpled on the ground. *And not-so-stunning view. Seriously just walked in and called out Ryder's name and he's doing someone in the master bedroom. Forget what time I said I'd be here or he really can't keep it in his pants long enough to welcome me?*

Yikes. Brielle wasn't sure how she'd handle that kind of awkward situation, but she wouldn't be crashing in someone's living room to begin with. Gavin had two roommates now. Chances were, they'd both have guys in and out through that living room to their bedrooms throughout his entire stay. At least with Lilac, he could shut his bedroom door to tune it all out.

"Whatever." Nora passed by with her plate in hand and started half-assedly scraping it all into the garbage. "You may be satisfied cleaning toilets for the rest of your life, but I'm not letting Mom lock me into being her servant forever like you."

"*Nora!*" Brielle watched as Nora added her plate to the stack and walked away, leaving the dishwasher unopened. "Mom doesn't *want* me to keep cleaning for her."

"You tell yourself that if it helps you sleep better." Nora grabbed her phone off the table and stomped out of the room with more sound than seemed possible coming from her petite, lanky frame.

Brielle shook her head and turned back to her phone, ready to add her own "woe is me" tale to the message thread. *If this is what it's like to have kids*, she thought, *maybe it's best I don't go searching for Mr. Right to start a family for the next decade.*

Even though Mrs. Tanaka was usually a Monday-Wednesday-Friday client, she'd been insistent she couldn't skip a holiday without making up for it the next day, so this week, Brielle had the pleasure of cleaning invisible dust off her shelves on a Tuesday as well. And to come back again the next day.

Mrs. Tanaka remembered her well—"the girl Tigger hates but Spark can somewhat tolerate"—and she remembered everything she'd gotten wrong at her house the summer before. She spent most of the cleaning session explaining for the umpteenth time how she liked everything cleaned, but that worked out well enough for Brielle. Mrs. Tanaka was keen on demonstrating, so, with the exception of emptying the litter box, she basically had paid Scrubbing Cherubs to have someone walk around the house with her watching her clean on her own. She'd insisted Brielle carry Spark around from one room to the next as they did—although that went far beyond her job description. Spark seemed to have aged overnight since the last time Brielle had seen him and had mellowed out somewhat, so he actually let Brielle cradle him in her arms without struggling to get free. She pet his head absentmindedly and he only tried to bite her twice in two hours. Not bad for a cat that used to hiss at her from across the room and tried to swipe at her whenever she was within range on the floor scrubbing. That was the cat who "tolerated" her, too.

By the time she pulled up to the condo complex—conveniently only a few minutes' drive from her house, so maybe she'd be able to get her Saturday half-days over with quickly—after lunch to meet the new client her mom had deemed "a handful," she was almost giddy about how well the Mrs. Tanaka job had gone. She verified the condo number and checked the notes: *Archer Ward prefers his own cleaning formulas, bring fresh sponges and garbage bags. He has a bagless vacuum to use—empty it every other day. His key is on Brielle's ring, but expect him there most days.*

Really? Expect him home in the afternoon in the middle of the work day? Brielle wondered if she was dealing with another retiree like Mrs. Tanaka, but then his mother would have had to be ancient, and he was still having her clean for him once a week. *And if he's there, why can't he just answer the door?* Brielle had a key to Mrs. Tanaka's place, too, but she was always there, so Brielle just rang the doorbell and Mrs. Tanaka let her in. She didn't like the idea of barging in on someone at an inconvenient moment.

Brielle found the right condo number, almost stumbling over what appeared to be a wooden ramp placed over the left side of the three stairs leading up to the two first-floor condos in the unit.

She slipped her bucket down her arm so it hung over her elbow and pushed the doorbell.

She waited.

No one responded. *Guess he has a life sometimes after all?* Brielle dug the key out of her pocket but wanted to make absolutely sure he was gone before she entered, so this time she knocked, shouting, "Scrubbing Cherubs, here to shoot your home with the arrow of cleaning power!" She hadn't made up the slogan, obviously. And luckily, no one was ever home to hear it. (She didn't bother saying it with Mrs. Tanaka—the woman always said it herself.)

She shifted her bucket again and moved the key toward the lock when the door swung open hastily.

"Don't you have a key?!"

Brielle stared in shock, the key still in her hand out in front of her. It was almost perfectly lined up with the poor guy's eyeball. He was in a wheelchair. One of those "sporty" types of wheelchairs with the wheels bent inward somewhat. There were two canes sticking out from the back of his chair.

And he was gorgeous. He couldn't have been much older than her. His clipped, sandy blond hair belied a slight wave to his locks. He had the shadow of a beard despite the relatively early hour and Brielle assumed he'd just gone without shaving for a day or two, but somehow the hair and beard came together for that too-perfect "messy" look.

"Apparently you do. You're just mystified as to how to use it."

Right. The key. In her hand. Pointed at his light brown eyeball.

The man—Archer, Brielle assumed—shook his head as he gripped both wheels and backed up into the hallway, spinning around adeptly in the limited space and hightailing it down the hall to the living area. He didn't so much as look back. "You can start in the kitchen," he said, and that was that.

Brielle felt horribly embarrassed—she wished her mom had *put something about his disability in the notes*! She hadn't meant to inconvenience him. This was off to a lovely start.

She sighed and closed the door behind her, dragging her bucket down the hallway. At the first opening, she could see the living room, which bled over into the kitchen. Archer sat in the living room against a table by the window, and Brielle headed for the small area with the stove and refrigerator. She wondered how he could easily maneuver in a kitchen so small. It looked like when the dishwasher door opened, it'd take up half of the area's floor space. That was probably why there was a small stack of dishes in the sink. That wasn't too odd for Scrubbing Cherubs to do. They did just about any household task that involved cleaning. She'd even been to a few houses and apartments without a dishwasher at all and had had to scrub the dishes herself.

She opened the dishwasher to see if it was empty or full.

"Dishwasher's broken," called Archer from across the room. He didn't even look up from whatever he was staring at on the table. "I would have thought Deena would have told you that."

Brielle grimaced and grabbed for the dish soap that sat atop the sink. She wondered how he could even reach the sink to do this himself if he wanted to. No wonder he had someone come clean every day. She felt bad for ever thinking poorly of him for it.

Brielle cleaned the dishes in silence for a few moments until Archer cleared his throat. "Where's Deena?"

He hadn't exactly given her a chance to introduce herself. "I'm taking over your home for the summer." She shook a plate and grabbed one of her towels from her bucket to dry it. "My name's Brielle. Brielle Reyes."

"What's wrong with Deena?"

Brielle stacked the dried plate on the counter, wondering if she should bother having him give her a tour of where everything went or if that would incite his anger and she'd have better luck simply peeking in all the cupboards until she figured out what went where. "Nothing. She just has other clients. I've been off the job for a while and I needed new clients."

"You mean she complained about me and the new girl got stuck with the job no one else wanted."

Wow. Suffer from self-confidence issues much? Brielle felt bad for thinking that. He was disabled, after all. He certainly had more going on than most jerks to excuse his behavior. Brielle felt bad for thinking of him as a jerk, too. "I haven't even spoken to Deena. But I'm sure no one's *complained* about you." That was a lie. There had to have been something to get her mom to use the dreaded term "handful." It was the absolutely worst term she'd used to describe any of her clients, and there'd been a few doozies that would have made Brielle resort to words of a much stronger flavor.

"Sounds like your company is a real team-driven effort. Great communication."

Brielle put the spoon she'd grabbed from the sink down with a loud clank. *What does that even mean? Is there no answer that would please this guy?* She cleared her throat and picked the spoon up again, willing herself not to bore holes into the back of his head with her eyes from across the room. "I don't know if that's supposed to be some kind of insult, but it's a great business. We're all independent, but we also know we can go to the owner with *any sort of issues*." She grit her teeth, trying to stop herself from hinting that he'd caused issues after all. "The owner just doesn't believe in sharing her clients' personal business unnecessarily is all. No need for the rest of the team to know everything. *Some* clients appreciate that." She tackled the frying pan next. There was caked-on cheese, and Brielle wondered if he was really a grilled cheese kind of person or if the cheese was from a burger or something. She looked at the oven behind her out of the corner of her eye and wondered how he comfortably fried anything when his head would come only a couple of feet above the stovetop.

"I hope the owner is as attentive to her clients' complaints."

"Of course." Brielle shook the pan over the sink and glowered at Archer's back. *Is he going to complain about the key thing? Mom will be disappointed in me, maybe, but she'll understand when I point out how she didn't fully explain the situation. So good luck trying to get me 'in trouble,' buster.*

Almost as if he felt her eyes on him at that moment, he backed up and turned around, wheeling himself closer to the kitchen. He nodded at her as he pulled beside her. "Because you're lucky I'm not allergic to animals."

A chill ran through Brielle's body as she gently put the pan down. *What is he—?* She looked down at her Scrubbing Cherubs shirt, ignoring how tightly it clung to her moderate curves for once, to see what Archer must have noticed: It was covered with cat hair. *Covered* with cat hair, all the way down her chest.

"Oh! I'm so sorry. I have a lint roller in my car, I should have—"

"It kind of says something about a cleaning company when the cleaners themselves are untidy."

Brielle felt as if she'd been slapped. He had a point. But he was also being so rude about it. Still, her mom would kill her if she lost a six-days-a-week client like this. Brielle's gaze wandered over Archer's head as she examined the place. It was nice enough but pretty small. She wondered how he *could* afford $50 a day. "It was a client's cat," she said, nervously taking in the living room. She knew there was no excuse, that she was just sloppy, that the time away from the job, her distracted mind, had made her less sharp when it came to the details. She'd even gone to lunch like that. Yuck. "I came here afterward and—are those sketches?" She zeroed in on the table where Archer had spent the past few minutes.

Archer scrambled back across the living room, far faster in his wheelchair than Brielle had ever thought possible. "I'll thank you for not gawking at my personal effects."

Well, excuse me. "I'm sorry," she said, taking a deep breath. "I just thought it was interesting. So you're an artist?"

Archer crouched over his table and picked up a pen. "Yes."

"Well, that's neat." Brielle was glad that despite Archer's clipped tone, she seemed to have shifted the conversation away from her slovenly appearance. She stepped out and looked around the living room, spotting a few framed works of art—one of a pretty fall country scene, the other of a beautiful woman looking over her shoulder. "Did you paint those?"

Archer looked up from the table. "No."

"Oh." Brielle dried her hands on her apron. She took a survey of the room as she walked around, watching for areas that might need dusting and trying to pinpoint the garbage cans. There was one next to the kitchen area and one overflowing with crumpled up paper between his drafting table and his computer desk. Brielle felt stupid for wondering why there wasn't a desk chair in front of the desk at first. In fact, there was only one small loveseat, period, in front of the TV. Even the small dining room table only had one chair, and it was shoved against the wall, out of the walkway. Brielle shook her head. "I'm going to run to my car, get that lint roller—"

"Don't bother. You've already spread the fur and dander all over. What's a few more strands?"

Brielle bit her lip as she stared at the back of Archer's head. He had hair that was perfect for ruffling. Daniel had hair like that, although it was a much darker color.

You told yourself you never thought about Daniel without reason, didn't you?

Brielle removed the roll of garbage bags from her apron pocket and pulled out a single bag, preparing to empty the trash bins. She crouched beside Archer to grab his overflowing basket. "Should I recycle these or—?"

"Good god, woman!" Archer jumped in his chair and slammed the pen in his hand on the table. He scowled down at her. "Can you not sneak up on me?"

"Okay..." Brielle raised an eyebrow despite herself. She'd just been talking to him; he knew she was behind him. "Sorry?" She started grabbing for the papers that had fallen out of the basket. A strange drawing poked out of the corner of one of them—it looked like a huge fist. She unfolded it quietly and saw what looked like the rough sketch of several comic panels featuring a man in a superhero outfit in combat with a large, bulking alien. "Oh my god!" she said, before thinking better of it. "You draw comics?"

Archer reached over to snatch the paper out of her hand. "Personal effects, remember? Just do your job!"

Brielle frowned. Part of her felt like he got extra sympathy points for being in a wheelchair, but she also felt like he was working overtime to destroy those extra points and obliterate the empathy she had for anyone until they proved unequivocally that they were a jerk. "I'm sorry," she said, shoving the rest of the crumpled papers into her garbage bag. "I just thought it was interesting is all."

Archer snorted and picked up his pen again.

Brielle took that as her cue to get out of there and clean the rest of the place. She didn't speak to Archer again for upward of an hour, simply finding where the dishes went through trial and error and examining the spare closet nearest the door to find the vacuum. Good thing it was there, too. She wouldn't want him accusing her of "rifling through his personal effects." Honestly, he talked like someone from a century ago. Maybe because he didn't have enough chance to work on his socialization staying at home all day and what little chance he had, he totally blew.

There wasn't much remarkable about the sole bedroom and its connecting bathroom, other than there were grab bars on the wall and the side of the sink. Even the bed had those grab bars that went up and down that you saw in hospitals. There was a half-bathroom in the hall on the way to the bedroom, too, and that had the grab bars as well. He was a little untidy, but the place was hardly filthy. Of course, that was what happened when you had someone in to clean every day. Brielle figured she'd only need to do the dusting every other day to stay on top of it, although she did it that day since she'd missed the holiday and who knew how thorough a job his mom did on Sundays.

By the time Brielle finished in the bedroom and came out to say she would see him—regrettably—the next day, she found Archer near the front door, bent over on his chair.

Brielle watched him warily and grabbed her bucket from the kitchen, making sure everything was in place, hoping he'd get back to his table and not say another word. But he was still there in front of the door. She'd have to walk by him.

"All right," she said, clearing her throat. "I finished everything for the day, so I'll see you tomorrow." She held up the key to his condo as she got nearer. "I'll be sure to come in a clean shirt and let myself in." She winced. It didn't seem like a good idea to *remind him* of her failures.

Archer grunted. As she approached, she had to lift her bucket up to avoid hitting him as she squeezed past. His pants were rolled up and one of his legs had a brace on and he was struggling to put the brace on the other leg. Despite his top half being rather buff— his arms especially—his legs were awfully thin. So skinny, he looked sickly. Brielle immediately felt dumb for even thinking that.

Archer swore under his breath as his hands slipped and he had to tug his brace closer.

"Do you need any help?" Brielle bent over, grabbing for his leg.

"No!" Archer dropped his brace like a hot potato and gripped his wheels, backing up to put space between them. "Don't *ever* do that!"

Brielle's head snapped up; she felt tears welling in her eyes and swallowed them hard. He was right, of course—that had been inappropriate of her. It was invasive. She felt so stupid. But still, did he have to be *so* cruel about it? She'd just meant to help. "I'm sorry," she sputtered. She bowed a little, unable to look at Archer and deal with that rage on his face. She couldn't believe she was getting *this* upset. Even Daniel didn't ever get her *this* upset. "I'm sorry," she said again, bowing. She didn't even know why she was bowing. It felt so dumb.

She scrambled for the door knob. "Sorry," she said again, quietly.

She cleaned two more houses in blessed solitude afterward, trying to stop the tears from falling as she scrubbed, and spent the hours until her mom got home Facebook messaging with Lilac and Gavin, only somewhat really there in the moment to deal with Lilac's tales about how amazing Florida was and poor Gavin's upset about his jackass of a boss. More than once, she started typing: *"Wait until you hear about the jackass client I cleaned for today..."* But she kept hitting the back space button as she pictured Archer's face. She felt as if she'd violated him. And she probably had. She didn't really tune into the conversation until Gavin mentioned that Pembroke hadn't responded to any of his messages, and that she'd been acting weird that graduation weekend so he couldn't just fluff it off as her being busy.

Brielle tried to remember the last time she'd really talked to Pembroke. It'd been about Daniel. When things had gotten bad, she hadn't run to Lilac and Gavin—she knew they wouldn't be sympathetic, that there would be too many told-you-sos. So Brielle pulled up Pembroke's profile and DMed her about her day.

CHAPTER FOUR

Archer hadn't been alone with a woman so close to his age in years. He hadn't been alone with a woman so beautiful in forever. (And no, he wasn't going to count his mother, no matter what others said.) That first older cleaner he'd had when his mother had signed him up for the service had made things awkward enough, but to suddenly send him someone who looked like she'd stepped off the pages of a perfume ad (well, despite the cat hair and the cheesy attire) without even warning him? His life was always a joke, but it never failed to surprise him just how many ways life could mess with him.

And now he'd just made her cry. He'd made a grown woman he barely knew cry. (She'd tried to hide it, but he could see those striking dark brown eyes glistening as she left.) What was he, a ten-year-old bully?

He sat in his hallway a long time after that, cradling his chin in one hand he leaned on his wheelchair armrest, his half-affixed brace forgotten. His phone buzzed a few times—had enough time really passed that he'd be missed already? He'd given himself half an hour to get to the park on the north side of the complex that only took him five minutes to wheel to on a good day—but he didn't dig it out of his pocket to look at it.

He couldn't get those glistening eyes out of his mind.

She was *not* what he'd been expecting when he'd opened the door. He'd thought he'd find that Deena woman with excuses that she'd lost her key, he'd pictured the headache of having to have another one made—or more likely, asking his mother to have one made. He'd made it *quite clear* to her last week that he wasn't to be disturbed while he was working, that it messed with his concentration. If he'd had to ask his mother to get another key made, he'd have had to see her before Sunday. Either that or he'd have had to keep letting Deena in all week, tearing himself from his art, wheeling all the way to the front door to be gawked at by the help like some oddity. Although he supposed he could have left the door unlocked for her. Who cared if some thief walked in? He had nothing he cared about for them to take. So long as he locked it before his mother came on Sunday, she wouldn't even know and they wouldn't have to argue about it.

That had all gone through his head before he'd torn open the door to find a key mere centimeters from his face. Mere seconds from making him half-blind on top of everything else.

But the woman holding the key was absolutely the last thing he'd expected to see.

He'd noticed the cat hair almost right away—but he couldn't help it. She'd looked about to pop out of that gaudy shirt with the atrociously stupid design—not that she had the biggest breasts he'd ever seen, but with her top practically acting like a second skin, it was hard not to be drawn to the pair of breasts just about eye height for him. He'd had to stifle a laugh to discover they were covered in white and brown fur—a cleaning woman who could use some cleaning? He'd had to shake his head to clear his mind of the images of himself in the bathroom *cleaning* the poor woman he'd just met.

Jesus, how did any straight man do it? Spend more than a few seconds around a woman like that without losing track of everything else he had to do?

He'd tried to do his best to keep it all professional, although he'd found it difficult to have the conversation he'd had almost immediately with Deena—to be as quiet as she could be and to keep questions to a minimum. He didn't want to speak with this one more than necessary, to say something wrong. To—*God*—invite questions about what he was doing.

Thanks to movie blockbusters and all that, many women these days were cool with comics. To a point. It was one thing to see a bunch of real-life hunks on the giant silver screen once every few months and quite another to collect comics—to be *a part* of the industry. He'd had enough teasing from girls like her all his life. He'd been into comics since before it was hip—had, somehow, with more help from his parents and social services than he'd like to accept, made a meager living out of it.

Few people knew what a rare accomplishment that was. Few women in the dating pool would think it was a big deal at all. They'd more likely view it as a negative.

But who was he kidding? He wasn't going to be dating anyone. He didn't need to be dating anyone. The only benefit of dating someone would be to shut his mother up whenever she talked about introducing him to the daughter of a woman she'd met in the grocery store or suggested he mingle more with people "like him" to meet a woman "like him" who'd understand. How him having *someone* would help put her "mind at ease."

He had nothing against dating a woman with a disability, but it was the way his mother phrased it that made it so unappealing to him.

Although he wondered if his mother would be so "at ease" if he started dating "the hired help." He didn't even know why she insisted they come every day—was he really that much of a pig? Sure, he let things go a few days when he had a deadline approaching, but if it weren't for Pauline complaining about it once or twice to his mother when she called to check in—because Pauline was a private duty nurse, and Archer's parents were footing the bill, so apparently that made it okay to share information about him like he was a five-year-old child—he was sure his mother wouldn't have been struck with the idea to hire a cleaning service. "Pauline isn't there to pick up after you, you know!" she'd said. "Besides, with how little you get out, would it kill you to have more than Pauline's and my faces to see throughout the week?"

Archer pointed out that he had two-times-a-week basketball games with the guys, but that wasn't good enough, apparently.

Speaking of, his phone was now ringing instead of buzzing. *That's no good.* Only one person *called* him. Everyone else texted.

Sure enough, he saw the call from "Mother" and let it keep ringing until his main screen popped back up. He swiped aside some texts from Jayden about where he was at, how they were starting without him, how they were getting worried—holy crap, it was an hour after he was supposed to be there; he'd been *sitting in his hallway thinking about a cleaning woman for an hour and a half.* Then the phone rang again.

He took a deep breath and ran a hand over his face. If he didn't answer now, she'd show up. He was in for an earful either way, but it was better when it at least wasn't face-to-face.

"Yes, Mother?" he said, the too-smooth-innocence he injected into his voice at odds with the frustration of the day boiling inside him.

"Why didn't you answer my call?!"

It was just half a minute ago. My god, woman. "You know I play basketball on Tuesdays."

"So I'm meant to *assume*, but I got a call here just a minute ago that you hadn't showed up and you hadn't let any of them know you weren't coming, and I just about had a heart attack! I—oh, watch it!"

I'm going to kill Jayden. I'm a ten-minute walk away. If you're that worried, why don't you come check on me before you call my mother? Jayden wouldn't even have had his mother's number if she hadn't insisted on coming to the park for a couple of their informal games and handed her number out to every single player there, urging them to call her if anything ever went horribly awry. He'd wanted to melt into his chair and take the chair with him through the asphalt into hell. Archer put the phone on speaker and started picking up odd noises from the call. Honking and a repetitive clicking. Like a turn signal. "Are you on the phone while driving?"

"No—yes—I wouldn't be normally!" At least she had enough sense not to pretend she wasn't being hypocritical for long. "But you didn't let me know you'd be skipping your game—"

"There was no reason why I'd *have to*!"

"But when I get a *call like that* and you don't even answer!"

Archer cradled his head in his hand. "Okay. I'm sorry, okay? I'm sorry you got a call like that. I'm sorry my friend worried you. I'm sorry I didn't let him know not to be worried."

"You know how I get—ooh!" She shrieked as a loud squealing sound erupted.

"Mother?" Archer felt himself break out in a cold sweat. He'd just lost track of time, he'd just taken a short moment to feel pity for himself, and his mistakes had put her in danger. "Mother!"

"I'm okay. I'm fine." A pounding sound, like she was hitting the steering wheel over and over in frustration—something he'd seen her do more than once or twice. "I just started going before the light turned and—" A loud horn blasted.

"Mother!"

"Oh, fuck you, jackass! You never had a bad day?"

Archer raised his eyebrow despite the fact that he had no audience. He couldn't help it when it came to her. She was normally so uptight and proper. Not that he'd never heard her speak like that, but only the very worst of occasions usually called for it in her eyes. "Mother, can you pull over, please?"

"I am. I am. I'm right by the Starbucks by your condo. I'll pull in there."

Shit. She's less than a ten-minute drive away. She'll never be turned away now. Archer cleared his throat. "Okay. Okay, pull in—" He winced as he heard another loud horn blast. She didn't swear this time. She just laughed like she'd become unhinged. "Mother?"

"Just a moment, dear," she cooed. Her voice had a singsong quality that was quite disturbing between the cackling laughter.

The clutch gear shifted and she likely pounded the steering wheel again. "I'm in the parking lot, all safe and sound."

Archer let out a breath. "Okay."

"Okay."

"Maybe go inside—take a break before you go back home—"

"No, I'm coming over. I'll grab you a coffee. Caramel macchiato?"

"You don't need to come over."

"Nonsense." An unbuckling of a seatbelt and the door opening. An incessant dinging.

"Mother, you forgot your keys," said Archer, knowing exactly what that ding meant. "Or you forgot to turn off the headlights, but more likely you forgot—" A door slam. "Mother?"

"Yes?"

"You left your keys in the ignition, didn't you?"

"Oh." She must have been peering through the window. "I guess I did."

Archer pounded his palm against his head. "And you locked the door by hand on the way out, didn't you?"

"You know I don't like the honking it makes when I lock it with the remote! Everyone *looks at me*."

"I told you you could get that disabled—"

"I don't have time to take it to a mechanic or whatever I'm supposed to do."

You have no job, woman. You are obsessed with checking in with me. You have plenty of time. "Okay," said Archer, exhaling loudly. "Did you put a spare pair in your purse like I asked you to?"

"Of course I did, I... Oh."

"Oh?"

"My purse is still on the passenger's seat."

"Why did you get out of the car and lock it without even grabbing your purse?"

"I was *talking to you*! I had the phone in my hand and I just... I forgot, okay? I was *scared to death* because of you!"

"All right." Archer massaged his temples. "All right."

"I hope you realize how *scared* I was—"

"I do."

"You *know* I don't like you changing plans without letting me know."

"I *know*, but you're really overreacting."

"Overreacting? When you're... When I didn't even want you to move out on your own anyway!"

There it was. The feeling of anger, guilt, and embarrassment all rolled into one. "We're not having this discussion again. We agreed—"

"*You and your father* agreed—"

"I'm twenty-five years old!"

"But you're not like... other twenty-five-year-olds."

She never believed in me. She never saw past this. She's known me my whole life, has been there since the beginning and... She still can't stop seeing me as somehow less than other people. He took a deep breath. He knew her prejudices, her domineering, all came from a place of worry and concern. He knew she wasn't perfect. But they'd settled into a routine he thought was better for them both. He didn't need to shut her out of his life entirely, as long as she acknowledged some boundaries. And today was his fault. Sort of. "Go inside and order some coffee. Sit down and take a deep breath."

She sobbed. "I can't order coffee. My purse is in the car!"

"No, remember, I told you your card is accessible on your phone?"

"On my phone?" She paused, probably pulling the phone away from her ear to examine it, as her voice got quieter. "How do I do that...?"

Archer had shown her at least twice before. There was no way he'd have the patience or capability to tell her how without being there to show her again. "Ask the baristas!"

"What?"

Archer spoke louder. "Ask the baristas!"

"All right, all right." Her voice got louder. "No need to shout."

Archer hit the back of his head against the wall several times. "I'll call Dad and have him bring a spare—"

"No!" She sounded flustered again. "Don't call your father—"

"He can bring a spare key—"

"*No.* He can't know about this." Know about her rushing over to their son's place in the middle of the week or locking her keys and purse in the car? Probably both.

Archer sighed. "I'll call a locksmith."

"Could you get Pauline on the line? Maybe have her bring you over?"

Archer shook his head, even though no one was there to see it. "Pauline is my nurse, not my chauffeur. You were the one who told me she wasn't my maid."

"But this is different!"

"She also has a life and I don't need her here at all hours." He wanted to say that he didn't have a spare key anyway, but he knew he did. His mother locked herself out too often not to have one here—or she'd do it on purpose to use it as an excuse to stay longer.

"I have to go now," said Archer.

"But I don't know what to do."

"Coffee. Or maybe tea would be a better idea. Use phone to pay. Ask barista how. Wait for locksmith."

"Archer—"

"I have to go and let my friends know why I wasn't showing up. Right? They'll be worried about me."

"Why *didn't* you go? You never told me."

"I'm getting off now. I'm going to call a locksmith and then my friends, so you'll probably just get sent to the voice mail if you call again." He hung up, even though he heard her call his name once more.

When she called back a few minutes later, he still hadn't called the locksmith or texted Jayden. He hadn't finished putting on his brace or taken the other one off. He just let it ring.

CHAPTER FIVE

Pembroke still hadn't responded to Brielle's DM. Granted, it'd only been a day, but that wasn't like her. Even when they never saw each other over the summers, she'd always responded by the next morning at the latest.

Brielle wanted so desperately to talk to someone about her big mistake with Archer. She wanted to vent about what a jerk he was, too, but mostly she just wanted someone to tell her it was okay and she'd made a mistake, but it would all be forgotten and it would soon be better.

She couldn't tell her mom. Oh, no, she would be in so much trouble. Even if she wanted to confront her about not *warning* her to begin with. But then she wondered if her mom had just been trying to be politically correct. Because it shouldn't have mattered, right? It didn't matter. Still, she just would have liked to have known. So she wouldn't have kept embarrassing herself left and right with him.

Nora wouldn't understand. And she was hardly outside of her room when home from school anyway.

And Lilac and Gavin had had so much to tell her about their own adventures—actual adventures, not this bs nothing-changed-in-my-life post-graduation existence Brielle was experiencing—

that Brielle couldn't find the right moment to add her own thoughts. Lilac was on cloud nine in Florida, even though she wouldn't say much about the job itself, and Gavin loved the work, even if his co-workers were apparently almost as much of a drawback of his new life as living in close quarters with two very active roommates. To tell the truth, Brielle had started tuning them out after a while and let them chat back and forth on the thread while she browsed the Internet with a numb mind.

She'd spent the evening Googling how to interact with disabled people and felt stupid doing so. They were just people—Brielle *knew* that—so what was there to know? How was she supposed to act any differently? Everything she read said she wasn't basically. By offering to help him with his brace, she had violated that line of not treating him any differently—and plus, she didn't know him well enough to offer to help with such an intimate gesture.

She'd meant well, but that didn't matter.

Disheartened, Brielle had considered lying to her mom and asking for the next day off, but she knew that would open up a whole can of worms about responsibility and her job search—cripes, she hadn't looked for a job since last week, assuring herself she was just excited about graduation and she could afford to take "some" time off—so she cleaned at Mrs. Tanaka's (tuning the woman out most of the time) and her once-weekly clients' in the morning, barely stomached a half salad for lunch, and then went to Archer's, making sure to let herself in with the key. Her fist hesitated over the open door. Normally, she'd knock to announce her presence even after letting herself in, but maybe then he would think she *hadn't* let herself in and feel the need to come to the hallway, all bent out of shape and railing at her—

She took a deep breath. She was driving herself crazy. "Scrubbing Cherubs, here to shoot..." She let the motto die on her tongue. She really, really didn't want him to hear her say that again.

But he wasn't there. After all her worry, after all those derogatory thoughts about how he never left home (before she knew his situation), and he was gone on her second day.

He hadn't left too much of a mess, so cleaning went fast and she was gone before he returned.

Wednesday evening Brielle spent applying for jobs. Mostly secretarial jobs. There was one at a museum several states away, but she wasn't sure she could manage moving across country without first saving up more money. Then again, it wasn't like she had a great shot anyway. In all her years at college, she hadn't managed to figure out exactly what it was she wanted to do after, even if she'd ruled out a few things. So she never got the internships or forged the connections she needed to get a job like that.

She applied anyway, knowing she was simply sending the cover letter and resume into a void.

Thursday morning was her first morning back without stopping by Mrs. Tanaka's and it was refreshingly peaceful not to have to speak to anybody before lunch. She thought about skipping lunch entirely and going for a walk in the nearby park—it'd been a long time since she'd done that—but her growling stomach had other ideas, even if it was still agitated by dread.

When she went to Archer's and he wasn't there again, she was partly relieved and partly puzzled. Although it was clearer than ever now how inappropriately she'd behaved—his absence seemed to attest to that—he shouldn't have to avoid her in his own condo. If he'd called her mom to ask for a new maid, she was certain she'd hear of it, whether or not her mom could easily pull that off at the moment. No, he hadn't registered a complaint. He'd just taken to leaving before she got there so he wouldn't have to deal with her.

She was so certain she'd never see him again despite going to his condo practically every day that while cleaning the toilet, she actually screamed when she heard the sound of footsteps and a woman's voice coming from the living area.

"...Hello? What?" A middle-aged woman wearing navy scrubs poked her head around the open door of the bathroom. "Are you... all right? Are you... Who are you?"

Brielle let go of the toilet brush. "Brielle," she said, clearing her throat. "I'm the cleaner."

"...I told you I didn't want to rush back, that there was someone—"

Archer wheeled into view behind the woman. He stared at Brielle for a moment and his face reddened as he looked down. "Yeah. The cleaning lady is here this time of day."

"*House cleaner*," said the woman, staring down at Archer like he was a child she was chastising.

"Sure, yeah." Archer wheeled backward into the hallway. "Cleaner."

The woman shook her head. "You have to forgive him. He's woken up on the wrong side of the bed for the past ten thousand days."

Whoa. Brielle's eyes widened.

The woman chuckled and extended her hand. "I'm Pauline, Archer's nurse."

Brielle reached her hand out, noticed the yellow rubber glove, and quickly removed it before taking Pauline's hand in hers. "Brielle."

Pauline pulled her head back and glanced over her shoulder, but she didn't make any effort to lower her voice. "So you're the reason why Archer has been so insistent he get out lately? That we spend ten more minutes at the grocery store?"

Brielle winced. She heard pounding and cupboards opening from the kitchen down the hall.

"You don't know what you're talking about!" Archer's voice echoed down the hallway.

Pauline laughed again. "Normally, I'd thank you for pushing him to get some fresh air once in a while. But I knew something was off when he insisted he needed another fifteen minutes to choose which flavor ice cream to buy. He hates spending time in the grocery store."

"You say that," yelled Archer, "and yet last week when I insisted on just grabbing the first pint of ice cream I saw, you complained for days that it was pistachio."

Pauline shouted down the hallway, "Pistachio isn't a proper flavor, I'm sorry."

"Sure, sure. Just vanilla and chocolate. I suppose you see no need for entire aisles of flavor."

"Not when the classics will do, no." Pauline turned back to Brielle, grinning. "I'm normally not here this late, but he's been insistent we go out and who am I to say no?"

Brielle grimaced. "That was probably my fault."

"Was it your fault or were you simply the cause?" Pauline gave Brielle the onceover and a knowing look, but Brielle didn't feel like she was in the know at all.

"Enough, Pauline," called Archer. A cupboard door slammed so loudly, Brielle jumped. "Don't you have another patient to get to? Isn't that why you were so insistent we get going?"

"I was insistent we get going because I felt like we were about to grow roots." She laughed and checked her Apple Watch, swiping at the screen. "But it is indeed about time I got going." She nodded at Brielle. "Nice to meet you, Brielle."

"Likewise." Brielle cleared her throat. *Don't leave me alone with him.*

But the nurse had already turned the corner. "Stay cheerful, sunny!" she cried. Brielle heard Archer grunt, followed by the front door opening and closing. The place got eerily quiet. After a moment, Brielle slipped her glove back on and picked up the toilet brush. She finished cleaning and then kept scrubbing a few minutes longer just because she couldn't stand the idea of going out there yet. She listened for Archer's slamming around the kitchen to end and once it did, she waited a few minutes more.

Then she decided it was now or she was going to have to lock the door and camp out in his guest bathroom forever. Which would be decidedly more awkward anyway.

She gathered her belongings and headed out into the living area. Archer was in front of his computer this time, a tray table Brielle had never noticed before pulled out to reach about his lap area. He held a digital pen in his hand and it kept making loopy movements on the digital tablet, although Archer's eyes never left the monitor.

Brielle almost walked right out the door without a word. She wondered if that was what Archer would have preferred. It was what she would have preferred... If the tension between them wouldn't keep eating at her forever.

But it was also the wrong thing to do. It certainly wasn't the professional thing to do.

She cleared her throat. "So... Um... I'm finished for the day."

Archer nodded but didn't look away from the screen. "Congratulations...?"

Brielle's face soured. She didn't know how she'd been in this guy's presence for maybe less than three hours and already she found him as aggravating as Daniel. It took her months—years, probably, if she was being honest—to start really being annoyed by Daniel. And yet somehow this guy was annoying in a different way —not outright crude, just... Beastly. Yes, that was perfect. He was just like the beast in *Beauty and the Beast*, all sullen and incapable of saying anything that could possibly be construed for kindness or even civility. At least not as far as she was concerned.

Brielle felt an anger surge inside her she only thought Daniel capable of arousing. She dropped her bucket, letting it hit the hardwood with a clatter. "I wanted to apologize for the other day."

Archer sighed and put his pen down. He backed up in his chair and it was the first time Brielle got a good look at the drawing on the screen. It looked like he was inking a pencil sketch digitally.

"No, don't bother," said Brielle quickly, scrambling to pick up her bucket, which she oughtn't to have dropped *quite* so loudly. "I just wanted to say I'm sorry, and I'll try as hard as I can to be quiet and not disturb you at all from now on, and you don't have to worry about structuring your day to avoid me—not that you can't leave whenever you want anyway, but if that *was* the reason you were gone the past few days—"

"Whoa, whoa." Archer wheeled closer, taking one hand off its wheel as he neared to make the universal palm-faced-down hand gesture for "calm down." He paused in front of her and ran his hand through his hair and over his face. Brielle found the movement surprisingly alluring, like he'd casually flicked on the light switch to her libido. "I don't want you tiptoeing around my house, afraid I might explode at the slightest sound."

Brielle stared down at him blankly. He *had* met himself, hadn't he?

Not that he likely saw himself the way she did.

"I'm sorry," he said, quietly. He looked at the floor.

"What...?" Brielle spoke more out of confusion than from not having heard him. She'd heard him.

"*I'm* sorry!" he said, loudly this time. He gripped both wheels tightly, although he didn't move, and he looked up at Brielle with the most amazing puppy dog eyes. How such a hot guy could have little baby puppy dog eyes, she didn't know.

"But I—" began Brielle.

"I was rude to you your first day."

Brielle gripped her bucket handle with both hands and tapped the toe of her sock against the floor. "I shouldn't have touched you. I'm sorry."

"You barely did..."

"I wasn't even thinking; I just thought you might need help..."

They both stared at each other for a moment and then flicked their gazes to the floor at just about the exact same moment.

Archer coughed a little and Brielle looked back at him in time to see his Adam's apple bob. "That type of thing can be a sensitive subject for people like me."

Brielle shook her head brusquely. "I totally understand. I didn't even think—"

"I know you meant well." Archer did this odd thing where he rolled forward and back a little, just barely the space of a half a foot. "I put my braces on almost every day, though. So... I don't need help, even if I might struggle."

Brielle nodded. "Of course. And even if you *did*, I should wait for you to ask for help before I just give it to you."

Archer laughed and it made him look like a totally different person. Forget Beast, he was like a hunky Prince Charming. "Which I would have never done because I barely knew you."

Brielle bit her lip. "Right. Understandable."

"So... truce?" Archer stopped his wheelchair "pacing" and folded his hands over his lap. He was wearing a dark gray polo and what looked like black workout pants and Brielle suddenly wished she could see how tall he'd be beside her. Like that made any sense or made any difference. (She would date a shorter guy regardless.)

Brielle gently put the bucket down and extended her hand. "No truce necessary. Just... a fresh start."

Archer's lips moved just slightly, like he was fighting a huge grin. He took her hand in his. "That sounds even better. I'm Archer," he said, finally letting that grin show.

"Brielle." She shook his hand and leaned back slightly against the counter that separated the kitchen from the living area. The eagerness in his pale brown eyes was actually making her knees buckle.

CHAPTER SIX

Archer hadn't felt this good in weeks. Months even. Maybe years, if he was being honest with himself.

Maybe ever?

Which was astonishingly stupid. There was *no reason* to be happy. His life hadn't changed. Not really. He just was no longer not speaking to his cleaning lady. (*House cleaner*, he corrected himself.)

Like that was a great accomplishment. The fact that he was ever avoiding her to begin with was actually a depressing enough thought to sour his mood considerably.

He'd been mad at his cleaning lady. His cleaning lady, whom he'd known for about an hour at that point.

He really was pathetic. And not because he had a disability— he knew plenty of amazing people like him through the in-person and online support groups his mother used to make him join. No, the feebleness was all him.

His pace slowed considerably as he headed toward the park to meet up with Jayden and the guys. Jayden had gotten an earful from him when he'd called to explain Tuesday's mix-up about avoiding contacting his mother until *after* he'd confirmed seeing Archer on a stretcher and absolutely at no other point in time ever, even if he'd been abducted by aliens in the midst of a hook pass.

Brielle hadn't spoken much when she'd come today. She'd just been... so much happier. She'd radiated happiness *vacuuming*. *Emptying trash*. Archer wished he could ever be so happy doing things that people typically considered soul-sucking grunt work, yet here she was... Content.

She hadn't disturbed him at all, but he'd found himself unable to focus, upcoming deadline or not. He'd purposely had his back to her—although he'd fought against every instinct he had to slink away by at least greeting her and thanking her when she was finished—but he'd kept redrawing the same line over and over. It wasn't just that it wasn't good enough, it was that he couldn't picture the scene properly in his head. Every time he'd tried to focus on the superpowered man with a plan (he didn't write the comic, he just drew it—no one could blame him for that tag line), he'd kept picturing what she was doing based on the sounds alone. Putting dishes away was easy, only he hadn't just pictured her putting dishes away, he'd pictured her standing on her tiptoes and stretching to reach the top of his cupboards, that too-tight shirt of hers riding up and flashing a spot of bare skin at her waist line. (Which was ridiculous since he knew only the things he almost never used were stored that high because *d'uh*, he'd have a tough time reaching them, so she wasn't putting anything away that high up.) Then there was scrubbing in the bathroom. She was on her hands and knees in his vision. A little grunt and a moan. *Whoa.* He'd pictured her someplace else entirely. No, he could be *absolutely certain* she wasn't lying alone on his bed. Bed comfort testing was not in the service contract. Bed comfort testing was not something one paid for if one wished to be on this side of the jail cell.

He should have talked to her more. If she was going to distract him that much without even trying, he should have just said the hell with it and given into it.

He knew almost nothing about her.

It probably wasn't right that he spent so much time fantasizing about her lately.

"Hey, look who decided to show up!"

Archer hadn't even noticed Jayden appear behind him or heard him bouncing the basketball down the sidewalk. He'd passed the parking lot Jayden and most of the guys usually used since few lived so conveniently close. He patted his hands against his wheels hard for good measure. He had to get his head in the game—in more ways than one. "Someone had to stop you from sending my mom into a tizzy, right? Had to get here plenty early this time."

Jayden twirled the ball on his fingers. *Show off*, thought Archer. "Hey, I said I was sorry about that, man." He looked over his shoulder to nod and shout "hey" at a few more guys who walked past them.

Archer sighed. "I know you are. I just..." He clapped his hands together once loudly. "I just wish I didn't have to overthink everything, have to basically get permission to do anything not planned in my day."

"I feel you. If anyone else hadn't showed up, I'd have texted him once and that would have been the end of it, whether he responded or not." Jayden shrugged. "Life happens and all that."

Archer smirked. "But with me, you decide it's necessary to call in the bomb squad?"

"You, you're..." He nodded at him and looked him once over, as if taking in his form in the chair for the first time.

"I have a disability; I'm not dying."

"Yeah, yeah, my bad." Jayden cocked his head and stopped the ball from spinning by gripping it tight with both hands. "She really that bad?"

Archer nodded. "She's really that bad."

"Sorry." He tossed the ball in the air a few times and caught it each time. "I would have checked on you myself, but I forgot where you live."

"Right back that way!" Archer gestured at the sidewalk behind him with both hands, like he was an air traffic controller showing a plane where to land. "Straight down this sidewalk. Like ten minutes. You can't miss it."

Jayden shrugged. "I knew it was in those condos, but I didn't know *which one*. You've only had me over like once, dude."

Archer leaned over just as Jayden went to catch the ball again and snatched it out from under him. "Fine. My bad. Just... Next time, it's preferable you go from door to door knocking in lieu of calling my mom, okay?"

"Roger, roger." Jayden grinned and nodded toward the court. "Ready?"

Archer spun the ball over his fingers—perhaps not as adeptly as Jayden had, but at least the ball didn't go rolling off elsewhere—and then dropped it onto his lap, his hands on his wheels. "Are *you*?" He took off toward the court.

Jayden had to jog to catch up. "So why *were* you gone Tuesday? You never said."

Archer finished saying "hey" to the rest of the guys and passed the ball to their friend Lawrence before peeling his shirt off and tossing it onto one of the benches on the side of the court. "I wasn't aware you were my keeper, man."

The game started and Jayden, Team Shirts today, guarded Archer so there was no escaping him. Jayden spoke between looking over his shoulder to see if the ball was in danger of getting to Archer and shuffling around the court to make sure it never became a possibility. "I'm not. I'm just... curious. You were sick?"

"No." Archer leaned around Jayden's torso to track the movement of the ball, trying to subtly edge his way toward the opposing basket.

"You had a deadline?"

"Always." Archer made a sharp turn with his wheel, jutting out just enough beyond Jayden's range of grasp. "But I've been making good progress this week."

"Okay, then I'm about stumped. I know you have no social life, so... *No*." Jayden actually stopped in place, a look of astonishment on his face. Archer wondered if he'd given something—not that there *was* much there—away, some quick flit of the truth of his thoughts, considering the way that girl wouldn't get out of his mind. "You had a date!" shrieked Jayden. "That's why you didn't want your mom involved—"

"Nope." Archer used Jayden's utter distraction to lean out and catch a pass from Darrin. He grinned and dodged away from Jayden, using his chair to block him as he wheeled with one hand and dribbled with the other. "I don't need to have a date to not want my mom involved, and I promise I'd send a text if I was canceling because of a girl."

It'd taken Jayden an extra beat to get back into the game and that was all Archer needed to make the shot.

Jayden jumped, but he wasn't quite close enough to make a difference.

The ball hit the rim and rotated all the way around... And rolled right off. So much for an epic rim shot.

Jayden laughed and did a little victory dance, like he had anything to do with it. "So close. *So close.*"

Archer groaned and dismissed him, digging into the bag that hung on the back of his chair for his bottle of water. He took a sip as Scott dribbled, knowing he'd probably have to step in any minute to guard Jayden. He quickly popped the spout of the bottle back in place, his last sip still swishing in his mouth, and turned around to drop the bottle back in the bag.

He dropped it right onto the court floor. And he practically spit his water out to boot. He had not expected to see *her*.

"Nice!" shouted Jayden, who sure enough, now had the ball in play.

"Yo, Arch!" shouted Darrin, clearly disappointed. "Get your head in the game, man!"

Scott ran over and picked up Archer's bottle, dropping it in his bag for him.

"Sorry," said Archer, running his forearm over his mouth.

"No problem." Scott clapped his hands together several times.

"All right, all right, all right, let's do this—aw!" He clutched his hair as Jayden took a shot and made it.

Somehow he'd gotten clear across the court and Archer hadn't even moved an inch.

"Time, time!" Darrin grabbed the ball and held his hands out together in a 'T' shape. He called over the Skins, more than half of which seemed like they wouldn't be out of place posing for the model photos that decorated those cheap bags of underwear. Archer grabbed his own shirt from the bench to rub the sweat off his brow, his face flushing at how pathetic he must look beside them.

He tried to listen to what Darrin had to say, but his gaze kept flickering to the park bench just twenty feet away from the court. The bench on which Brielle clearly sat, her Scrubbing Cherubs shirt abandoned for an even more revealing spaghetti-strap tank top.

"Hey, Arch? ARCH!" said Darrin.

"What? Sorry?" Archer felt dazed.

"You all right, man?"

"Yeah, I..." He rubbed his face with the front of his shirt for the second time in half a minute.

"You didn't hear a word I said, did you?"

Archer shook his head like a dog after a shower and clapped. "No, I'm in this. Let's do this!"

Only Archer couldn't get his head in the game. It wasn't *entirely* his fault that his team got utterly trounced less than an hour later, but he was confident he wasn't winning any MVP awards if there were such things for a bit of casual park basketball.

The guys still shook hands with each other—in that casual, swing your arm widely and come in for the hand smack kind of way—and talked shit about next time, but Archer wasn't even able to focus on that. His arm hung out kind of limply, accepting each smack halfheartedly.

"Rest up next time, bro," said one of the guys. Archer didn't even remember which. "Got to get your head in the game."

"Yeah," he said. His gaze drifted for the first time in quite a while to the bench. He hadn't let himself check since he'd first noticed her, but he could almost *feel* her eyes boring through the back of his head the rest of the game. Only she wasn't there anymore.

He laughed to himself. He'd been stressing all game over it when she'd probably left like a minute after he'd noticed her there. Probably just as soon as she'd noticed him on the court. He couldn't blame her. He'd had half a mind to bolt himself, but he figured it would draw more attention to himself if he did.

He was an idiot for even worrying about it.

"See you next week!" Jayden nodded at Archer as he headed back toward the parking lot, this time cutting through the grass for a more direct route.

"Yeah." Archer nodded, his damp T-shirt crumpled in his fists.

"Don't hold out on me, bud!" Jayden called over his shoulder just as he passed the bench Brielle had been sitting on. "I want to know first thing next time if you have a hot date!"

Archer winced and tried to politely smile, but the smile was lost the instant he noticed Brielle wandering toward the bench from the park bathroom—how she stopped and looked from Jayden to Archer and back, clearly having heard Jayden's pointless jab.

Archer's blood ran cold and he slumped his shoulders, turning his chair toward the path that would lead him home.

CHAPTER SEVEN

Brielle knew she'd chosen the worst possible time to pee. But how was she supposed to know when a basketball game was going to end? She'd never cared to watch a game before today.

And she'd already held it for so long at that point. She'd figured she could be in and out before the guys went their separate ways.

No such luck.

She saw the group breaking up as she approached and her heart sank. Then again, what did she intend to do? Strike up a conversation with Archer? Why on earth would she even bother? Sure, she could say "hi" and everything, but what was she expecting?

Maybe it was a good thing he'd already left.

"Don't hold out on me, bud!" called some guy a few steps in front of her as he headed for the parking lot. "I want to know first thing next time if you have a hot date!"

Brielle raised her eyebrows. This felt awkward. It felt even more awkward when the guy smiled at her and winked before turning around.

But nothing was as awkward as noticing the person the guy was actually talking to—Archer.

Brielle stared. She wanted to nod or something or wave, but she was pretty sure she just stared.

For one thing, he was *still* shirtless. And boy did that look good on him. He was just slightly sun-kissed, just the softest bit tanned. His chest muscles really had no business being that defined. And thanks to the sweat glistening off him, he looked like he'd been oiled down, ready for the taking.

She might have bit her lip at the thought. But she was certainly still just staring.

So it was no surprise he turned and started wheeling away a short while later.

Brielle sighed and sat back down on the bench. It had been a little surprising when she'd sat down earlier and absentmindedly stared over at the court and found a guy in a wheelchair playing—and that guy being the one guy in a wheelchair she knew.

Then again, it wasn't that surprising. She'd driven there—even though if she were being honest, she definitely could have walked from her house, except there weren't sidewalks or paths the entire way and she hadn't felt like walking in traffic in her frame of mind —and she knew it was a short distance from his condo complex. Much closer to his condo than to her house even—and when she thought about it, she was sure there was even a sidewalk leading to it. But she honestly, totally wasn't hoping or expecting to find him when she'd set out for it.

She'd just wanted some fresh air and some peace of mind.

She'd been in a great mood after another day of cleaning Archer's without all of the awkwardness. Even Mrs. Tanaka has been downright pleasant to be around because her favorite cousin's daughter had called her the night before or something—Brielle wasn't even sure, as she'd only been able to half-hear her over the sound of the vacuum and the scrubbing.

By the time she'd gotten back home to Nora grumpily draining a pot of noodles in the kitchen and her mom on the phone with one of her employees at the kitchen table, Brielle was ready for her first weekend post-college to be amazing. She had to clean Archer's place, sure, but that wasn't such a bad thing anymore. And then she'd be free to catch up on shows she'd missed because of finals and packing and every other crazy thing from the past few weeks and maybe she'd even spend some time reading—she hadn't read for fun in forever—and waste time online and see how the gang was doing after their first full week of "real" adulthood (although Pembroke still hadn't answered her—the thought of her ignoring everyone was a bit of a downer).

Nora slammed the pot on the glass plate protecting the counter. "On. War. Path," she said as she flicked the stovetop fan off.

Brielle cocked her head, but Nora just shook the strainer of noodles back into the pot and crossed her arms, sulking against the cupboard and staring daggers at their mom.

Their mom put her hand over the speaker on her phone. "Girls! The sauce!"

Nora groaned as if she'd been asked to pick up an axe and chop firewood for the household as she flicked the burner with the sauce pan off and carefully lifted the cover to stick the mixing spoon in. She shouted and shook her hand when a bit of bubbling sauce spurt at her despite her efforts. She smashed the cover back on and tossed the spoon at the spoon rest, getting sauce everywhere. "I'm not even *hungry*," she snapped, rinsing her fingers in the sink.

Their mom laughed on the phone, oblivious to the mini drama show her youngest was putting on several feet from her. "Okay. All right then. Thank you, Deena." She hung up and dropped the phone on the table, her face suddenly ashen as she massaged her temples.

Brielle dropped her purse by the hallway to the bedrooms and removed her half-apron. "Something wrong?"

Nora leaned over the counter beside the sink and examined her nails, probably looking for damage from the sauce incident. "There's *always* something wrong in the ever-so-exciting world of indentured servitude."

Their mom looked up, gesticulating widely above her head. "*Nora*, I've had it up to here with your attitude today."

Nora scoffed and raised her hands out to either side. "Then *why* would you want me here all summer when I can be out of your hair for a month and a half?"

"I've explained this to you. One, we don't have the money to spare for that camp—"

"God, you're acting like I'm off to a camp for drug addicts instead of wanting to do something to better my life. *Lita* understood and said she'd pay for half of it!"

Brielle almost forgot that Nora still video chatted with their grandmother—their father's mother—in Puerto Rico on occasion. She used to herself, but she hadn't in ages. She hadn't really had the interest in it. Their dad was never involved, just their *abuelita*.

Their mom stood up from the table. "No. Oh, no. I'm not asking that poor woman to chip in for anything. She has enough to deal with cleaning up your father's messes."

"Again, Mom! Again with the cutting down Dad!"

Their mom grabbed the pot of noodles and dropped it on the table. "You don't know the half of what happened between your father and me—"

Nora grabbed the pan of sauce and tossed it down on the table next to the pot of noodles, droplets of sauce splaying out at the rough handling. The splatter made it seem as if someone nearby had been punched in the nose and had spurted blood everywhere. "Oh, I've heard *plenty* about it from Lita!"

Their mom opened her mouth and seemed about to speak but closed her eyes a moment, holding up her index finger. "I don't want to get into this with you, Nora."

"You act like he was a *wife beater*, but he wasn't!"

"I *never* said he abused me!"

"Lita said you lied about that and that was why Dad left!"

Brielle could almost feel her heart thump out of her chest. Had this been going on all the time since she'd gone to college? She didn't remember things being quite so heated between her mom and sister when she'd last been here for holidays or the previous summer.

Their mom turned that pointer finger accusingly at Nora. "I never *once said* to *anyone* that your father beat me, and if your grandmother is saying that's what *he* said, then one or both of them are liars! Which doesn't surprise me!"

"You don't even *know* Lita! You never went to Puerto Rico to visit her, not even once, despite being married for nearly a decade!"

"Your father didn't *want me* to meet his family, probably because he was *still married* to a woman there and I didn't even find out that our marriage was a sham until I'd been with him for eight years and had had two daughters!"

Even though her mom had told Brielle the truth in private when she'd turned eighteen, it still kind of blew when shrieked like that at high volumes. She'd asked her mom if Nora knew, and she said she would wait until she was older. Brielle did *not* think this was the right moment for that revelation.

Nora clenched her fists together at her sides. Her lip was shaking and tears were threatening to spill out from her eyes. "You're lying! Lita said you were a liar!"

Their mom crossed her arms. "Did she mention your father's real wife to you?"

"No, because you're just a hateful, bitter old woman who just wants me to stay home so I can work as your slave like Bri does!"

Brielle wasn't sure that being in her late forties qualified their mom as an "old woman." But as soon as she thought that, she realized she was being the adult in the room, and she wasn't quite sure she was comfortable in that position.

Their mom crossed her arms and bit her lip. She looked about to cry, too. "You *don't* know what you're talking about!"

"Yeah, I do, and I'm *going* to that camp. You can kick me out of your house if you want to, but I *won't care*. I'll go live with Lita."

"In Puerto Rico?"

Nora was already heading toward the hallway, the dinner uneaten. Their mom trailed after her. "Your grandmother has *no legal right* to you, and if you do run off to live with her, I can report you as a runaway and have you back here before you can blink!"

Nora spun around, practically knocking Brielle over. "When I'm eighteen, I can do anything I want."

Their mom scoffed. "Sure. If you have the money to do it."

"Oh, I *will*," said Nora, heading to her room. "Because I'll be certified multilingual and I'll actually have a chance to get a *good job*, not be a floor scrubber!" She slammed the door behind her.

Brielle watched the closed door for a few moments, staring at it even after Nora blasted a Taylor Swift tune like a scene straight out of a movie. *I was never* that *bad, was I?* Brielle really didn't think she was.

"Where's your job offer, huh?"

For a second, Brielle thought her mom was shouting it at Nora in response to finding that "good job" because she'd be multilingual. (Multiple members of the Scrubbing Cherubs' staff were multilingual—about half were immigrants—so Brielle failed to see the correlation.) But when she turned, she found her mom full-out glowering at *her*, like she'd just been the one to insult her mom's business and make her scream about her marital failure.

"What?" she said, stunned, although the gears in her head were already turning to make sense of the question.

Her mom tossed her hands in the air and rolled her eyes. "The offer for the job you're supposedly looking for. The job hunt that's *supposed to be your priority!*"

Brielle was so taken aback, she actually took a step back. "I've been busy... Working..."

"Yeah, so have we all." Her mom stepped over to the table to grab her phone and then snatched her purse off the counter along with her car keys. She sniffed audibly, obviously trying to stop herself from crying, but Brielle was too hurt to care much at the moment. Her mom left out the back door, letting it slam behind her almost as loudly as Nora's bedroom door.

The steaming pot of pasta and the smaller pot splashed red with sauce sat lonely in the middle of the kitchen table as Brielle heard her mom's car exiting out of the garage and driving away. (Brielle was relieved she'd parked on the street as usual, so her mom didn't come back in in a foul mood demanding she remove her vehicle from her path.)

Brielle felt her own well of tears filling up and swallowed hard. *Screw it*, she told herself. *I'm not letting her take it out on me.*

She ignored the cooling dinner and went to her room to change before making her own getaway.

⁂

Staring at Archer play for almost an hour had been enough to empty her mind. In a good way.

Even from that distance, she could tell he looked *really good* bare-chested and covered in sweat.

Sitting back on the bench after he'd left without so much as a word, she stared after Archer, watching as he almost vanished from sight.

Some impulse raged in her. The same kind of impulse that had made her follow Daniel down his dorm room hall months after she'd already known he was bad news because he'd given her some look, said something halfway flirtatious, and she'd been lonely and tired from all of that studying and writing she'd been doing for weeks on end.

So it was a bad impulse, she knew, but she pushed the guilt down anyway and ran after her cantankerous client. "Archer!" she called more than once. She got louder as she picked up the pace in order to catch up to him.

Is he actually moving away from me faster *now?*

She hesitated, not wanting to bother him or break the tenuous working relationship they'd managed to hash out between them, not wanting to seem desperate.

Which after weeks—*months* of getting no action—she kind of had to admit she was.

Damn it, she thought. *Please tell me I'm not turning into Lilac.* Take away the endless assignments and constant research, though, and her brain did seem to wander to more sensual things apparently.

Not that the job hunt was much less mentally taxing than school at this point.

Her foot caught a crack on the sidewalk and she stumbled, crying out.

Archer stopped and spun his chair around in time to see her hopping on one foot to regain her balance. "Hi," she said after the fourth dorky hop.

"Hey," said Archer. He was panting and looked like he'd just had a cooler of water dumped over his head. "You okay?"

"Yeah," she said, putting her hands behind her back and shuffling her foot. "I just..." She pointed back to the bench. "I was sitting back there and I saw you and I thought I'd... say, 'hi.'" It sounded really stupid when she said it. "I didn't know you'd be here—I mean, I know you live near here, but—"

"You didn't think I'd be into park sports, considering the wheelchair?"

She shrugged. "No, not that. I mean... This is just the closest park to my place, too. And sometimes I just need some fresh air and peace, you know what I mean?"

She wondered if Archer really did know what she meant since he had his peace alone in his condo and seemed to find camaraderie here in the park.

He nodded, though, his gaze drifting off somewhere behind her. Brielle felt eager to fill the silence and said the first thing that popped into her head. The stupidest thing, she would soon think. "So... 'Hot date'? That guy said you had a hot date."

His face grew three shades darker and his Adam's apple bobbed perceptively. "He was just kidding. Trash talk."

Brielle wasn't sure "trash talk" meant what he thought it meant, but she could certainly tell he meant the guy was teasing him. "Oh," she said, interlacing her fingers in front of her abdomen. "That's good." *Dumb, dumb, dumb.*

He raised an eyebrow and looked into her eyes for the first time since he'd spun around. "It's *good* I don't have a hot date?"

"No! I mean... Of course not. I guess." She laughed nervously.

"Well, I've never had one." He swallowed.

"A hot date?"

"A date at all. Not really. Not if you don't count a pity dance date in school."

Brielle frowned. She hadn't meant to bring up such an uncomfortable topic with him, hadn't meant to insinuate anything. She supposed he was a bit old not to have been on a date—although Pembroke wasn't much better, but she was a girl at least and guys typically didn't patiently wait for "the one" to walk into their lives —but there was his disability to consider. It was definitely rude to question him further on that point. Maybe he couldn't even... Maybe he didn't want to date because of where it might lead and maybe he couldn't go that far. Her own face darkened at the picture that had just popped into her head. It wasn't her business anyway.

"I *can*... date," he said as if reading her mind and deciding to censor her thoughts somewhat, considering there were kids just a few hundred yards away. "I just... haven't." He cleared his throat. Then he laughed, his face stricken as if she'd caught him in an embarrassing admission. "It was always just easier not to try. I can't even picture how I'd kiss a girl comfortably."

Brielle's cheeks blazed harder. "You've never been kissed?"

He stared at her. "Well, I mean... Not more than a peck on the cheek. From... relatives." The ground seemed suddenly far more intriguing for him to look at. He was squeezing the life out of that shirt with both hands. Brielle was just glad he hadn't thought to put it back on.

"Would you like to try?" Brielle could feel the heat on her breath. She knew she was being bold, knew this type of interaction was awakening something inside her she usually managed to keep hidden. *God, if Lilac even knew, she'd never stop teasing me.*

Startled, Archer jumped a little in place and looked around. "With who?"

Laughing, Brielle crossed one foot in front of her other one.

"With me. I don't exactly have permission to grant on behalf of anyone else."

Archer tried to look up at her, but his gaze kept flicking to whatever he found so intriguing behind her. "When? How?"

She shrugged. "Right now." She tentatively took a step forward and put her hands on either side of him at the edge of his armrests. They were shaking a little, but she could feel that warmth surging inside her from that place below her stomach. She *needed* this right now. She needed to have a small taste of him. "Like this."

There was no pulling away from her eyes when she was this close. He looked as surprised at what she was doing as anything.

"Would you like to?" she asked, breathless.

"Yes," he said softly.

She leaned forward, tilting her head slightly as he turned his to let her that close. When she was sure she'd make a skilled landing, she closed her eyes and tapped her lips to his. They were a little chapped, a little rough, but they gave way to the slight pressure she put into the kiss as she deepened it. Her back and neck strained just slightly from holding the position leaning over him, but she dug her nails deeper into the sides of his armrests and pushed harder, parting his lips to let just the tip of her tongue inside him.

More, her idiotic mind commanded her. *More. More.*

But the screeching laugh of a child across the park reminded her of where she was, of her relationship—or lack thereof—with this man, and she pulled back, laughing. "Sorry," she said as she let his chair go and took a step back.

He swallowed again and ran his fingers over his lips, almost like he was trying to catch the ghost of her kiss. It drove Brielle wild. She wanted to do it again. Wanted to lean in once more... Instead, she started walking backward, pointing over her shoulder. "So, yeah... Um. Yeah," she said, her sex drive apparently shutting down the communication center in her brain. "I should get back. I left my purse at the bench." She laughed at how obtuse that was of her, and what a dumb excuse it really was to walk away from a hot guy she'd just kissed. "See you. See you soon." She pantomimed vacuuming. "When I come clean," she added, in case he got the wrong idea.

She didn't even wait to hear any response at all he might offer, just turned around and took off for the bench.

Fortunately, no thief had made off with her purse while she'd been gone. She didn't have much cash in there, but it would have sucked to have to cancel her cards and replace her phone. Her phone buzzed almost as soon as she confirmed it was still in there—a video chat invite with Lilac and Gavin. She would have thought they'd be too busy with their hectic, really-grown-up lives to bother with it. But they were all freshly graduated—only the test of time would tell if they'd really stay in touch.

"Hey," said Brielle, breathless, as she accepted the invite and their faces popped up on her phone screen. She had a sudden pang of how her mom would be mad if they went over family data plan limits, but it wouldn't be long before she'd make her pay for her own plan regardless. Plus, her mom kind of deserved it right now.

"Bri!" Lilac reached out toward her phone camera and made smoochy noises. From the background, it looked like she was in her room at her aunt's. "Help me!"

Her tone was whiny and not exactly panicked, so Brielle wasn't concerned for her safety.

Gavin rolled his eyes. He was sitting on a couch. Brielle had to wonder if he actually had the place to himself for once. "Miss Big Bazongas is being harassed by Earl. Like that's such a big surprise."

"Earl?" asked Brielle, totally out of the loop, her mind still lingering on that kiss.

"The guy I work for at the resort." Lilac pressed closer to the camera with a haggard face. She pinched her fingers together. "He's *this* close to like dropping a pencil in front of me and touching my butt when I'm bent over to pick it up, I'm telling you."

"Gross," said Brielle and Gavin at the same time.

"But he's like... He's walking that line perfectly. Making me feel uncomfortable without ever giving me anything I can actually complain to anyone about." Lilac sighed. "And actually, I don't even know *who* to complain to since, like, he's my boss and I don't know who *his* boss is."

"Tildy Tapir," said Gavin, entirely unhelpfully.

Lilac scoffed. "I'll be sure to file my complaint to Ms. Tapir—right before I hop over to Disney World like a traitor and tell Gaston how my best friend back home first thought he might be gay when he fell madly in love with his two-dimensional six-pack."

"You were in love with the villain?" asked Brielle. Okay, he was hot for a cartoon, but she'd pictured Gavin as the more innocent type.

"He was fine as hell and he could sing like a badass. So sue me." Gavin shrugged. "I wore out that DVD so much, it got to be I could only watch *Beauty and the Beast* with my sister or at Grandma's if I didn't want to risk raising my parents' suspicions."

Because only a gay guy could like Disney, princesses, or musicals? Not for the first time, Brielle felt so sorry that Gavin had grown up with people like that.

Lilac massaged her temple. "Gav always has the worst taste in men."

Gavin gestured to the screen with both hands. "Says Earl's new girlfriend."

"Don't even," said Lilac, shaking her head. "Besides, if I'm going to be anyone's new girlfriend, it's going to be the guy in a Silly Sandgrouse suit."

"You're joking, right?" asked Brielle.

Lilac laughed. "Only half-joking. He's pretty hot once you get that doofus head off."

"There are actual live Gastons walking around the much better park next door"—Gavin held a finger up so Lilac wouldn't jump in to correct him—"and you're telling me Silly Sandgrouse is hot. Reality check, Li." Gavin brushed his bangs out of his face.

Brielle sat down on the bench once more, ready for a long conversation. "So how's your love life, Gavin?"

Lilac snorted. "Don't ask."

Brielle cocked her head. "That bad?"

"That *good*," said Gavin, grinning mischievously.

"Okay, now I want to know more," said Brielle, devoting her entire attention to the phone.

Gavin shrugged and avoided her gaze. "My roommates have a date here almost every night." He looked up and gestured back and forth with his hands as if tabulating the numbers. "Okay, between them, there's been a guy here every night."

Brielle winced. "You must be getting a lot of sleep with all that... activity."

Gavin stuck out his tongue like he was about to gag. "Yeah, well... One of their 'dates' decided to hang on my couch with me before heading off to the bedroom."

"Please tell me you didn't hook up with someone your *friend brought over to bang*," said Brielle.

Lilac gasped and giggled.

Gavin raised and lowered both of his hands in turn like he was weighing his options. "Is it really so bad if he didn't make it to the bedroom and decided to take me out for coffee instead?"

Lilac rested her chin on both hands and stared dreamily into the phone. "Aw, coffee. Not a drink. Not the bedroom, but coffee... Sure."

"I don't exactly have a bedroom to invite a guy to," said Gavin matter-of-factly. His voice lowered. "Until I settle in permanently, I have to entice a guy to invite me back to his place."

Lilac laughed and clapped her hands. "So innocent, this one."

"Besides, I'm not a one-night-stand kind of guy. So excuse me if I wanted to get to know him a little better."

Brielle could feel her face flushing. She wasn't exactly comfortable discussing her friends' love lives in *this much* detail. "How's the job, though? Think you'll have an offer by the end of the summer?"

Gavin's face soured. "I don't know if I want an offer. I'm

thinking of this as a resume-booster and hitting the classifieds in a few weeks to see if I can find something else in Chicago." He made the hitchhiker's thumb movement. "Otherwise, I'm just out of here."

"Oh, but what about coffee guy?" cooed Lilac.

"Shut it," said Gavin, but he was suppressing a smile.

"Why?" asked Brielle, confused. "I thought you were really excited about working there."

"His boss is a huuuuugggeee asshole," said Lilac. "Like, we've been having a competition for whose boss is the bigger asshole all week."

Gavin pointed at the screen. "No, you win that, hands-down. If Gabriel starts grabbing my ass, maybe there'll be an actual comparison." He pinched his lips together, thinking. "No, even then, you'd win. I don't know if Gabriel is married or not, but at least he's hot."

Lilac covered her mouth. "Oh *my god*, you never told me he was *hot*!" That seemed to make an actual difference to her.

"*Anyway*," said Gavin. "Bri, you've barely told us what's up with you. How's your week been?"

Brielle shrugged, not sure how much to say. "Not much going on. I've been cleaning. I've applied for a few jobs. My sister and mom are at each other's throats just about every day." She shrugged again. "I... Well..."

Lilac grabbed a decorative pillow from off-screen and hugged it. "Oo, please tell me this is boy-related."

Gavin shushed her and Brielle felt herself blush even deeper.

"It *is*!" said Lilac.

"Not really," said Brielle. "I mean, this guy I clean for is kind of super sort of gorgeous."

Gavin shook his head quizzically. "'Kind of super sort of gorgeous...'" He laughed. "That's even better than the compliments you first paid Daniel when he caught your interest."

"Don't remind me." Brielle huffed.

Lilac pounded her pillow. "Details, details!"

Brielle shrugged again. "Nothing to tell. I clean for him. We had a misunderstanding the first day and I thought I would die from embarrassment, but... We're cool now, I guess?" She didn't want to tell them about that kiss. Nope, she really didn't want to keep thinking about that kiss.

"What kind of misunderstanding?" asked Lilac.

Brielle tapped a finger to her cheek. "He's in a wheelchair and he was grumpy about me seeing his comic book art and I just... sort of crossed some boundary with him? I don't know." *Ha, speaking of crossing boundaries...*

"Wait a minute," said Gavin and he grabbed his phone from where he'd leaned it on the armrest of the couch. His face minimized as he tapped the phone screen and typed in a few things. Brielle wasn't sure what was going on and Lilac watched, mesmerized. "Archer Ward?" asked Gavin.

Lilac scrunched her eyebrows up. "Is that some kind of codeword I'm supposed to know or... some zoning info?"

Brielle's jaw dropped. "How did you know?"

"Super hot, disabled, comic book artist, from your hometown." Gavin tapped his head. "I have a good memory for these kinds of details." He shrugged. "Besides, he's only the current lead artist on *The Mystified*. Kind of sort of a big deal in comics circles. Kind of."

"I didn't know," said Brielle. She hadn't heard of that comic.

"Oh my god, Brielle's going to date a celebrity!" shouted Lilac.

"Kind of," said Gavin.

"We're not dating," said Brielle. It was true. One kiss didn't mean anything. Especially when she'd basically just sprung it on him out of nowhere.

Lilac looked thrilled as she hugged her pillow closer, doing a little dance in her chair. She stopped suddenly, her face serious. "But if he's disabled, how would you two—"

"*Okay*," said Brielle, loudly. "Change of subject. Has anyone heard from Pembroke?"

"No," said both, shaking their heads.

"I DMed her earlier this week," said Brielle, "and still,

nothing."

"Ditto," said Gavin.

Lilac shrugged. "I haven't reached out, but I included her on a few texts and she never responded."

"You're the closest one to campus," said Gavin, referring to Brielle. "She was a commuter, so she lives nearby, right?"

"You want me to drop by?" Brielle asked. She wasn't sure if that was the right thing to do or a total invasion of privacy. "I don't know..."

"*Somebody* ought to," said Gavin. "If it was simply a matter of her wanting to be left alone or being busy, she should just send us a brief text saying as much."

"Give the girl some space," said Lilac, shaking her head. "We just saw her less than a week ago. Maybe she's not even the type to care to stay in touch after graduation."

"We promised we all would," said Gavin.

Lilac sighed. "Yeah, just like every other group of college class-mates in the universe." She nodded at the camera. "How long do you think we'll even stay in touch? We'll get even busier with jobs, maybe husbands, maybe kids..."

"You're starting to sound like my grandma," said Gavin.

Brielle couldn't even check one of those off. She felt so behind.

It was starting to get dark. How long had she stayed out here? And she'd totally wasted the evening. She hadn't even applied for one job. She sighed. "I should get going," she said.

"Yeah, where are you?" asked Lilac. "Looks like a park."

Brielle shrugged. "Just getting some fresh air."

"Wow, pigs must fly these days," said Lilac. Always smarmy.

"Check in with me next week about Broke," said Gavin. "And sweep that comic book artist off his feet!"

"Look up how you have sex in a wheelchair—" started Lilac. Brielle quickly closed the app.

She was beginning to wonder if it wouldn't be such a bad idea to follow Pembroke's lead and cut off contact with her college friends.

CHAPTER EIGHT

Archer was halfway home when he finally decided he'd had enough of being a coward.

He was going to see her tomorrow. What was he going to do? Pretend she hadn't kissed him? Why had he just turned around and gone home instead of going after her?

But it was just a kiss. Well, it was *the* kiss to him, the one he'd dreamed of, the beauty offering it to him more gorgeous than he'd ever dreamed possible. But to her, it was just a pity kiss.

Just like his pity dates.

He'd sort of dated a girl from a support group back when he was a young teen, but that was just because their mothers had forced them together, mostly so the girl would have someone to go to her school dances with. Archer had quickly had enough with being gawked at as the two teens who'd arrived in wheelchairs and besides, he could barely talk to that girl, so that hadn't lasted long.

He'd flirted with whom he hoped was a teenage girl online when he'd been in high school. He'd been lonely, but after seeing so many exposés about child/teen predators as well as catfishers and all sorts of online scam artists, Archer had stopped pouring his heart out to LisaUnderFire97x from Colorado, who'd never quite seemed real regardless.

Besides, he'd never told her about his disability. He wasn't sure why.

In college, he'd mostly stuck to himself. He'd gone to some support and ally groups at his mom's insistence, but he was done. Closed off. He'd had other things to focus on. Besides, it had been embarrassing to think any off-campus dates might have to be chauffeured by his nurse or worse—his mother—because he couldn't comfortably fit in a typical small car his date might have. And then there'd been the fact that he'd have to ask her to drive and pick him up even if he did decide he wanted to squish in there. No. He'd considered asking his mother to help him get his license again, but he'd known how she'd react.

"Do you want me to never sleep again?" she'd said once.

The idea of him behind the wheel, no matter if he tried to explain how hand controls worked and how he'd be totally safe (at least as safe as any other driver, but with drivers like his mother on the road, that, admittedly, was only so safe), was enough to send her into a tizzy.

He was an adult now. Mostly. So he could theoretically do whatever he wanted. His dad would probably even pay for the car if he called him directly and hoped his mother wasn't within earshot. But he'd already moved heaven and earth to get her to be sort of okay with him moving on his own just twenty minutes away from her—and that was only by letting her pay for the nurse to visit him most days and for a cleaner to come every day and by letting her have that one "Sunday Funday Mother Day" he'd keep open for her visit.

And to tell the truth, his dad still chipped in with even his basic household expenses.

He loved what he did for a living, but he wasn't salaried. Which meant he didn't really make *that* much, even though he definitely made a lot more than a lot of artists. And he was just old enough to still be on his dad's insurance, but that would end next year and his mother was scrambling to figure out some kind of disability coverage he could get.

Maybe he could qualify for disability aid, too, but, he was sometimes embarrassed to admit, his parents were wealthy. Even if he technically didn't have to count them on any application for aid, he'd feel too guilty knowing he could just ask them for the money and there were other people in need out there applying who didn't have that luxury.

So he walked this fine line of being too dependent on his parents at his age and asking for just the smallest bit of freedom, the smallest bit of privacy.

He'd drive someday. But he wanted to enjoy this bit of peace between him and his mother for a while longer before he opened the next can of worms.

Besides, he'd never had anywhere he wanted to go. But now, thinking about Brielle and how he wished he could ask her out, to see if the kiss meant half as much to her, had been half as *amazing* to her, as it had been to him... He wished he'd fought for getting his license earlier.

But then you'd just be riding around in a car your daddy paid for like a spoiled sixteen-year-old. No, there was nothing he had to offer a woman who worked an adult job and probably had a hundred adult responsibilities.

He looked over his shoulder, but the park was now barely visible from where he sat.

Forget it, he told himself, and he wheeled himself back home.

Archer hadn't been able to sleep much Friday night. He kept tossing and turning, thinking of what to say to Brielle when she showed up to clean today.

He decided the best thing to do would be to let her bring it up first. Feel out how she felt about it.

But what if she was waiting for him to speak first...?

He thought and thought and thought about it until he was exhausted and could think no more.

Insomnia was going to make the evening's signing so much more miserable than he'd already expected.

He could barely focus on his work in the morning and didn't feel hungry enough to eat more than a banana for lunch. Pauline was coming later today to take him to the signing—it took all of his willpower and a matter of luck (his dad's country club had a dinner tonight his mother wouldn't miss for the world) to keep his mother from being the one to bring him—so he was alone, utterly, painstakingly, every-minute-like-an-hour alone, until 1:00 when he heard the key turn.

"Scrubbing Cherubs!" came Brielle's voice from the doorway. Archer noticed she no longer bothered with the silly motto.

He cleared his throat. He wasn't going to ignore her. That would be incredibly stupid. Even bleary-eyed and short on sleep, he could at least be a halfway decent human being. "Hello," he said, not looking up from his drafting table.

"Hi." Brielle made a small amount of noise as she put down her cleaning equipment. "Oh," she said after a minute. "Have you not eaten anything today?"

I guess she's not going to talk about it, either? Part of him expected that—proof it was just a pity kiss for her, even if it meant so much more to him—but he couldn't help feeling disappointed. He turned himself around halfway. "Dishwasher got fixed yesterday," he said. It was the truth, although it was only half the story.

"Oh, right." Brielle nodded. "You told me someone was coming." She looked around at the counter. "Still... My job here appears to be done. Not a single crumb or coffee stain or anything!"

Archer couldn't help himself. He laughed and maneuvered his chair to turn around completely. "You'd think you'd be happy you have less to do."

She shrugged. "I'm here for an hour, whether you're a slob or a neatnik. Some clients actually *clean* before their cleaners show up. I can tell. They think we haven't seen a mess before and they get embarrassed." She opened the dishwasher. "I can put things away at least... There's nothing in here."

Archer rolled over to the kitchen. "You got me."

Brielle cocked her head.

"I haven't eaten more than a banana since you were here last."

Brielle's eyes widened. "You didn't even eat supper and you played basketball for a couple of hours?"

"Oh," said Archer. "So you saw the whole game?" The game wasn't off-limits, so they weren't pretending the park hadn't happened... Just that the kiss hadn't.

"Practically! I didn't exactly expect to see you there, so I only started paying attention partway through, but—"

Archer rubbed one of his biceps. "Then you know how badly I sucked."

Brielle seemed genuinely flabbergasted. "I thought you were amazing."

Archer stopped scratching to stare up at her. "I didn't score a single shot."

"Oh," said Brielle. "I guess I didn't really pay attention to that. I'm not actually a big basketball fan."

Archer opened a drawer and rifled around for an energy bar just for something to do. "Neither am I, usually. I just like playing a couple times a week. It's good to get some exercise in beyond the usual therapy."

"Therapy?"

"Pauline helps me exercise almost every day. I... need to." He tapped his arm with his energy bar. "Side effects are building up half my muscles a little too much." He always felt self-conscious about how lopsided he looked. But he couldn't get the same kind of muscle development in his legs, even if he did work them out with Pauline.

"I wouldn't say *too much* at all." Brielle tapped her thigh and stared at the wrapped lunch substitute in his hand, clearly disgusted. "I can make you a better lunch than that."

Archer chuckled and tore the wrapper off. "You're my house cleaner, not my full-service maid."

"I don't mind if you don't." Brielle twirled a strand of dark brown hair that had fallen out of her ponytail around her slender finger. Coupled with the slight pout shape to her mouth, it was driving Archer crazy.

He ate the bar in just three bites, swallowing quickly, and went to back up to get out of the kitchen, but he started choking.

"You okay?" Brielle swooped in and lay a hand on the back of his shoulder, bending down to his level. Like when she'd touched his leg, he felt the heat wash over his face and he wanted to scream and push her away—but only because he *really* wanted to grab her and pull her onto his lap. "I'm fine," he choked, his throat dry.

"I'll get you some water," she said, grabbing a glass from the cupboard as familiarly as if it were her own home and filling it up from the tap.

Archer almost swore he felt an icy chill in the spots where her fingers had been, a coldness left by the lack of Brielle.

She handed him the glass. "So... What ingredients do you have?"

Archer took a sip and then cradled the glass. "Don't worry about it."

"All right," said Brielle, eyeing him suspiciously. She shut the dishwasher and then spun back around, her arms out and her eyes darting back and forth, as if figuring out what to do. "Oh, I..." She gestured behind Archer.

Right. Her cleaning supplies were behind him.

Not thinking straight in the face of those deep brown eyes, he set his glass down in his lap—not between his legs like he might usually, not on the counter or holding it in one hand—and backed up. As he turned the corner, the glass tumbled forward, splashing his lap and splintering as soon as it hit the ground.

"Oh my god," said Brielle. "Are you okay?"

Archer looked at his lap and then back to Brielle again and back at his lap. He wanted to sink into his chair. "Fine. Just wet."

"I'll get that for you." Now that he'd backed up enough, Brielle was able to slip by. "Careful," she said, stepping around the shattered glass with her white socks. Her long leg stretched over one of his wheels so she could get a better grip on her cleaning bucket.

Archer hovered his hands behind her ass, feeling awkward but sure it was better to catch her there than let her fall onto his wet lap.

"Sorry," she said over her shoulder, and the way she scrunched up her face was absolutely adorable. "Sorry," she said again as she maneuvered back into the kitchen, the bucket way above Archer's head. The barest bit of the pocket on the butt of her black plants brushed his fingertips as she did.

Archer clenched his wheels tightly. He suddenly, without delay, needed to get away from her.

"Um," she said, staring down at him, "about yesterday—"

"Have to change," he mumbled, backing up and heading down the hallway.

He shut the door to the bedroom behind him—never before feeling so frustrated that he had to wheel in, back up, and then turn around to get it closed without slamming it—and cradled his head in his hands, his elbows propped on his knees.

He was hard. With a woman just a few feet on the other side of that door. *Because* that woman was just a few feet on the other side of that door.

This wasn't like when he'd accidentally gotten that way in therapy—that had started as a preteen and it had embarrassed him to no end—he knew that was normal and he'd gotten better at not letting it bother him when it happened. This was because he *genuinely* wanted to be with this *specific* woman. He'd never been with a woman outside of his wildest fantasies.

He had it bad.

And he was losing track of time just sitting there in his wet pants, in his wet chair, thinking about her again, because there came a knock on the door what felt like two seconds later.

"Mr. Ward?" said Brielle from the other side of the door. "Are you okay?"

Snapped out of his daydreams, Archer laughed and wheeled over to his dresser. "I'm fine," he called loudly. "And please—call me 'Archer.'" He couldn't believe she'd *kiss* him but still refer to him as a "mister."

"'Mr. Ward is my father.'"

Archer froze, a pair of new pants still in his hands. "What?"

Brielle's nervous giggle echoed through the door. "Sorry. That's just what people usually say when, um..." She took a sharp intake of breath. "So I cleaned up the glass?"

Archer tossed the pants onto his bed and grinned. "Are you telling me or are you asking me?"

"Now you sound like my high school English teacher."

Archer grunted as he lifted himself to the side of his bed with the grab bars so he could change, then grunted again as he reached into his pocket to toss his phone onto the comforter.

"You okay?" he heard Brielle ask.

"Huh? What? Oh." He chuckled. "Yup. Spend enough time with me and grunting becomes background noise." He finished peeling his pants off, looked around for the towel he'd forgotten to grab before heading over, and shrugged, balling up the pants in his fist and using a dry part of them to pat his legs down. He tossed them across the room, landing a perfect shot in his hamper.

"Oh, okay," said Brielle. "So I'll... Um... Wipe down the counters and table and get to vacuuming out here."

Archer leaned toward the door, one leg through his pants. "No, you don't have to—" But he could already hear her walk away.

Since he hadn't even really used the kitchen since she'd last been here, Archer felt bad. He really didn't need daily cleaning, period—his therapists had always encouraged him to pick up after himself to begin with—but he had a feeling it put his mother's mind at ease. Just one more person checking in on him who could call an ambulance if he was lying on the floor, he guessed. He finished getting his pants on and then he sat there, trying to clear his mind, trying not to think about her.

It wasn't long before he heard the vacuum and figured he better get out there. He was nervous about tonight, but he still had a deadline next week and he needed to get in his daily quota.

He'd just repositioned his chair when he heard a loud crash, a sound like an engine being choked, and a scream.

"Brielle?" he said, his heart thundering. "Brielle!"

Damn this chair, he told himself as he positioned his arms and swung himself back in. Thanks to his nerves, he fumbled. He'd forgotten to lock one of the wheels and that half of the chair pushed backward with his sudden weight. He almost slid right down, chin first, into the seat, but he managed to catch himself, wrenching his shoulder and hitting his forehead with his canes, which he kept in the bag at the back of his chair.

"Damn it!" he said, aloud this time. He really wasn't supposed to walk without his braces, but he *could* and he had—mostly when there was a therapist with him. *Screw it.* He pulled both canes out and set them in front of the bed steadily. He couldn't stop thinking about what could have possibly happened. The vacuum was still running, but it was making a sort of pathetic sound, like it was on its last legs. He pictured Brielle on the floor, unconscious, blood pooling. He *had* to get there, damn it, and make sure she was okay.

It took him a few tries, but he pulled himself up using his canes and stood still, trying to decide whether to head toward the door and walk out there or to simply walk in front of the chair so he could lock it and sit back down. Part of him wanted to *run* out there, but he'd never even gotten close, not even in a treadmill harness.

There weren't a lot of days lately that he cursed the fact that he was born with legs like these—that was just how he was, even if it had a whole share of problems few others had to deal with—but today was one of them.

Phone, he thought, realizing it was still on the bed—out of reach if he got into his chair to grab it. If she needed him to call someone, he wasn't going to be a lot of help without it.

He gritted his teeth and walked back to where he came from, shifting one cane under his arm to grab hold of the phone and slip it into his pocket. His arms—easier to work out than his legs, but still never as reliable as he'd like them to be—ached, even after or maybe because of the workout he'd given them the day before.

The vacuum shut off just as Archer let out one of his loudest grunts in months. Archer breathed hard, the muscles in his arms, legs, and chest hurting. He needed to calm down. Breathe in, breathe out.

A knock came at the door. "Mr.... Archer? I'm sorry about the noise. The vacuum sort of *exploded* a little, I don't know why—I might have missed some of the glass when I picked it up. Um, if you want, I can file the issue with my mom and then we can talk about a replacement." She stopped speaking and knocked again. "Archer?"

Archer opened his mouth. He wanted to speak, to tell her it was all right, to breathe in relief that she was fine, too. He felt stupid for picturing her unconscious on the floor, for imagining himself some kind of savior.

But it all hurt and right now, all he could do was breathe.

"Archer?" The door creaked open slowly and Brielle's svelte fingers hooked around the edge as she peeked around the corner. Her jaw dropped and she shoved the door all the way open. "Are you okay? You're... You can... Your face is flushed." She rushed to his side, her hands hovering out around him, but she pulled them back quickly, searching his face for an answer. His legs were shaking. He'd gotten up too quickly.

"My chair," he managed. He cleared his throat and pushed through it despite the pain. He wasn't about to undo what little progress he'd made with her after their disastrous beginning. "Please."

"Right!" Brielle jumped up and clapped her hands together before rushing to the chair. She pushed it into place behind him—

not without an effort, since one half was still locked and she had to lift it up—and stood back. "Should I...?"

"Locks," said Archer. "On the sides."

"Oh!" Brielle bent over, her loose hair hanging over the side of the chair. She fumbled around with the lock on one side until she figured out it was already locked, then locked the other. "Okay," she said, whipping her loose hair over her face with one hand.

Archer shifted himself slightly and then let himself collapse into the chair, tossing the canes against the bed. He took a deep breath and ran a trembling hand over his face. It felt hot to the touch. He'd been one second away from a full-out panic attack.

Brielle leaned toward him and clenched her hands together, almost as if she were stopping herself from reaching out to touch him. "Can I get you anything? Should I... Should I call for an ambulance?"

Despite everything, Archer laughed, shaking his head. "No need."

"Your... nurse?" Brielle leaned closer, and that loose tendril of hair swung down again. She tucked it behind her ear, driving Archer crazy. "Do you need medication or...?"

Archer cradled his face and took a deep breath. "I'm fine. I just..." He went to move his chair and scrunched his face up in pain. "I moved too fast and I pulled some stuff." He opened one eye and then the other to find Brielle staring down at him, her hands clasped together almost as if praying, her face panic-stricken. "Maybe you can get me some ibuprofen. In the top drawer in my bathroom."

Off on a mission, Brielle scrambled into his bathroom, appearing with the bottle just a moment later. She handed it to him and was off again, this time coming back with a glass of water before he'd even managed to shake a couple of pills from the bottle onto his hand.

She gave him a beautiful smile, although it was fleeting. "I won't make you drop it this time. Promise."

He let her exchange the bottle for the glass, staring up at her the whole time. "You mean, I won't make *you* clean it up." He tore his eyes away and swallowed the pills, downing the whole glass.

They stared at each other for what felt like a full minute. She reached for his glass and he handed it to her, but then she still stood there, staring.

"So," he said. "The vacuum?"

"Oh!" Brielle looked shocked. "Right." She kept looking over her shoulder as if the vacuum might sneak up on her. "I'm so sorry! I don't know what happened. I heard some of the glass, I think, but I don't know how that basically caused the engine to catch fire—"

"*Catch fire?*"

Brielle jumped. Archer hadn't meant to speak so loudly. Her palm bobbed up and down as if to reassure him. "Well, it sparked. Then the whole thing got black. I panicked and ran for a glass of water, and then I remembered there was fire extinguisher in the front closet, and *then* I remembered I should at least *unplug the dang thing.*" She winced. "I'm sorry."

Archer opened his mouth and then closed it, thinking.

Brielle seemed to mistake his hesitance for condemnation. "I... This has never happened to me before, so I'm sorry, I don't know exactly how we file a complaint with—"

Something struck Archer, something she'd said earlier. "Your mother?"

"Oh," said Brielle. "Right. I guess I said that." She threw her shoulders back. "My mom owns the company."

"I thought the owner's name was... Clark?"

"Leah Clark. Yeah, we have different last names. She went back to her maiden name after the divorce. She built her business practically from scratch after my dad left."

Archer was impressed there was such fire in her eyes. She seemed so proud of her mother and well she should be. "Keeping it in the family then?" That reminded him too much of his situation with his dad—of how his dad would have liked things to be. He pushed the negative thoughts down.

Brielle bounced her head back and forth. "Sort of. Although Mom is liable to fire me any day now."

"Because of this?" He gestured toward the doorway and the surprisingly explosive vacuum somewhere far behind her. "I doubt it was anything you did. Don't worry about it. I'll just get a new one."

"No, not because of that alone, but thank you. Really." Brielle swallowed. "I feel bad, though."

Archer glared at her, hoping he appeared commanding. "Don't." He didn't want to say what she might have guessed just by how often she was called to clean for him—they could afford to buy a new vacuum. His parents certainly could anyway. It made him feel bad to think that way when he'd thought of her as working for minimum wage, of taking the first job she could find— although he supposed maybe she was better off than he'd expected since her mother owned the company.

She nodded and didn't say anything more. She shifted, probably about to leave him to clean up that mess, but Archer wasn't about to let her go.

"Why will you be fired?" he asked, genuinely curious. "You do a great job."

"Thanks." She smiled and tucked that piece of hair behind her ears again. Did she *want* him to pull her onto his lap? His shoulder ached just then, almost as if in punishment for his dirty thoughts. She turned around and put the glass down atop his dresser, then pulled the hair tie out of her ponytail. Her long, dark hair cascaded around her shoulders for a moment as she gathered it back up. She placed the hair tie in her mouth and bit down, her lips curling seductively.

Okay. I am definitely about to do something I regret. Pushing through the discomfort, he slapped both wheels and backed up a little, then moved forward a little, his own version of pacing. He stared at her feet. "Do you have an obnoxious client somewhere who's been complaining about you?" He couldn't help but offer a faltering smile. He knew she probably thought he was that obnoxious client if anything.

"Not that I know of... No, I should say no. Mom would definitely let me know if that was the case." She finished readjusting her hair and sighed.

Archer cocked his head and patted the corner of the bed beside him. "Sit down and tell your old uncle Archer what's going on."

She grinned. He felt like an idiot, but he'd made her smile, so maybe the silliness wasn't half-bad. She looked over her shoulder. "I should clean that mess—"

"It can wait. I can even help."

Brielle hesitated, bouncing on the balls of her feet and biting her lip. *God, woman, will you stop being so delectable? I'm sore all over and I really can't take it.*

"Unless you have somewhere to go right away after your hour's up..."

"No," said Brielle, shaking her head. "No plans at all today." A brief, impulsive thought shot into Archer's mind, but he knew it was really stupid of him. She practically collapsed onto his bed, the energy deflating out of her like she was a popped balloon. "Well, I *ought* to be spending hours scouring for jobs and drafting a dozen cover letters, but..." She left the rest unsaid.

Archer wove his fingers together and wrung them to distract himself from his naughtier thoughts. She was just at the foot of the bed and she was wearing the unsexiest maid costume he'd ever seen. But damn, did that ugly shirt cling to her. She could she make anything sexy. "Because you're getting fired?"

"Mom *said* I could work for her company as long as I need to. To save up and make sure there isn't a hole in my resume." She grimaced. "Although I've had to spin a bit of what I do so it doesn't seem like I've only cleaned since I was a teen."

"Like... helping a person with a disability?"

"No!" Brielle looked shocked and put one hand at the base of her throat. "Oh, god no. I wouldn't exploit you like that. I don't even... I don't do anything special for you."

Archer shrugged. It definitely wasn't something you could put on a resume, but he'd call waking up his shriveled heart "something special" indeed.

"No, I just mean like... Helping with scheduling, consulting with management, that sort of thing."

"How is that a spin?"

Brielle's face grew sheepish. "Mom is a one-woman show. I couldn't offer her much help that way if she wanted it."

"So why the job hunt?" Archer twiddled his thumbs and stared down at them, suddenly not sure he could keep looking at her when she was this close. "Our town too boring for you?"

"Not really. Or... I guess." Brielle tucked her hands under her thighs and turned her attention to the artwork his mother had painted that hung over his bed's headboard. "I don't really care where I go, as long as I have a job I sort of like."

"You don't like cleaning?" Archer felt like an idiot as soon as the words left his mouth. Because cleaning was sure to be many people's aspiration in life? God, he sounded stupid.

Brielle laughed, swinging her ponytail over one shoulder. "I actually could clean the rest of my life, so long as I had to do something. But I mean, I did study history and philosophy. I should probably do something with those subjects. And besides, Mom doesn't want me to stay in her house or keep working for her."

History and philosophy? He'd had no idea. He didn't know *what* he'd thought she was interested in, but that wasn't it. "Well, that blows," he said, not sure what else to say. "How long have you been job hunting?"

"Just a few months. I graduated last weekend."

"Oh!" She was younger than he'd thought. Not that he thought she was ancient, it was just... She *exuded* sexiness. He tended to associate that with *experience*. Now he felt really dirty. "Congrats."

Brielle shrugged. "Thanks." She raised her eyebrows. "Years of school loans and maybe at this rate, job hunting ahead, yay." She studied the painting again, clearing her throat. "Do you have an art degree?"

Archer nodded. "Yup. Mother wanted me to pursue a master's, but I had no need for it. Mother also enjoys painting. She did those." He pointed at the art above his bed.

"Nice," Brielle said, looking back at them. Then she glanced at him, the curiosity plain on her face. "How did you get a job drawing comics? That's so cool."

It was Archer's turn to feel sheepish. "Thanks." He wasn't sure if she really thought that, but she seemed genuinely interested. "It's a... long story." She didn't seem deterred. "Well, it sort of started the... opposite way of yours? I didn't want to work for my dad's company and he wanted me to work for him. Or... he would have."

"Would have?"

Archer swallowed. He didn't know why he was telling her this. "Well, he owns a construction company."

"Oh!" said Brielle, gasping. "Ward Construction! I see their trucks all over."

Archer laughed. "Yeah... But I bet you don't see any workers in wheelchairs in them."

"Oh," said Brielle, suddenly sad. "Oh, I... Yeah. I see." She paused. "But couldn't you help behind the scenes? Like in the office?"

"Probably." Archer ran a hand over the back of his head. His muscles were doing better. The pain reliever was probably kicking in. "But it's not like I had much interest in all that anyway. Besides, I think Dad's happy to keep me out of sight, out of mind." He gestured around him. "I owe half... No, more than half of everything to him throwing money at me to keep me out of the house and keep me quiet."

"I'm sorry..." Brielle bit her lip again and Archer had to go back to his wheelchair-pacing. "Guess we both have parents who don't want us to live at home?"

Archer scoffed, gripping both wheels hard in a lock. "You haven't met my mother yet."

Brielle stared at him, questioning. He wondered why he'd said "yet," but he knew his mother—she was bound to show up sometime she wasn't supposed to. "Hey," he said, trying to change the subject, but his voice was already shaking, "if you're really not busy today after we finish up here..." He lost his nerve.

Brielle's eyebrows arched. "I'm not!" She sounded almost like she was sure he wouldn't believe her.

"I... have a signing today. At a local comic shop." *Why the hell would she want to go with you to a comic shop? Not exactly the most welcoming place for a woman—particularly a woman this hot.*

Brielle's face lit up. "I'd love to come! I'd *love to!*"

Crap. Archer had been so caught up in the moment, he'd forgotten why he'd stayed away from dating to begin with.

Pauline was going to have to be their driver.

CHAPTER NINE

Brielle wondered if it would have been easier to just Google map where this shop was and to meet him there. She wanted to go home and change anyway. (Archer had been surprised to learn she lived just a few minutes from his condo. *Pleasantly surprised*, she might even dare to say. As if proximity made any difference to anything.) But Pauline had shown up before Brielle could leave—they'd lost track of time when cleaning up the mess of the dead vacuum—and she'd insisted Brielle come back to the condo after Archer's therapy exercises and that they'd all go together.

Archer's face wasn't that hard to read when Pauline offered the ride. He so clearly preferred Brielle's idea, but Pauline was a force to be reckoned with.

So now she was in the passenger seat of Pauline's van in front of Archer in the one and only seat behind her. Pauline had strapped Archer's chair in—apparently some of her patients just continued to sit in their chairs when she had them in her car, but Archer had insisted on sitting in the van's bucket seat. It had taken him a short while, but Pauline's vehicle was equipped perfectly to make it easier for him with grab bars and a ramp that lowered so he could make the step up.

Archer's face had turned a deep shade of red the entire process, which would have made him look more endearing, except that Brielle was worried he was ill from the exhaustion.

"Do you read these funny books? *The Mystics?*" said Pauline, her eyes focused on the road.

"*The Mystified.*" Archer sounded like he was about to laugh. "Come on, Pauline, you know this."

Pauline looked both ways before she executed a turn. "Excuse me if I can't follow all the things you kids do these days."

"You're like twenty years older than me," said Archer. "If that. Stop acting like an old woman."

Pauline waved a hand in the air, dismissing him.

But he continued. "They had comics in 'your day,' Pauline. Comics *before* your day."

Pauline nodded and slowed the van down, glancing over her shoulder to switch lanes. "If they don't have an actual Chris Hemsworth to look at, they aren't worth my time." She flicked her eyes to the rearview mirror. "Well, I mean, your *art* is always well done..."

"Sure, sure," said Archer. "Blame the writers."

The car fell into a slightly uncomfortable lapse of silence and Brielle felt compelled to fill it. "I prefer Loki to Thor."

"Ah," Archer said. "One of *those* women."

Brielle felt like he'd punched her in the gut. *So after all this, he's one of* those *guys, huh? Going to complain how all women love the bad boy and he doesn't have a chance because he's "so nice"?*

"What's that supposed to mean?" asked Pauline, more like a chaperone than ever.

Archer slapped his knees. "Nothing," he said. "Just... I guess she likes tall, dark, and handsome."

"Or more like pasty and evil?" said Brielle, unable to help herself. She felt relieved that was all he'd meant. "Not that I love the evil types in real life, let me assure you. But villains are where it's at in fiction."

Archer snorted.

"What?" Brielle turned around, ignoring the seatbelt now

digging into her shoulder. He was grinning, but he tried to hide his grin in his hands.

He stared at her, the mischievousness in his light brown eyes sending shivers down her spine. "Will you settle for slightly naughty?"

Brielle whipped her head around so fast, she practically got whiplash. She could feel her face coloring.

"Okay, you two. Grandma Pauline is still here, you know. She can only take so much pheromones floating in her direction."

Brielle buried her face in her hands. She'd known the guy for less than a week. This was ridiculous!

"*Pauline*," said Archer. "Be cool."

Brielle really, really felt like she was riding with her boyfriend and his mom on the way to junior prom.

Still, she didn't think she was imagining things. Even if Daniel —god, why did she too often think about Daniel?—had made it crystal clear much earlier he wanted her in his twin XL dorm bed. Other than with him, she didn't have much experience, so she wasn't sure how one normally did this thing. Other than she knew this situation wasn't exactly normal in its own right—not that Archer could help it.

Besides, he was so handsome and could sometimes—reluctantly—be charming, so he'd probably had a dozen opportunities to date even if he relied on a personal nurse driver. He just must have not wanted to.

He probably had fangirls waiting for him at this comic store right now, ready to jump him.

That was an image Brielle couldn't shake—only she was imagining herself holding up a poster board saying how much she loved him, herself waiting in line to shake his hand, herself crawling onto his lap.

A flush of heat from her midsection roared up and down her body. She needed to change the subject like yesterday. "I'm not a huge comic reader or anything. I mean, obviously, I've read *some*. But I haven't heard of your comic, sorry."

Archer didn't even hesitate. "No apologies necessary. It's not an entirely unheard of comic, but it's not exactly mainstream, either."

Oh. Brielle had been worried he'd be one of those comic book guys who think anyone—a woman especially—who only sees superhero movies is somehow "lesser than." "I should have asked to read a trade," said Brielle, happy she had Pembroke in her life to teach her words like that. Even though she never in a million years thought she'd meet a comic book artist, let alone maybe, possibly, date one. She cocked her head. She wasn't even sure she'd seen any in his condo.

"That's okay," he said. "I've only been on the book a few years." He sniffed. "You can look at one tonight."

Brielle had to stop herself from burying her face in her hands. Somehow, Archer acting like he didn't want her to see his book—then contradicting himself—was the most adorable thing she'd heard in ages.

Her phone buzzed and she fished it out of her purse to make sure it wasn't her mom, but it was just Gavin sending a photo of himself and his date, both looking hot and hipster-y in some kind of tight quarters café. Brielle had texted her mom earlier that she was going out, but all her mom had said back was, *Ok.* She was still waiting for the hammer to come down and the lecture about not looking for jobs.

She *had* looked for some that morning. She'd applied for three or four, although nothing really spoke to her. She'd finally gotten back *one* reply from the jobs she'd applied to the week before, thanking her for her application and stressing that there were many qualified applicants.

She didn't know what was worse: the few outright rejections, the "we got your stuff, but just so you know, you're probably not going to be good enough" emails, or the frequent, frequent dead silence. She'd had one Skype interview for a historical society in Iowa of all places about a month ago that went nowhere. That was actually the only interview she'd scored at all so far, and it'd come so early into her job-hunting process that she'd assumed this whole job-finding thing would be easy. Ha.

"We're here," said Pauline. She scoffed. "Not a lot of accessible parking." There weren't any parking spots, period. There weren't many uptown, where all the buildings seemed a little worn, like they were built back in the days of horses and carriages. But there were a lot of cars parked up and down along the block.

"Pull around the back," said Archer. "The owner said he'd open it up for me."

Pauline actually cringed as she pulled into the back alleyway. "This doesn't seem shady at all..." She stopped in front of a door next to a dumpster, ignoring the "No Parking / Cars Will Be Towed" sign and shifting the car into park. "Sorry about the lack of space. I need more on this side for the chair." She looked over her shoulder. "No offense, hon, but once I make sure you're situated, I think I'll spend the next couple of hours at that Starbucks we passed."

Archer unbuckled his seatbelt and waved a hand. "You can go home if you want. Don't worry about it. Mother will pay you the full extra three hours, but I doubt I'll need you again until it's time to go."

Pauline pulled the keys out of the ignition and hit some buttons, opening the door beside Archer and the door beside his wheelchair automatically, extending the ramp. "Nonsense. What's waiting for me at home? A husband who promised to give me a night off from two very dramatic preteen children. Let them bond with Dad for the day. Mom's getting her mocha."

Pauline exited the vehicle and started reaching for Archer's wheelchair and Brielle scrambled out of her seat, shoving her phone back into her bag. She had to be careful to hold her door as she opened it and slid out so it wouldn't hit the dumpster. She actually exhaled audibly when she managed to sneak out and shut the door without dinging it, like it'd all required physical exertion.

Looking at Archer slowly sliding out of the vehicle with the help of the grab bars, she felt bad for even making a peep.

"Can I help?" she said, wondering if that was the wrong thing to say.

Archer laughed, grunting, and nodded behind him. "Hand me my canes?"

Brielle reached under his extended arm, her face brushing his side as she grabbed hold of the canes. He felt warm and she had to fight the temptation to bury her face into him for more than a couple of seconds.

"Here," she said, backing up to give him more space.

He rested up against the first extended step of the ramp, taking the canes from her with one hand. He stared up above her head and laughed, gesturing upward.

Brielle slapped her hands above her head and felt how her hair was sticking up. Had his shirt been covered in static? She often did his laundry, so if it was, it was her fault. She swallowed and smoothed her tresses down, probably stroking her hair more times than was necessary.

Archer looked away as he slipped his arms through his canes—they kind of wrapped around his forearms when he used them—and swung his brace-covered legs down one at a time. "Can you... Um, go in from the front? And ask someone to open the door?"

Brielle jumped, clapping her hands together. "Okay." She felt relieved to be useful. She scrambled around the van, smiling awkwardly at Archer as she plastered herself against the wall and passed mere inches from him before heading down the alleyway. Turning the corner, she passed a couple of guys in comic book shirts who gave her a onceover as she headed for the door.

She'd wanted to look nice for Archer, but she didn't think dressing to the nines was a good idea for a comic book shop. So she'd just thrown on her nicest (albeit tightest) jeans and a slightly wrinkled flowery Boho top still in one of her boxes from her dorm room. Still, she felt like a freak as she stepped inside and saw the crowd gathered there. More than one group of people—almost all in comic book or flannel shirts, although some of the women had cute animal hats on as well—stopped talking to watch her warily as she headed for the busy cash register.

Brielle cleared her throat. "Um, excuse me…"

The guy behind the counter looked her over from top to bottom. Twice. "End of the line's that way." He handed a receipt to the guy in front of him along with a pen for him to sign. Brielle got a look at the stack of books the guy in the Pac-Man shirt was buying: all *The Mystified* except for one called *Wheels*.

"She's not *buying* anything," muttered Pac-Man guy as he signed the slip.

Brielle bristled. She'd discussed this before with Pembroke—that feeling that you weren't allowed to enjoy something if you didn't show up dressed for the part. (And sometimes not even then if you might be confused for a hot cosplayer.) She'd been to a comic shop before with Pembroke, a much nicer one in their college town, thank you very much.

Brielle ignored Pac-Man fan. "I came with Archer—Archer Ward? He asked me to get someone to meet him at the door."

That made everyone within earshot stop what they were doing. The cashier and the customer were both still clinging to the same receipt as they stared at her, wide-eyed, their hands frozen mid-movement.

"Oh," the cashier finally said. He snatched the receipt from the customer and picked up a phone. "George? Can you come to the front—pronto?"

The customer grabbed his bag and slinked his shoulders, stepping around Brielle and muttering something she couldn't hear. She watched him sit in one of the few empty folding chairs at the back of the store set up in front of a desk with stacks of graphic novels on it. There was a big cardboard cutout of a superhero Brielle only recognized from Archer's crumpled-up drawing.

So the guy had gone from outright contempt to muffled loathing. That's what happened when you dissed someone who'd shown up with the guy they were all here to see.

The cashier went back to ringing up the line of customers—the next guy was also buying *The Mystified*—and Brielle stood there, resting her hand on her cross-body purse, trying not to tap her toes and come across as impatient. But the truth was, she felt uneasy in such a place without Pembroke, and Archer being the only person she knew there made her feel even more awkward.

"What's up?" asked a middle-aged guy with short-cropped gray hair and countless visible tattoos. He even had big round black discs in his earlobes that made his ears bigger.

"This... lady," said the cashier, gesturing to Brielle with both hands like she was a display on *The Price Is Right*, "says Archer Ward is waiting at the door."

"Oh!" The middle-aged guy jumped and held out his hand. "George."

Brielle took it and shook. "Brielle."

George gestured over his shoulder. "Follow me."

Brielle did, excusing herself a few times as they slinked through the too-big-for-the-too-small-store crowd, although George just sort of sucked in his breath and maneuvered through them without saying anything like a ghost sliding through unnoticed. He stopped only at the front of the rows of folding chairs briefly, nodding at the front row, which had eight seats with sheets of paper tossed haphazardly on them reading, "Reserved." The only person on that side of the aisle in the front was a rather severe-looking woman who looked more out of place than Brielle did. She sat there, her legs crossed, in crisp slacks and a silky top more at home at a cocktail party, a pair of designer sunglasses resting on top of her head. Her attention was focused solely on her phone, which she kept in a case like it were an e-reader and prodded at with a stylus. "You can sit here during the presentation," he said. "How many others did Archer bring with him?"

"Tw—" Brielle started to say, then remembered Pauline was leaving for the next few hours. "Just me."

George nodded and strode over to the chairs, scooping up two of the "Reserved" papers and crumpling them in his hand. "The rest are for my staff," he explained. They'd just barely taken three more steps toward a door leading to the backroom before two girls in adorably eye-catching Batman and Wonder Woman dresses squealed from the line of people standing to the side and rushed to take those two seats.

Once George got to the "Employees Only" door, he held it open behind him, revealing a mountain of boxes, a couple of computers with figurines perched all around them, a bathroom, and a couple of lockers in the back. Brielle took hold of the door and was about to follow when she glanced to her right and saw Pembroke.

"Pem?" she said, her jaw dropping.

George stopped ahead of her. "I'll head on back to let him in," he said, and Brielle nodded.

She hesitated, wondering if Archer was really expecting her to show up with George or to chat with him before his presentation began. It seemed the right thing to do—she could hang with Pembroke later, assuming she was here for the signing, which she seemed to be, as she was currently reading a volume of *The Mysti-fied*—but there was this niggling worry at the back of her mind, the shock at seeing her friend after almost a week of dead silence. "Pembroke?" she said again, and she finally looked up.

Her eyes widened. She shut her book and slipped back behind the line of people.

"Pembroke?" called Brielle, and she let go of the backroom door to follow after the skittish young woman.

She almost lost sight of the oversized cargo pants and the tight black T-shirt she knew belonged to her diminutive friend, but Pembroke's thick-rimmed black cat-eye glasses and blue-streaked hair made her easy to spot, even amongst so many others with just as much indie fashion style.

"Excuse me," Brielle kept saying, finally letting out an exasper-ated sigh, holding her breath, and just shoving forward through the crowd. She grabbed Pembroke by the shoulder and spun her around. "Did you seriously just try to avoid me...?"

Pembroke's gaze flittered up to Brielle's and she adjusted her glasses with the hand not holding on to the book, rolling her shoulder out of Brielle's grasp. "Sorry," she said, almost too quietly to be heard.

"What?" said Brielle, slouching down to hear her better over the noise.

Pembroke straightened her back. "I said I'm sorry, okay?"

Taken aback, Brielle stepped on a guy's foot. "Sorry," she said, over her shoulder, feeling the full fury of the greasy guy's glare. Ugh. This close, it seemed apparent the guy was way overdue for a shower.

She grabbed Pembroke by the arm again. "Can we go somewhere to talk? Somewhere quieter? Like outside, maybe?"

Pembroke swallowed visibly as she cradled her book to her chest. A receipt stuck out like a bookmark. "The panel is about to begin. I don't want to miss it."

Brielle frowned. "You came all this way to see Archer?"

"It's only an hour away." Pembroke said. "Archer Ward doesn't do much traveling, so his rare appearances are usually within the vicinity of his hometown."

They both stared at each other for a minute. "What are *you* doing here?" asked Pembroke at the very same moment Brielle asked, "But why did you come here without letting me know?"

"I forgot you lived here," said Pembroke, holding her book higher up to her chin and practically pouting.

Brielle gripped her purse over her abdomen where it hung, grunting when someone trying to make her way across the room bumped into her from behind. She spoke loudly to be heard. "Why haven't you answered any of my messages? Or any of Lilac's and Gavin's?"

Pembroke wagged an eyebrow. "Lilac hasn't sent me any. A handful of 'look at me, I'm so perfect and fun and flighty' photos she tagged all of us into, but nothing besides that."

"Okay," said Brielle, shaking her head. It was like dealing with a ninth grader. She almost made Nora look mature. Almost. "So what? Gavin and I have been trying to reach you..."

Pembroke shrugged. "I haven't been online or on my phone much."

Brielle cradled her forehead in the tips of her fingers. *Then how did you know Lilac hasn't sent you many messages?* she wanted to say. But she clearly wasn't getting anywhere here.

"Wait," said Pembroke, studying Brielle suddenly as if she were an alien species, "is that disabled guy you mentioned cleaning for, the one who made you put your foot in your mouth so to speak, actually *Archer Ward?*"

"So you *have* read my messages!" Brielle clenched her fists at her side. "You were just ignoring them!"

"I've been too busy to write, okay?" Pembroke pushed her glasses up her nose again. "And I didn't think you'd want to talk to me anymore."

Brielle cocked an eyebrow. "Why wouldn't I?"

Pembroke bit her lip and shrugged. She really was one of Nora's peers. The quieter, more sullen, stubborn variety. She grimaced. "How could you not tell me it was *Archer Ward* you were talking about?"

Brielle crossed her arms. "Maybe I would have if you'd bothered to return my messages." She looked over her shoulder, taking in the packed store. "Besides, I didn't know he was famous at first."

"'Famous' is a bit of a stretch," said Pembroke, "but yeah, I guess. *Within a certain community.*"

Brielle frowned. There seemed to be an accusation there under Pembroke's words, the kind the two of them used to vent about—the "you're not welcome here, faker."

Pembroke tapped her fingers against the back of her book. "Did he actually... *invite* you here?"

"Yes," snapped Brielle, actually feeling herself raise her nose in the air. "I'm actually one of his *guests.*"

Pembroke scrunched her nose. "Why would he invite his *cleaning lady?* That he's known for a week... Oh my god." She covered her mouth and hissed. "Have you *slept* with him?"

"Don't be crass," said Brielle. She didn't much like this post-graduation Pembroke. Or maybe that was how Lilac had seen her all along. Quiet but judgmental. Off doing her own thing and looking down on anyone who thought that dating was actually something humans did, not something to be completely avoided. So instead of admitting the truth, she let her draw her own conclusions. "That's none of your business."

"I wasn't sure if he could even..." Pembroke gestured with one hand, not very clearly, but there was little else she could mean.

It was Brielle's turn to scrunch her nose. "You know, I don't get—"

"Ladies and gentlemen," called a voice over an overhead speaker. "If you could take your seats—or your places, really. Sorry there's practically standing room only. We're about to get started."

Pembroke pushed past Brielle to make her way back to the presentation area.

Brielle squared her shoulders and squeezed through people to walk beside her. "This isn't over," she hissed. "I'll talk to you afterward."

Even though Pembroke nodded, Brielle wasn't very confident she'd heard her.

CHAPTER TEN

Archer often asked himself why he did these things in the weeks leading up to his events. He *really* wasn't sure why he did these things when they made him feel so... Looked at. Examined. Unreal.

But he knew that a part of him really liked it. A part of him liked moving his world beyond Pauline, his mother, and his basketball buddies. A part of him liked to see the people who sent him fan messages in person. (Fortunately, any trolls who sent him messages seemed reluctant to venture out to meet him face-to-face. The closest he got were some rambling people who thought he had a textbook knowledge of the comic and could follow every long-winded conversation they had about the story—which was also not even up to him.)

He'd made it both exponentially worse and exponentially more thrilling by inviting Brielle along. He still couldn't believe he'd done that... And that she'd accepted.

He sat in his chair in the alleyway alone—it'd taken a bit to convince Pauline she didn't need to wait there with him like a parent dropping an elementary school student off, and besides, her van was kind of in the way of the door swinging out—tapping his knees, trying to calm the discomfort he felt for so many reasons.

Finally, George opened the door and grinned, shaking his hand.

"Thanks for coming, man."

"Thanks for having me."

George stepped out into the alleyway so he could hold the door. "Careful of all the boxes. We tried to clear a path."

Archer grimaced as he navigated his chair through the mess of a backroom. He didn't say anything, though, because he appreciated the extra effort George had gone to, even if he felt like a towering pile of boxes might fall down on his head at the slightest wrong move. And since this was the second time he'd had a signing here, he was used to the tight space.

"Your girlfriend saw someone she knew, but I told her where to sit."

Archer stopped moving at that, realizing he'd just chalked Brielle's absence up to her waiting in the audience. Then he realized George had just called her his "girlfriend." "She's..." he started, then realized how juvenile it would sound if he insisted she wasn't his girlfriend. And was it so bad that George thought that hottie was his?

Wasn't that maybe, just maybe, within the realm of possibility soon anyway? If he could get over his reservations and actually make his secret fantasies a little less secret.

But she was planning to get a job out of town. And he was... He was different. Not worth slowing some woman's life down or outright derailing it.

But then again... Did it have to be something serious? Couldn't they just enjoy each other's company... for now?

Archer swallowed. But that was it. He *didn't* want to enjoy her company just for now. He'd only known her a week and it was stupid to even imagine anything long-term—he'd never imagined himself with *anyone* long-term—but he knew one thing:

When she left, she would take a little piece of his heart with her.

He could handle that if his love was unrequited. He could handle that if he never knew whether or not his love was requited. But if they gave into these feelings he had, the feelings he sort of, maybe, thought she might be developing for him, and then they had to go their separate ways?

His heart would shatter beyond repair.

He shouldn't even be encouraging her.

George didn't notice Archer's sudden crisis of conscience. He plastered himself gently against the boxes to shift around Archer. "You're right on time," he said. "Let me check with the front and see if we should get started."

He left Archer alone in the backroom. Archer paced with his wheelchair, pushing the wheels back and forth. He'd been so consumed by the idea of being in a relationship that he'd almost forgotten George had said Brielle hadn't come with him because she'd met someone she knew. Who did she know at a comic book store? She seemed mildly interested in comics, but... What if the person was a guy?

He really didn't know much about her, did he?

Archer wasn't sure how long he spent there. He didn't even feel like checking his phone. He heard "ladies and gentlemen" over the loudspeaker, followed by some more mumbling, and then George opened the door to the store.

Archer felt like a rock star.

A rock star in a no-name town with several hundred fans instead of several hundred thousand, but a rock star nonetheless.

He waved and did his best to smile as he sent his wheels rolling, eager to make use of the meager free space they'd left for him. Staff members actually held the line back with their arms extended, like they were keeping fans from jumping him. (More likely, they were keeping fans from standing in his path to the table so they wouldn't get their toes run over, but Archer's fantasy decided not to acknowledge that.)

He rolled past the cutout of The Mystified, alter ego of Derek Diggerson, and up to the small mic at the table that had some of his works on display. He cringed a little to see *Wheels* there, but the comic store probably needed the opportunity to sell out whatever backlog of copies they'd ordered years ago when it had come out.

"Thank you," he said, clearing his throat. An electric shock practically ran through him. They'd seated Brielle right in front of him. Brielle, with those too-tight-jean-covered legs crossed so perfectly, with that top that moved like water over her whenever she shifted, revealing a deep dip of her perfectly-toned skin.

Her mouth was parted slightly, her eyes focused on him.

If it weren't for the fact that the girls beside her suddenly squealed, and his gaze roved over the row, he might have totally missed that his mother was sitting right next to Brielle.

Thankfully, George sat beside Archer and led the panel, asking all the questions and helping re-direct Archer's focus when his panic started overtaking him. He wasn't sure how he would have gotten through it otherwise. Actually, almost as soon as it was over, he barely remembered *how* he'd gotten through it. It was like he blinked, was enveloped by this feeling like he wasn't even there in his own body, and then it was over. Now the interested customers were lining up to have him sign their books.

His gaze kept flitting to where Brielle and his mother were sitting, but the line had already blocked them from view.

Not seeing them—not knowing if now that the presentation was over, his mother was asking Brielle questions—was worse than seeing them after all.

"We *love* your work! Do you remember us?"

Dazed, Archer looked up and realized he'd instinctively took the latest volume of *The Mystified* from a young woman's outstretched hand, that the girls who were sitting in the front row just a few seats over from Brielle were now standing in front of him.

"Sorry?" he said, willing himself to focus. He slid the book in front of him and picked up a black Sharpie.

The girl on the left practically bounced. "We've met you before. We came to your signing here last year."

"Oh." *Smile, Archer, smile.* "Thank you!"

The girl on the right opened a copy of *Wheels* she had on her, and sure enough, it was already signed and already had a drawing of his main character scribbled on in green marker. He cringed, but he tried not to let it show. He hated looking at his old work, and *Wheels*—panned the Internet over for its "contrite" and "clunky" story, the one comic story he'd ever written himself—was the worst offender.

"Gini?" he said, reading the book inscription.

She shut the book and giggled. "He *remembered*!" she gushed.

Oops. Is it too late to tell her I read the book inscription?

George leaned over and whispered, "Just a few minutes with each, if that's okay?"

"Oh, right." Archer shook his head. "Do you want a quick drawing...?" He looked up, waiting for the other one to tell him her name.

"Becca," she said, her lips souring just a little. "Sure. Derek's cat please."

Archer laughed. He hadn't even meant for the animal to be that cute, but it was a fairly frequent request. He wrote a note thanking Becca for her readership and signed his name, grabbing a brown Sharpie to start the sketch of Lina, The Mystified's (Derek Diggerson's) feline friend.

"Um," said Gini, "I asked this last year, but... Are you married?"

Archer's pen stopped moving. "No...?" Why was he framing it like a question?

Gini squealed and glomped on to Becca's shoulder. Becca rolled her eyes. "But there was a woman in the 'Reserved' section who doesn't work here..."

"That was probably his *mom*," insisted Gini.

"The *other* woman, the one spilling out of her top."

Archer sputtered. Actually *sputtered* out loud. It wasn't even like Brielle was *that* busty. Yet he clearly wasn't the only one drawn to her cleavage.

Gini looked over her shoulder, wincing. "Oh. She's not there anymore."

Archer's heart sank—not that he expected her to leave without saying anything to him, even if she had another ride home. It would make Monday awfully awkward if she did.

Archer quickly finished up Becca's drawing and slid it her way, smiling again. "Thank you so much for your support," he said, blowing on the page to help dry it. He winked. "Maybe I'll see you next time."

Becca cradled the book to her chest, beaming, stepping slightly aside to let Gini through. Gini reached into a tote bag she had over her shoulder, rifling through what easily looked like half a dozen books, and plunked the latest *The Mystified* down in front of him. She slid her signed copy of *Wheels* behind that, looking up at George. "They said we had to limit it to two copies signed, and at least one had to be bought here." She dug into her tote and waved a receipt around. Archer noticed an identical copy of the latest *The Mystified* still in her tote as she shifted things around. "So I was hoping you could sign my *Wheels* a second time?"

Pushing down his feelings of disgust at his own work (without which, he reminded himself, he was unlikely to have gotten *The Mystified* gig), Archer smiled and reached to put *Wheels* atop the pile to get signing it out of the way.

Gini actually leaned forward and placed her hand atop his as he did. "You don't know how many times I've read *Wheels*. You don't know *how much* it means to me."

Archer cleared his throat and tried to gently pull the book closer to him to free his hand. "I'm so glad to hear. Thank you." He'd gotten a few messages from people like that, especially other people with disabilities, which, he had to admit, made him feel just a little bit proud, despite the problems with the work.

It took some doing, but Archer did manage to free his hand and open the book. "Which character should I draw this time?" he asked, writing a second note on the page across from the first.

"Do you want to get coffee after this?" asked Gini.

"*Gini!*" Becca slapped Gini's arm playfully.

"What?" Shrugging, Gini readjusted her tote bag strap. "I want to tell him how much the book means to me, and this guy who works here keeps staring daggers at me, so I figure we should step aside and let the rest of the line get their autographs."

Archer just stared up, shell-shocked. He'd be lying if he didn't admit he'd seen a *few* fans online talk about him being attractive—if he didn't admit that made him feel good, despite everything, even led him to daydream about a gaggle of hot fangirls surrounding him, and Becca and Gini weren't that bad-looking at all, far from it—but he'd never had to deal with these kinds of compliments outside of the comfort of his own head. If he'd detected flirting at any of his previous signings, it didn't really mean much because no one had outright said anything.

"I, uh, have plans," Archer mumbled. He quickly scribbled a squirrel—it was important to the plot of *Wheels*, and he'd already drawn Todd, the main character—and blew on it before sliding it back to her.

"How about another day?" asked Gini, undaunted. Her eyes sparkled. "I live just a couple of hours away."

"You live a couple of hours away?" asked Archer, opening up her other book to write an inscription. His usual "thanks for your support" message seemed awfully dull and dumb in this situation, but he scribbled it anyway. "And you came all this way?"

"More like *six*," said Becca, and it was her turn to get playfully slapped by Gini.

"I can make the trip for *you*," said Gini. She raised her eyebrows in such a strange, seductive way that it was all Archer could do to focus on the generic drawing he added of Lina. When finished, he didn't even blow on it before closing the book and pushing it back at Gini. When he dared to meet her stare again, he swore she looked like an eager puppy.

"I, uh..." Archer's gaze roved around the store. He found her. Brielle was over in the corner behind some of the crowd milling around, standing but looking unfazed by the crowd around her. She had her wrist looped through one of the shop's bags, which looked heavy with purchases, and she was engrossed in a graphic novel. He wasn't sure from this distance, but he was pretty sure he recognized *Wheels*. Of course she'd be reading that one.

Still, she was reading his work. She'd *bought* his work. He could have gotten her free copies if she'd asked.

He turned back to Gini and smiled. "Thank you, but no. I have someone." He didn't have to explain more. Let her think what she would. The "someone" he had was just someone he couldn't stop thinking about. Someone he would give anything to be with—in theory—if he just knew it weren't impossible.

"Told you," said Becca.

"Oh," said Gini, clearly disappointed. She gave him a faltering smile. "But I can still give you my number—"

"Thank you, ladies," said George, leaning in front of Archer to sort of stand between them. "But we have a long line here."

Gini's face soured as she looked George up and down. She gathered her books and walked away, and Archer lost sight of the pair in the crowd.

He signed for over an hour without incident, although he had a strange, fluttering feeling whenever one of the women especially seemed overly enthusiastic—not that anyone else outright flirted with him the way Gini had. Every few people, he caught a glimpse of the front row and saw his mother still sitting there, her lips pursed, engrossed in her phone. He kept glancing to the side as well to keep an eye on Brielle. She stayed there reading for quite some time, although he was sad to discover she'd moved and he lost sight of her about forty minutes into it.

He tried to focus on the fans. It was why he was there, after all. He hadn't arranged this signing to show off to Brielle—he hadn't even known she existed less than a week ago—but he had to admit that a small part of him really wanted her to be impressed. And that wasn't fair to the people who'd traveled to meet him today.

He let go of all of his anxieties and all of his distractions and just enjoyed interacting one-on-one with his fans and their crazy theories and their genius-level memories about every detail of everything he'd ever worked on. It wasn't until he found himself in front of another cute girl—this one with those 1950s-style glasses that were all the rage again among hipsters and a streak of blue hair—that he remembered this wasn't just any other signing.

"Do you want them personalized?" he asked, referring to her copies of *Wheels* and *The Mystified* volume 18.

"Sure, thanks." She spoke so softly, it was hard to hear her over the roar of the crowd behind her. There wasn't anybody left in line, but he knew George often scheduled these types of things to coincide with sales and tabletop games, so the size of the crowd had barely diminished.

"What's your name?" he asked.

"Pembroke," she said.

"That's a pretty name." Archer was sure he wasn't imagining the slight flush on her cheeks. He started writing his usual message. "Which character do you want a drawing of?"

"Oo," she said, gaining more confidence. "That's really hard for me to decide!"

Archer grinned, tapping the copy of *Wheels*. "Well, you get one per book signed. And they don't have to be from the same series. I could do Derek or his cat or even Superman or your grandma if you have a picture..."

Pembroke laughed. The smile lit up her face, and Archer could have easily seen himself falling for her if he were ten years younger. "Then I'll have both Todd and the squirrel, please," she said, referring to the protagonist of *Wheels*.

Now it was Archer's turn to blush. He couldn't help but think of how his critics wondered if Todd was just a self-insert character. They weren't entirely wrong. But half the world seemed to say "write what you know," while the other decried anyone who wrote a Mary Sue (or Gary Stu, in his case). He hadn't mastered the right balance, and besides, writing wasn't his strong suit. He was halfway through drawing Todd's wheelchair when Pembroke spoke again. "Um... Have you been dating Brielle long?"

Archer felt like she'd just dumped a glass of cold water over his head. "You know Brielle?" He glanced back to where he'd seen her last, but she was still missing. Or she'd morphed into a man a head shorter and with twice as much girth flipping through the latest *Captain America*.

"We went to school together." Pembroke fiddled with the handle on her plastic bag. "Um, college, that is."

This girl is the same age as Brielle? He'd pegged her for seventeen at the oldest. Suddenly, he felt incredibly relieved. "You're the friend she saw when she got here?"

"I guess?" she said. She looked over her shoulder, maybe looking for Brielle, but she didn't seem to find her, either. "We didn't talk much before the panel started."

Archer finished his drawing of Todd and blew on it, trying to seem as casual as possible. "Did she tell you we were dating?"

Pembroke's lips pinched. "Not explicitly, no. But I knew she was your cleaning lady, and she said she came with you... And after the messages she sent me about you, I just assumed the two of you would wind up dating."

Archer's eyebrows arched as he smoothed the title page on the copy of an older volume of *The Mystified*—the first volume he'd done the art for, actually. "Now I'm curious."

"What?" said Pembroke, clearly confused. "The messages?"

Archer's Sharpie halted at the top of the page. He tore his gaze away. "You said they led you to believe we'd be dating. You've got to admit, that's pretty intriguing..."

Pembroke clutched her plastic bag. "I probably overthought them," she mumbled.

He wanted to keep prying, but it was clear he wasn't getting anywhere with her. Besides, anything he said might get back to Brielle. If he wanted to know, he should really just ask the woman herself. He focused on finishing his drawing, trying not to think about Brielle and how much he wanted to ask this girl.

"Um, she was really worried she'd been rude to you," said Pembroke, unbidden. "That first day."

He winced. It was like a punch to his gut. He suspected—he

basically knew—that first day hadn't gone well, but he'd tried to move past it with Brielle. It hurt to have it confirmed again. He blew on the drawing and pushed the book toward her. "Well, we, uh, talked about it."

"Oh, good." Pembroke smiled, flustered. "That's... good. Um, thanks." She scooped the books up and cradled them against her chest.

"Thank *you*," he said. She stared a bit longer—she may have shared that look he'd seen in Gini's eyes—before nodding and turning to leave.

"Hey, babe." A guy sidled up to Pembroke from somewhere in the crowd. "You see your... comic guy? Ready to go?"

George said something to Archer, but he was, wrongly he knew, too intrigued by the couple next to him to fully pay attention. They were just a few steps away, so it was hard not to hear them, even with the buzz of the crowd in the store.

Pembroke spoke so quietly, even her boyfriend didn't seem to hear her. He hunched over. Archer found his khakis and polo shirt a little at odds with his surroundings, although there was something about that ever-present smirk on his face that helped it make more sense. "What?"

"...*go*," hissed Pembroke, more loudly. "We have to go. Like this second."

Now Archer was really intrigued.

"...Is that okay? Archer?"

Archer snapped his head back toward George, noticing for the first time that his mother was no longer seated in the front row. "What? Sorry?"

George stepped around the table, moving several piles of books closer to him. "Can you sign these to keep in the store for selling later?"

"Oh, sure." He picked up a Sharpie again.

"Thanks, man." George left, heading toward where groups were already setting up several tabletop games.

"Okay, okay, chill." The guy next to Pembroke looked

disgusted. He scanned the crowd and put an arm around Pembroke's shoulder absentmindedly.

"Stop. Not here." Pembroke shrugged her way out of the guy's half-embrace, going so far as to shove his arm away.

He looked down at her like she'd slapped him. "What? So you're going to pretend we're not dating whenever we're in public? I don't care if you saw her. *Let* her see us." He put his hand back around her.

"*Stop,*" said Pembroke, shrugging herself out of his reach, moving farther away this time.

The guy looked like he wanted to slap *her.*

"Hey," said Archer before even realizing he'd been outright staring at them. He wheeled around the table to get closer to them. "She said to stop."

The guy stared down at Archer and then laughed. "You're serious? You think you can take me or something?"

"Not every conversation needs to be a pissing contest," snapped Archer. He looked at Pembroke. "You okay?"

Pembroke adjusted her glasses. "Yeah, I just... I want to get out of here."

"Why don't I call someone over—"

"Mind your own business!" said the guy, stepping between Archer and Pembroke. He sized the man in the wheelchair up and down, one hand clenched, almost like he wished he could hit Archer but knew he could never get away with hitting a man with a disability. It was the old "would you hit a man with glasses?" to the nth degree. "This is my girlfriend, and I wasn't doing anything to hurt her—"

"No, you were just making her extremely uncomfortable. And she told you so. And you went ahead and did it again anyway."

The guy opened his mouth.

"Daniel?"

He turned and Archer followed his gaze as well.

Brielle stood behind Pembroke, her plastic bag hanging limply from one hand.

CHAPTER ELEVEN

As if finding Pembroke and having to deal with her acting like Brielle had stabbed her in the back somehow wasn't crazy enough, then there was the matter of the older woman she sat next to who asked her if she worked for the store. When Brielle said no, she asked her if she was *really* a fan of her son's work because she looked almost as out of place as she did—Brielle hadn't known what to do other than to say "yes," silently thank god that the presentation started quickly so the woman stopped talking, and then jump up almost the moment it was over to hide in the corner of the store to avoid any more questions. She just wasn't ready to speak at length to *Archer's mother*.

She'd spent a while staring at Archer from afar, watching him interact with his fans and light up with such a smile, she almost forgot she'd ever seen him as anything but cheerful and charming. She felt like an idiot just slack-jaw staring, though, so she quickly ran to buy a copy of every one of Archer's books for sale there (the line was much better after the presentation than before) and took her spot back in the corner, burying her nose in the book that most caught her eye—the one about the guy in the wheelchair. She noticed as soon as she opened it that Archer had written, not just drawn, that one, so it made her even more eager to devour it. She kept looking up to see Archer sketching, smiling at fans, and laughing. She knew she didn't imagine the women and maybe even a few men flirting with him. She couldn't blame them. She wondered if half of them were only here because he was hot, not just a good artist.

But soon, she was actually genuinely engrossed in the book. She kept turning the pages, reading about Todd and his squirrel and knowing how odd that sounded in her head, but it was really a gripping tale. When she finished, she looked on the side of the book for a volume number and was disappointed that there wasn't one, so the chances of a sequel seemed slim. She put the book down and pulled out her phone to Google more information, but she saw a text from Gavin.

His date had gone poorly... To say the least.

Brielle wondered if hearing about Pembroke would cheer him up.

She texted him back. *So sorry. I need to hear more details. Bad timing, I know, but I'm out and I ran into Pembroke. She's acting weird.*

Brielle could see Gavin start typing almost immediately. *How so?* Brielle felt bad that they weren't talking about his problem, but she supposed Lilac would be there for him later. She wasn't responding to the group conversation right now.

She ran from me, Brielle typed, her frustration causing her to type a little harder than usual. *Literally tried to escape from me after we made eye contact and I called her name. Then she wouldn't talk to me. She said she'd gotten my messages but thought I wouldn't want to talk to her anymore.*

Brielle was getting more annoyed the more she thought about it. A girl bumped into her without even saying sorry and she decided to head to a less congested part of the store to finish her conversation. She spared one last glance at Archer—he still had a bit of a line left, including, she noticed, Pembroke herself—and retreated toward a hallway leading to the bathroom.

Gavin sent a frowny emoji. *She's hiding something.*

What? Brielle typed. *I don't get why she'd even think I'd be mad at her. For not answering my messages? I didn't think I was being ignored. I assumed she was busy. Although now I KNOW I was being ignored.*

Where are you? How'd you run into her?

Brielle entered a wink emoji. *Sort of on a date? With Archer. He invited me to a comic book signing he's doing in town. Pembroke's apparently a fan.*

OMG!! How could you not tell me you were on a date?

I may have been exaggerating. It's not an official date. We've never been alone once the whole evening. His nurse even drove us and... I sat next to his mom.

Awkward. Gavin paused. *What'd she have to say?*

We didn't talk much. She doesn't even know who I am or that I know her son personally. I just wasn't ready for that conversation.

Go introduce yourself. It's going to be more awkward later once he introduces you and she realizes you sat next to her without saying anything.

Brielle typed a line—*You're assuming there will be a time when he introduces me...*—and then erased it. A big part of her was hoping, maybe even assuming, there'd be a time like that anyway.

I'm going to wait, she typed instead. *I know the types of questions she'd ask and I can't deal with any more moms judging my career prospects or lack thereof.*

That bad with your mom, huh?

You don't know the half of it, she typed. But she knew that made it all sound so much more dire than it was. *Anyway, I should try to catch Pembroke before she leaves. Any advice?*

Gavin typed for a bit and then paused. *Just tell her I miss her and if she gives you more attitude, I'm going to drive back up there and shake some sense into her.*

That eager to escape Chicago already?

You don't know the half of it.

She and Gavin probably were overdue for a heart-to-heart. But there was so much going on. She typed her farewells and decided to make her way back to the line to see if she could catch Pembroke before she left. She took only a few steps toward Archer's table, though, before she saw... Daniel.

Daniel. In a comic book store. He'd never had the slightest interest, had made fun of Brielle for even halfway entertaining Pembroke's excited ramblings about the latest release of this or that issue.

"Daniel?" Brielle said his name before she could stop herself, like he was Rumpelstiltskin and saying his name aloud would make him vanish in a tantrum.

Daniel whipped around and smirked at her. "Ah. Hello, Elle."

Brielle noticed as Daniel shifted that Archer had been behind him and he was staring up at Daniel and Brielle in utter puzzlement.

Daniel slid his arm around Pembroke and Pembroke looked at the floor. He was clearly gloating without even saying anything.

"Pem?" Brielle said, stepping closer. "What is going on?"

Daniel ran his free hand through his hair. "What's going on is this is my new squeeze." He squeezed her shoulder on cue, as if reveling in the pun.

Despite wanting to ignore his existence, Brielle looked up at Daniel. "*She's* your fiancée?" Brielle kept glancing back and forth between Pembroke and Daniel, waiting for either Pembroke's embarrassed face or Daniel's smug one to morph into something that remotely made sense. She'd spent graduation with Pembroke. Well, some of it. Daniel hadn't been in the picture.

"No, that bitch broke my heart." Daniel leered down at Pembroke, side-hugging her tighter. "Broke picked up the pieces."

Oh, gee, I wonder why. "You were still engaged a week ago." Brielle readjusted her cross-body purse's strap, suddenly irritated immensely by the way the strap dug into the side of her neck.

Daniel shrugged and nuzzled Pembroke's neck. He had to bend over quite a bit to reach it, so he looked ridiculous. Pembroke leaned away, avoiding his kiss.

"Give me a break," said Daniel, his mouth twisting. "Why do you care so much about people seeing us? You're making me look like an abuser." His mouth soured around the word.

Archer wheeled forward and Brielle couldn't help but feel

swoony at the determined look on his face. "Then maybe you should stop acting like one, okay?"

"Lay off," said Daniel. He looked at Archer and then Brielle and back again. "So are you a fan of this crippled douche, too, Elle?"

Brielle didn't even know how it happened. She didn't remember dropping her bag to the floor and then slamming her palm against Daniel's cheek, but her hand was out and it stung, and Daniel cradled his cheek and stared at her like she'd just raised the dead. "What the hell is wrong with you, you jealous bitch?"

He took a step forward and then screamed, bouncing with one foot in the air. He stared at Archer. "You wheeled over my foot!"

"You walked into me," said Archer, gripping his wheels tightly.

"I could *sue you*!" Daniel pointed at Archer and Brielle. "I could sue you both!"

"Try it." Brielle crossed her arms, feeling stronger than she had reason to.

"Messed up." Daniel shook his head, limping slightly as he shuffled around Brielle and made his way to the door. "You are all *messed up*. Get your own damn ride home, Pembitch."

As soon as he was out of sight, Brielle rounded on Pembroke. "Seriously, what the *hell*—" She cut herself off the moment she saw Pembroke dissolve into a puddle of tears.

Brielle thought about walking out on Pembroke right then and there, never knowing what the hell had gone through her head to date Daniel for even a week, to be so secretive and withdrawn over *Daniel*—big fucking mistake *Daniel*—and leave her to deal with the problems of her own creation.

But that wouldn't feel right. She owed Pembroke a chance to explain herself, to do better. She at least owed her a freaking ride in her time of need.

Only, she hadn't driven herself.

"I most definitely want to take her home, but..." Archer tapped his lips with his finger and Brielle tried to push aside all her thoughts about wanting to jump him. Wrong time, wrong place. "I'd feel terrible asking Pauline to drive an hour away and back this late at night. She's already on special overtime for me as is."

Brielle had a thought. "Plus, there's only the one seat in the back...?"

"I can sit in my chair in the van, that's okay."

"Don't worry about it," mumbled Pembroke, her eyes still glued to the floor. "I can call my dad or... Uber or something..."

"That would be one expensive Uber ride." Brielle sighed, waiting for Pembroke to look up and explain herself, but she didn't. "If you don't mind her riding back with us to your place, I can just take her back home from there once I get my car."

"What's all this...?" The older woman—Archer's mother—appeared out of practically nowhere, slithering through the dwindling crowd with a Starbucks coffee in her hand. "Archer," she said, gazing down at her son coldly, "did these ladies come with you?"

Archer ran a hand over his head, stifling a sigh. "Mother, this is Brielle and Pembroke."

Mrs. Ward shifted her purse and switched her coffee cup to her left hand in order to extend her right. "Charmed," she said as Brielle took it, although she didn't seem charmed at all. She took one look at Pembroke, still gazing at the floor, and forewent the handshake entirely.

Brielle straightened her back. "*I* came with Archer and Pauline, but I just wanted to give my friend a ride back home."

"Huh." His mom stirred her coffee with the little green rod sticking out of the small hole. "I just met Pauline at the Starbucks down the road and she didn't mention it."

Archer slapped his palm against his thigh. "Because she's not a gossip, Mother, she's my nurse and a friend. What are you doing here anyway?" Archer looked positively flabbergasted. "You promised me you wouldn't come."

His mom sipped her coffee calmly. "I said I had a charity dinner tonight."

Archer stuck his hands in the air, as if she were stating the obvious and it proved his point.

She shrugged. "I didn't say I was going to it instead."

Archer tousled his hair roughly and Brielle wanted to kick herself for thinking inappropriate thoughts within a few feet of one of his parents. "Does Dad know you're here?" he asked.

"Of course." The way she covered her face with her cup, the corners of her mouth twitching, made even Brielle suspicious of her declaration. "And I would cool it down, dear. I'm your ride home."

"*What?*" Archer looked as if he'd been punched in the stomach.

"I saw no sense in Pauline waiting around all evening in a Star-bucks, so I sent her home. I assured her she'd be paid for the full hours we agreed upon." She held her coffee cup aloft as her eyes scanned the room. "Don't they have a garbage around here...?" She wrinkled her nose as a display of rotting zombie statues caught her eye. "Ah." She stepped around the counter as if she owned the place and dropped the cup into a basket that must have been back there. The cashier stared at her as she did so, slack-jawed. She smiled and pointed at the group behind her. "My son is the star of the evening."

"Sweet Jesus," muttered Archer. He ground his teeth and whispered. "I'm so sorry, Brielle."

Brielle wanted to laugh, but the humiliated look on Archer's face stopped her.

"Mother," said Archer, clearly trying to keep an even tone to his voice as Mrs. Ward re-approached, "you can't just do things like this; we've talked about this!"

"Nonsense. Most people would be happy to have a mother half as attentive as me." She clapped her hands together. "I'll drive you both home. There's plenty of room in my van."

Brielle looked to Archer. "My car's at his condo."

"Oh." Mrs. Ward nodded, clearly considering Brielle's statement and assigning it more meaning than there was. "And you, dear?" she asked, staring at Pembroke.

Brielle nudged Pembroke's arm. "I live an hour away..." said Pembroke.

"I can drive her once I get my car," Brielle offered.

"Nonsense," said Mrs. Ward. "I love a long car ride."

"Heaven help us," said Archer, rotating his chair to get around his mom. "This is sure to be a *long* car ride indeed."

His mom nodded, turning after him. "Maybe we should stop somewhere... more accessible... so you can go to the bathroom before we hit the highway."

"*Mother. Please. For the love of God. Stop.*"

Brielle would have found the whole situation somewhat comical if it weren't so clear Archer was suffering.

CHAPTER TWELVE

If he had to choose between a slightly long car ride or his anger and embarrassment being the cause of his current nausea, Archer would have to wonder if it weren't a little of both. He always did get a little carsick. Although perhaps not that strangely, that did seem to abate somewhat when he could rely on Pauline to drive him instead of his mother. Pauline didn't make a habit of grating on his nerves.

Oh, boy was he regretting not pressing his dad to help him get his license and a car now.

Luckily, or not so luckily, depending on whether or not you considered what she *could* be talking about, his mother hadn't shut up about inconsequential aspects of her life, from the way Charlotte (whoever that was, Archer didn't remember) had made a big deal about Lucy's (also a name Archer didn't have a face to put to) dietary requests at a dinner the other day to her usual liquor store no longer carrying her favorite brand of white wine. She spent the first half hour droning on, Pembroke beside her upfront and Brielle in the back beside Archer, his wheelchair strapped in the trunk of the van. Every few minutes, he'd look over to Brielle and find her either staring out the window silently or, on occasion, even raising her eyebrows at something his mother had said. He wanted to apologize so badly.

But then he figured, well, he had told himself that acting on his desires with her would be foolish for so many reasons. Maybe a good, embarrassing few hours with his mother would be enough to slow things down. Surely (he hoped), it wouldn't be like when he and Brielle had had their awkward exchange the first day they'd met. They could still be friendly even after this spectacle, surely. It would just be enough to warn her away—far away—from getting more involved in his life than she already was.

"So where do you go to school, dear?"

Archer looked at the van's clock. *Nice. Only forty minutes into the drive does Mother even remember other people are in the car with us.*

"Dear?" his mother repeated, and Pembroke jumped in place, just realizing she might be talking to her.

"I graduated. I'm job hunting," she replied, quietly.

A rustling drew Archer's attention. Brielle drummed her fingers across the bag of books on her lap.

He felt bad that, thanks to his mother, she wasn't getting a chance to console her friend in the privacy she deserved. He still wasn't sure what was going on and what exactly had happened between the two of them, but it was clear that Daniel dick didn't like Brielle.

Which meant they'd either dated before or he'd simply really wanted her. That type of asshole never took the end of a relationship or a flat-out rejection very well. He shifted all the blame to the woman while his mouth betrayed the reality that he had nothing of substance to offer once you scraped away the good looks and whatever charm he'd turned on in the beginning.

The thought of that handsy asshole with his hands all over Brielle made Archer more nauseous. Brielle was upset—too upset. He was inclined to believe she and that Daniel had actually dated. There was no reason to be upset at Brielle over the idea—it was none of Archer's business, and she wouldn't be the first person burned by someone who turned out to be a grade-A asshole—but

Archer really, *really* wished now he'd taken a slug at the guy anyway. He may not have been able to reach his face, but he could have punched him in the dick.

He took a deep breath. He was better than that. But god damn it, that guy didn't deserve Brielle—or a cute girl like Pembroke, either.

He supposed Daniel didn't have either now, which was some consolation.

"Hmm, you might consider college," said his mother, oblivious as always that even if it were true that Pembroke meant she'd just graduated from high school, not everyone could afford higher education—or even saw the need for it. "Better prospects for a long-term job."

Pembroke cleared her throat. "I did go to college. I graduated last weekend. Biology major."

"Oh," said Mrs. Ward, clearly flustered. "You look so *young*." She took a hand off the wheel to pat Pembroke's shoulder affectionately. The car veered ever-so-slightly to the right. "But you'll be so grateful for that in a few years, believe me."

Pembroke shrugged. "We take the next exit," she said, as sullen as could be. Archer knew the feeling, although he suspected her mood had more to do with that jackass than his mother.

"The one that says—"

"The college," said Pembroke. "I live a few minutes down the road from it."

Crumpling plastic startled Archer a little and he realized Brielle had taken a chunk of her bag entirely into her fist. A little more effort and she'd probably twist the piece right off.

His mother took them off the highway and then merged with the light traffic to head east. "Well, a major in biology is a smart choice. I hope you plan to go to medical or nursing school now."

"No," said Pembroke. "Not really…"

Mrs. Ward took her eyes off the road for a bit to glare at Pembroke like she was gum found under her shoe. Archer ran a hand over his face, trying to relieve some of the stress with the massaging movements.

"Hmm," said Mrs. Ward. "I hope you'll reconsider. Although a girl like you with that bright, clear face... I suppose you could marry a doctor instead."

"*Mother!*" Archer could feel Brielle staring at him, but he couldn't look. He wrung his hands through his follicles instead.

"Oh, I don't mean anything by it. I asked her if she wanted to be a doctor herself, didn't I?" His mother pulled her visor down and fluffed her hair, even though it was dark out and the lights that went on around the mirror were distracting. Archer could feel his heart pounding a mile a minute.

"Besides," she continued, thankfully shutting the visor after half a minute, "there are still plenty of reasons to get at least a nursing degree. I know one man you can marry who's bound to inherit a respectable fortune who could definitely use a nurse for a wife." She stared pointedly into her rearview mirror.

"Mother," said Archer, swallowing, "if you could please stop bothering Pembroke..." He found himself looking at Brielle, the rest of his sentence lost on his tongue as she cocked her head, studying him. Did she just now realize he—well, his family, really—was well-to-do? Surely, she knew most people didn't have cleaners come six days a week.

Did that make her think less of him? Did that make him more attractive to her—did he even *want* any interest from her based on that anyway? Despite all the security and extras his dad's money provided, he didn't exactly feel like he was rolling in it. He simply... had the luxury to do things others couldn't through no action of his own. He hadn't earned that luxury. (Unless you counted by putting up with his mother's overzealous behavior.) And someone forced to clean houses to save up would probably not find that an endearing quality in a supposedly grown man.

"All right, all right." She readjusted the mirror, angling it toward Brielle. "How about you, dear? How do you know my son?"

"Take a right at the next traffic light," said Pembroke, cutting into the conversation. "The first house on the right side of the road."

The car went eerily quiet at that, but as his mother was executing the turn, she didn't seem aware that her question had gone unanswered.

Archer wasn't sure if it would be more awkward for Brielle to admit their connection or if he should just get it over with.

"Thank you," said Pembroke, unbuckling her seatbelt. "You really didn't have to go so far out of your way."

"No problem, dear," said Archer's mother as Pembroke opened the door.

"Pem," started Brielle, "please answer my messages—"

Pembroke turned around, clutching her bag to her chest, and nodded back at Archer. "It was nice meeting you."

Flustered, Archer looked to Brielle and back, the snub not going unnoticed. "You too... Thanks for your support. Uh, if you and Brielle need to talk about what happened—" But she'd already shut the door and walked away, heading down the driveway with her shoulders slouched.

The crinkle of the bag on Brielle's lap was hard to miss as she watched Pembroke walk away.

Laying a hand behind the passenger seat headrest to look over her shoulder as she backed out, Mrs. Ward spared a glance at Brielle again. "I still haven't heard about you."

Archer gestured toward Brielle beside him. "She's my house cleaner."

The van screeched to a sudden halt a little too quickly at the end of the driveway. "From that... Scrubbing Angels service?"

"Scrubbing Cherubs," corrected Brielle, cringing. She looked to Archer for confirmation on how to proceed, but he didn't want her to have to explain more.

"We have a lot in common," lied Archer, wondering if the only thing he knew they had in common was at least somewhat of an interest in comics and perhaps a little sexual tension. (The latter, of course, was mostly wishful thinking, but he didn't think it impossible.)

Brielle drummed her fingers on her bag as his mother frowned and finished backing onto the road. "I really liked your book," she said. "The *Wheels* one."

"Thanks." In the moonlight, Archer caught a glimpse of Brielle's smile and it was so dazzling, he couldn't tear his gaze away.

"I thought your cleaning lady was an older woman," said Mrs. Ward, completely ruining the mood.

"That was Deena," said Brielle. "She requested a swap in clients."

"Requested a swap...?" Mrs. Ward's voice went high-pitched.

Brielle bit her lip. "She wanted a change in shift, I mean. I came back for the first time in a year after going to school, and I was free to take on her clients."

"So you're a student?" she asked.

"I was," said Brielle. "I graduated with Pembroke." She nodded at the sign for the local college as they passed, although Archer's mother couldn't see it. "Right there."

"Congratulations," said the older woman, but there was a false note to the sweetness. "Were you a biology major too?"

"History and philosophy, actually."

"Oh," said Mrs. Ward. "And... do you plan to do anything with that or...?"

"Mother, can you please stop having an inquisition?" said Archer, certain he should step in if he wanted to prevent her from embarrassing him any further. As if that were possible.

"It's okay," said Brielle, but even in the dark of night, it was clear her smile was strained. "I'm currently looking for a career. I've worked at Scrubbing Cherubs every summer since I was sixteen, so I thought it could hold me over and help me save up for whenever I move."

"You still... live at home?"

Archer didn't know why she said it so disdainfully, considering she wanted him to still be home and he doubted he could afford to live on his own without his parents' help.

"Yes," said Brielle, nervously laughing. "But I did graduate only last weekend."

"What kind of work are you looking for?" Mrs. Ward asked, taking them back onto the highway. "I'm not sure what a history or philosophy major might do, other than teach history and philosophy."

"I thought about it," said Brielle. "But I didn't think I was suited for it."

"Then why the major...?"

"Mother—"

"I just find the subjects fascinating," said Brielle. "I've been applying to basically any entry-level office job. As far as using my majors, well, I applied for a few museums, but no luck so far."

"I imagine they want people with PhDs for that." Archer's mother drummed her manicured nails on the wheel.

"There are some lower-level jobs," said Brielle, her head bowed as she played with her fingers on her lap.

"You know, I know somebody who works at the Field Museum of Natural History." Mrs. Ward took a breath. "I should call him up for you."

"Mother, please don't interfere with—"

"Oh, that'd great!" Brielle spoke so quickly and with such excitement, even though it was like she'd stabbed Archer in the back while smiling about it.

"Give me your info before you leave," she said.

"I will," said Brielle, and she looked so happy, Archer felt bad for even feeling hurt that she was so anxious to leave town and what little they had behind.

"Good-bye! Good luck, dear!" Mrs. Ward waved to Brielle as she tucked the piece of paper she'd written her name and number down on into her purse. Archer watched the paper greedily, realizing his mother now had Brielle's contact information and he'd yet to get it. He had the Scrubbing Cherubs number, and he knew it was likely Brielle's mother would answer, but that would be one of the most awkward conversations he'd ever had.

Archer waited until his mother had opened his door and the two of them stepped inside completely. Of course she'd insisted on stepping inside for "coffee," even though tomorrow was her day with him, it was getting late, and she'd already had coffee earlier from Starbucks. Once she shut the door, he spun on her in the living room of his condo. "What do you think you were doing?"

Dropping her purse on the kitchen counter, Mrs. Ward turned on his Keurig. "Well, that's a fine way for you to thank me for going out of my way to help your friends this evening."

"You promised me you weren't coming tonight."

"I promised nothing of the sort."

Archer wheeled closer, trapping his mother in the kitchen. "You *implied* you were going to a dinner with Dad."

She grabbed one of the K-Cups out of the small open jar he kept them in and took down a couple of mugs from the higher-up cupboards, where she kept the things she liked to use when there. "Do you want any?" she asked, making herself a cup.

"No, Mother, I don't want coffee at ten o'clock at night. I want..." He rubbed his temple. "I just... want some privacy once in a while."

The sound of the Keurig as it finished brewing was so loud, it called to mind the cartoonish depictions of old-fashioned tea kettles practically about to blow. Something his mother said went unheard beneath the noise.

"What?" said Archer, his tone short and clipped, his hand flying back down to his lap.

She was in tears as she gestured around. "What do you call this? This place? This life your father and I provide for you? I *wanted* you home. I don't see why you couldn't do your drawings at home."

Archer blew out a deep breath. "I know. I'm sorry. That came out the wrong way, but—"

"And I try to make sure you're okay, even when I'm not here." The Keurig, briefly quiet, started growling again as it tried to keep the water still left warm. "I make arrangements with Pauline for your therapy and extra needs and to get you out of the house on occasion."

"I know, I know, I appreciate it. But tonight was me getting out of the house, me doing something on my own—"

"It was you having a *book signing* and not wanting your own mother there! What kind of mother would I be if I didn't go and support you?"

She didn't even *read* his comics, he was sure of it. She'd tried reading *Wheels* once, but she had no interest in *The Mystified*. Not that he cared. "You'd be a mother who respected her son's request."

She looked as if she'd been slapped and she flicked the Keurig off to quiet it mid-growl. "You never said I *wasn't* invited!"

"I thought I didn't *have to* only because you told me you had a dinner tonight!" He slammed his palms on his wheels. "I was outright going to ask you *not to go* until you said that."

Water flowed freely down her cheeks. "I thought you *wanted* me to go. You wanted me to cancel my plans to go."

"No!" Archer wrung his hands through his hair. "I'm *glad* when you have a life outside of me. I *want you* to do things for yourself."

"You didn't disinvite your father!"

"I don't have to! He'd never come!" He swallowed then, the words harder to articulate than he'd thought.

"Oh, but *that* causes you pain?" She was shaking so hard, her limbs were trembling. "But me being nothing but supportive of you, fostering your art skills, giving up *so much in my life* to take care of you, *me* you don't want around?"

"I didn't ask you to!" Archer found it difficult to stop the tears from welling in his own eyes then. "I didn't ask to be a burden. I didn't ask to be born this way."

"I never said you were a *burden*." She wiped the tears from her face with two of her fingers squeezed together.

"But I am. I get it." He backed his wheelchair up to give her more space in his tiny kitchen. "Look. I think it's healthier for the both of us if we see less of each other."

She sniffled, crossing her arms and not bothering to wipe her dripping nose. "You *allow* me to only see you once a week."

"I think... That's a good amount." Archer winced. He didn't like hurting his mother, but damn it, she drove him crazy.

She stepped past him, ignoring her mug of coffee. "I'm done paying for that maid you're sleeping with."

His jaw dropped. "I'm *not—*"

She swiped her purse off the counter, not noticing or caring that a small slip of paper fell out from the open top as she did. "You're so independent, you can clean your own place."

"Mother, please." Archer followed after her down the hallway to his front door. "Don't be upset."

She twirled around to face him. "So what's gotten you more upset? Me telling you to clean your own stuff or me being upset?"

He felt as if she'd put him in a vice, asking him to choose two equally bad answers, not even recognizing half of the real issues at hand. "I don't want you upset. I also don't want you getting Brielle in trouble for something she *didn't do*."

She threw her hands in the air. "What do you take me for? An idiot? Fine." She opened the door quickly. "This annoying *idiot* will leave you alone, as you requested. But she's not financing your intimacy, either." She slammed the door shut.

Although he'd dreamed of telling her off for ages—of saying worse things, even—he felt nauseous. It didn't quite feel real.

But a huge part of him didn't care.

He locked the door, even putting the chain up, which meant that she wasn't going to be able to let herself back in.

A thought struck him. The paper that fell out of his mother's purse... Depending on what it was, he might just summon the courage to act on his impulses, screw the consequences.

CHAPTER THIRTEEN

Despite the terrible, terrible evening Brielle had wound up having the night before, she still felt like she'd had the best evening of any of her friends.

One week away from graduation and already life was in shambles for her closest friends. She didn't even have it in her to talk about Archer or the weirdness of getting a ride from his mom—neither of which was terrible, really, it was mostly how things went down with Pembroke that worried her—with Lilac, who was in tears on Skype. Lilac wouldn't talk much about it, other than to lament the fact that she'd ever done such a reckless thing, that she wished she'd taken the summer off and stuck to the teaching job in Minneapolis like she'd planned, that she'd been stupid to do this stupid thing. Brielle had hardly known what to say other than to tell her to take a deep breath and wait until some more time had passed before she made another rash decision.

Lilac had not taken kindly to the *"another"* rash decision and she'd cut the call earlier than planned, barely hearing anything about Brielle meeting up with Pembroke.

Gavin sighed after she said goodbye. He looked haggard, like he hadn't slept in days, and Brielle was fairly certain he was in a closet.

"I'm sorry," said Brielle, slumping forward on her desk in her room. She was fully aware the room looked like a mess behind her, complete with piles and piles of half-opened boxes (throughout the past week, she'd dig around for something and not bother to unload the rest). She just didn't really care.

Gavin shrugged. "I'm worried about Li," he said. "But I'm also worried about Pembroke. And you too. What do you mean, she was dating Daniel?"

Brielle tucked a piece of hair behind her ear. "She *was* dating Daniel. Despite him having a different fiancée last week. But I think that's over now."

"I wish she'd answer my messages," said Gavin.

"Mine too." Brielle's lips soured. "I told her she didn't have to cut me off because she made the same mistake I did—albeit just a little bit shittier since she had a friend to clarify what a dick he was —but that's it. I've got too much else to worry about. If she doesn't answer, I don't... I don't need that kind of drama in my life."

Gavin smirked. "You did have a friend to tell you he was a dick."

Brielle grinned. "Shut up," she said without malice. "Okay, but you didn't literally have firsthand accounts to testify to that."

"Didn't need to fuck a dick to spot one." Gavin rolled his eyes.

"Touché. And apparently I needed to *screw* him several times before I could see the light." Brielle let her gaze wander to her bedroom door, but the house was eerily quiet on the other side of it. "But isn't it... Just... Too weird? Did Pembroke even go on a *single date* all of college?"

Gavin twiddled with what looked like a decorative piece of yarn at the end of a hanging scarf. "She was too shy, I guess."

"She never wanted to talk about it. I thought she might be gay."

"Not all late bloomers are secret gays..." Gavin shook the scarf toward his phone as if admonishing her. "I thought she might just be... Not interested? Or too scared to take a risk?"

"After yesterday, who even knows. Maybe she dated all the time and just didn't feel close enough to us to tell us." Brielle ran a finger over the top of a framed photo on her desk of her and her high school friends, including her high school boyfriend she'd dated for a year and a half, once a huge part of her life and whom she hadn't thought about in ages. Almost as if to signify that, the photo was covered in dust. She didn't talk to any of these people anymore. Not really. No more than an occasional reaction to a Facebook post. Was that what was going to happen to her and her college friends?

Brielle peered closer at her friend, trapped in a literal closet. "But enough about that. You worry too much about everyone else. Anything you want to tell me?"

The scarf stopped flapping as Gavin squeezed it. "Nope. Just a bad date."

"I'm sorry," said Brielle. "You were so excited."

Gavin shrugged and started tugging on the scarf again. He didn't even flinch when it fell down over his face. "It's fine. Maybe I don't always have my dick-seeing glasses on."

Brielle laughed. "The image you just put in my head."

"Shush," said Gavin, but he was smiling.

"And the job? Still a nightmare?"

"Yup." His lips grew tight.

"That all you have to say about that?"

"Yup."

"Okay," said Brielle, feeling a bit disappointed, but she knew Gavin didn't like to talk much about his own problems. He almost never talked about his own problems. But he worried obsessively over his friends', which made him a perfect match for Lilac, who was perfectly content to only worry about her own.

Sure enough, he redirected the conversation back away from him. "Do you think Lilac was... assaulted?"

Brielle felt the wind knocked out of her. She'd been so used to Lilac's hysterics, she hadn't even considered that Lilac might have had more than a wildly fluctuating fit of conscience to blame for it. "Has she told you—"

"No," said Gavin. "It's just... a feeling I have. Probably that asshole Earl."

Brielle waited for him to say more, but he didn't. She didn't want the world to rest on his shoulders, but she didn't feel like it was her place to intervene in Lilac's case. "Then keep at her... gently, okay? Let her know she can talk to me too."

"I will." Gavin wrapped the scarf around his neck and shook his head as if to clear it.

Brielle smirked. "Cold in that closet?"

"It's the windy city," he said, posing for the camera. He bonked his head against the wall as he flung back and both Brielle and Gavin burst out laughing, even as Gavin rubbed his head. He smiled sheepishly. "There's no other place for some privacy here." Almost as if on cue, Brielle heard some muffled voices in the background of the video and the light trickling in under the door shifted slightly as someone's shadow crossed in front of it.

"What about the bathroom?"

Gavin shook his head at her, like she was a poor, misguided child. "You have *not* spent time in an apartment with three hot gay guys, so I will forgive you for not understanding that the bathroom is practically the busiest room in the apartment."

"Other than the bedrooms?" said Brielle, feeling saucy.

Gavin flung the edge of the scarf toward her in a parody of a femme gay stereotype. "Oh, you did *not* just go there."

Brielle raised both her hands outward, as if to apologize, but she was smiling all the while. "I'm just going off the picture you've painted for me."

"Yeah, well, you're not too far off." His face soured. "But *I* don't have a bedroom, so I can't exactly be sure."

"You're not the jump-into-bed kind of guy."

She seemed to have struck a nerve. "So everyone tells me."

Brielle winced. She waited for him to explain more, but he had nothing more to say.

"Do you think—" she started.

"But what about your comic book hottie?" said Gavin at the same time.

Just as she got a text:

It's Archer. I got your number from my mother. Are you free today? Do you want to go on a date—just the two of us this time?

"Uh," said Brielle, minimizing the video chat and staring at the text. "He just asked me on a date."

<hr>

"I'm sorry I don't really have anywhere else to take you." Apologizing for what had to be the twentieth time in the five minutes since he and Brielle had set off for the park, Archer rolled his wheels again and again with such finesse, it was practically a struggle for Brielle to keep pace with him.

"I don't mind." Brielle caught sight of the tote bag on Archer's lap, not for the first time. He'd offered to meet her at his condo and go with her to the park, where he promised a lunch. She wondered what he'd made—and if she was going to have to clean it up tomorrow.

Why was that even a thought that had crossed her mind? She still wasn't used to thinking of herself as anything but his house cleaner. Even after the chaotic comic book signing.

"I'm sorry, too, if you thought it was rude of me to message you. I know you gave your number to my mother, but—"

Brielle laughed. "You're sorry you asked me on a date?"

"No." His face reddened. "I just thought... I should have asked you in person."

"Kind of more awkward to ask when I'm elbow-deep in yellow rubber gloves, right?"

"About that..." Just as they finally reached the park, Archer slowed and turned around to face her. "I'm afraid my mother is canceling my service."

A warm breeze rustled through the late spring air, but Brielle still found herself shivering as she grabbed a chunk of her hair to prevent it from hitting her eyes. "Did I... offend her?"

He grimaced. "No, I think *I* did."

"Does she think we...?" Brielle pointed to herself and to Archer, unable to voice the rest of it.

Averting his gaze, he tapped his wheels again. "Maybe. But that's not why. It had nothing to do with you."

If it had nothing to do with me, why does she think I'm dating you and then coincidentally decide to fire me? She pointed to a picnic table that sat under the shade of a giant oak tree. "Do you want to talk about it?"

"Oh? Right. Sorry." He pivoted and headed toward the table, gesturing toward his lap as he pulled beside it. "I'm already sitting, but I should have thought you'd be more comfortable if I didn't make you stand..."

Brielle felt a mixture of emotions as she took her place at the table. Giddy because of the date. Nervous about why his mother had canceled the cleaning service. Happy because maybe it was better if she didn't socialize with one of the service's clients anyway. Apprehensive about what her own mom might say when she found out. And she certainly hadn't found out yet, or Brielle would have heard about it. "Don't worry about it," she said, to herself as much as to him.

"Oh, wait!"

She paused halfway crouched to the bench and watched as Archer dug into his tote bag and pulled out a vinyl tablecloth, followed by a blanket. He arranged the blanket nicely on the table bench beneath Brielle, patting it when finished.

"Thank you," said Brielle, tossing her hair behind her shoulders as she sat. She helped Archer lay the tablecloth out across half of the picnic table, grinning as she thought about how cute but pointless protecting the worn and weathered table from their mess was. Folding her fingers together, she leaned her elbows on the table and watched, wide-eyed, as Archer pulled a fake-looking candle out of his bag and turned it over, flicking it on with a switch. He glanced sheepishly out of the corner of his eye at her and placed it on the table as far as his arm would reach.

"What else have you got in that enchanted bag?" joked Brielle, crossing her legs and staring at him. His cheeks were definitely a deeper, adorable shade. She couldn't believe this was the same guy who'd almost frightened her last week. Suddenly, she felt more in charge, like he'd crumble at the slightest bat of her eyes.

A burst of warmth spread through her abdomen all the way down to the bench beneath her. She uncrossed and crossed her legs again and took a deep breath, fighting the first thing that popped into her mind.

"You sure are spicy under the sheets," said Daniel, his hands practically pawing at her back. She was so hot at that moment, so lost in herself, that she almost didn't hear him as she moaned and rocked, pulsating against him beneath her.

"My little Latin lover," he'd said, nuzzling into the crook of her neck.

That memory was like a splash of cold water to the face. She was never going to tell another guy about her heritage again—although her last name kind of made it obvious. She had to clutch the edge of the tablecloth to will her heartbeat to slow as Archer pulled out two plates, two glasses, and a set of utensils from his wonder bag. *You barely know him*, she told herself. *And you don't even know how... If... How it would work with him.*

Still, there was a checklist of things she found appealing, so long as she pushed the memory of their first meeting to the back of their mind. Endearingly shy but able to stand up to jackasses when needed. Clearly interested in her without making her feel like a piece of meat at the market. Creative and talented—she'd almost cried reading *Wheels*, and she'd stayed up late to read his other books, even if he hadn't written them—he'd brought the stories to life with his talent. A sense of humor at the right occasion. Likely well-to-do, although she felt guilty for even thinking about it. That made her think about how Mrs. Ward had promised to talk to someone about a Field Museum job, though, and how that would take her hours away, which also made her think about his mother, period. There were definitely hints of mommy issues.

Although she was sure a therapist would tell her she had her own list of issues a mile long regardless.

Besides, it'd been *months*. And if she were honest with herself, she'd stopped enjoying it with Daniel longer ago than that. He'd just been there, available. The second time they'd dated, she'd hardly even cared that his eye kept wandering.

She didn't mean to voice her thought as she watched Archer pull out two plastic sandwich bags and gently place each sandwich on a paper plate, but she did. "What...?" Brielle covered her mouth.

Stuffing the bags back into his tote, Archer's lips twitched sheepishly. "I'm... not the best cook? I mostly eat sandwiches."

"No, it's fine." She poked her wheat bread with one finger. "I just... You went to so much trouble to set the stage, so to speak, it was a bit of a shocker to finally see the big reveal."

Archer tossed the tote on the ground beside him and buried his face in his hands. "This was a bad idea." He thankfully didn't sound so much devastated as embarrassed.

"Oh, come on," said Brielle. She picked the sandwich up between her hands and took a bite, not even bothering to ask what was in it. She typically would eat anything. To her surprise, it was pretty good. "Huh," she said. "Looks can be deceiving." It was toasted and there was chicken on it amidst some cheese and vegetables.

Peeking back out from behind his hands, Archer laughed and picked up his own sandwich. "My own little twist on a chicken pesto sandwich," he said. He paused, the sandwich halfway to his mouth. "But I should have asked if you have any dietary restrictions or allergies."

"No," said Brielle, taking another bite of the sandwich. She stared at Archer as she chewed. "Really, you did fine. Relax. I think I could bounce a ball off those tense shoulder muscles."

That made his shoulders loosen and a smile appear on his face.

"Now I'm picturing in what circumstances you could possibly be bouncing balls off my shoulders."

She nearly choked on some lettuce. "I'm getting the feeling that that was an entendre, but I honestly can say I've never used any bouncy balls in the bedroom."

Archer's face looked permanently burnt at this point, his blush was so profuse. "That was..." He put his sandwich down and cocked his head. "I'm really bad at this, aren't I?"

She grabbed her empty cup and held it out to him. "Not *bad*, per se, but... Should I go fill this up from the water fountain or...?"

"Tea!" Archer bent over the side of his chair to grab at the tote. "I almost forgot." Unscrewing the top of the large bottle, he poured some unsweetened black tea into both cups. "Sorry if you're more of a sweet girl," he said, picking up his own cup and about to take a sip.

Brielle peeked at him over the rim of her own cup before taking a sip. "You're probably talking about the tea. But I don't know. Maybe in certain circumstances, I'm not always so sweet."

The cup in Archer's hand wobbled as he practically spit his sip back into it.

Brielle grinned from ear to ear. He was hers if she wanted him, she was sure of it. She kicked back her glass. *So what if you barely know him? So what if you have no idea where the future will take you— and be honest, you're partly hoping and partly terrified it'll just be more of right here. You're not thinking about marrying him or anything.*

But first things first. "So I'm being fired because...?"

"My mother is just..." said Archer, drifting off. "She gets an idea into her head and she passively aggressively does whatever she can to make sure I know she's not pleased with me."

"So she *does* think we're dating."

"She... I don't know. She might think we are. But I need to pick up after myself more and not rely on other people so much anyway."

A little alarm bell went off in Brielle's head. The "picking up after himself" thing seemed more like an excuse. *Mother Issues 101.*

But whatever. She didn't even have to see Mrs. Ward again necessarily. And without meaning to, the woman had actually made it easier for Brielle to act on her darkest desires. "Do you want to... um, go back to your place after this?" she asked. She hesitated, devouring the look of shock on his face as the cup practically slipped from his fingers. "Oh, it's your mother's day with you, isn't it? Maybe we can have a rain check."

"Nope! No, I mean... My mother isn't coming by today." Squished between his fingers, his cup started leaking some tea onto his hands. He jumped, looking down at the spot on his lap.

Laughing, Brielle fished some tissues out of her purse and handed them to him. She purposely brushed her fingers over the palm of his hand as she did, letting the tips dance lightly over his partially calloused skin. "This is going to become a habit with you, isn't it?"

"What? Oh." He stared down at his wet crotch. His legs were a little too skinny for the bulk of his upper body, but Brielle didn't care—it looked right on him. "I'll try not to make it one?"

CHAPTER FOURTEEN

That went amazingly well despite being a spectacular failure on so many accounts.

Archer stared at the dark-haired beauty sitting kitty-corner from him at the picnic table. He'd thought his half-assed attempts at making the meal seem more formal might come across as charming, might play well enough to get her to consider a second date.

He didn't know when—*if*, even—he'd ever have her in his bed.

She clearly had no reservations about not waiting.

When he'd found Brielle's number and email written on that piece of paper his mother had dropped, he'd considered it a sign.

He'd had no idea it was a neon-blazing, flickering, you-better-not-pass-this-up kind of sign.

He was *not* going to pass this up. The only problem was, he didn't just like this girl. He *really* liked this girl. If he didn't get to know her first or, god forbid, he really disappointed her behind closed doors—as was likely, considering he'd never hit a ball before in that analogy, let alone made it to even first base—he'd utterly and totally blow it.

But she was *here*. She was interested, despite how badly he'd messed up their first meeting, despite how crazy his mother was. And she was going to leave him soon anyway…

"Yes," he blurted out. "Um, yes, please, let's go to my place. But I…" He looked around the park and let his shoulders slink as he lowered his voice, even though the nearest other people were well over two hundred yards away. Still, there were kids around. And grannies. "I don't have anything to…" He gestured wildly. "I don't have a…"

"Condom?" Brielle looked amused and spoke at a normal volume. "I do."

"Oh. Oh…" Archer didn't *want to* feel jealous at the idea of Brielle sleeping with guys so casually she had a condom in her purse, but he sort of did.

"And I'm on birth control," she added. "So… we're good." She cocked her head. "You catch on quick, don't you?"

"What do you mean?"

"What if I just meant to go back to your place and talk some more?"

He felt his stomach drop. "Did—Did you? I'm sorry. That would be… No, that would be great, I'm sorry I…" He couldn't string two words together.

Covering her pretty red lips with a long-fingered delicate hand, she still couldn't hide the way her eyes lit up. "*I'm* sorry," she said. "You're just too easy to tease." Her nose crinkled. "I would have thought you'd have been more comfortable with flirting, being so…" She gestured toward him, as if that explained it all.

A burst of wind caused their plates to fly up, and Archer's still had part of a sandwich on it. Laughing, Brielle chased after them, picking up both plates and the sandwich and bringing them to a nearby trash can. Holding the sandwich over the can in midair, she asked, "I take it you're not eating this, right?"

"No." *I've kind of lost my appetite.* It was apparently possible to get this nervous about something *good.* He just couldn't help but focus on everything that could go wrong.

"There were soooo many women flirting with you yesterday,"

said Brielle, swinging her legs in those too-tight jeans around the bench to sit back beside him. "And maybe even some men, too."

"You're exaggerating."

"I am not." She pulled her phone out of her purse on the bench beside her, scrolling through her messages. "My gay friend even knew who you were because, and I quote, you're 'super hot.'"

She's been talking about me to her friends? Pembroke had mentioned that too. That was somehow more impressive to him than the idea that some stranger found him "super hot."

Something must have passed over his face because Brielle filled the silence as she tucked her phone away again. "You don't even know you're hot, do you? Or you don't even care?"

He shrugged.

"Okay, then, that's really hot, too." She bit her lip. "Not being so full of yourself you're in love with yourself."

"Is there anything I can do that doesn't make me hot to you?" he said boldly.

Her laughter was like a soprano's solo carried across the warm breeze. "But you're just the right amount of confident, too. So the answer, I guess, is no. Everything you do makes you hot."

If there was such a thing as dying from embarrassment, Archer might be the very first person to die from an assault of compliments. He didn't consider himself confident at all, but that self-defense mechanism he'd fostered growing up "different" from everyone else, that instinct to make it seem like he was cool and calm and on top of the world, often snuck its way through. Especially when he was nervous. And this woman definitely made him nervous.

"Okay, maybe we should cool it down a bit." Brielle wrapped both hands around her cup, and Archer scrambled to grab her more tea from the tote. She smiled and put a hand over her mostly-empty cup. "I'm good, thank you." Some of her hair whipped across her face and somehow the subtle movement of her tucking it back behind her ears made Archer want to reach over and cradle her face. "I really liked your books," she said, not meeting his eyes.

Which ones? he wanted to ask. But she'd mentioned *Wheels* in the car, and he was afraid to press further. "Thanks."

"No, I mean it." The plastic cup crinkled under her grasp. "I only read comics on occasion, but your art in *The Mystified* is outstanding. You give this..." She looked up and gestured broadly with one hand. "...sort of *real* feeling to even a story that's so unreal. And after reading *Wheels*, it makes sense. It's such a grounded story—even with the talking squirrel."

"You're making me blush," said Archer, although that was long past being obvious. He felt a stab of guilt for ever even thinking she might be one of "those" girls with just a passing interest in comics thanks to hunks in superhero movies. That didn't seem to be the case—and even if it were, who cared?

"So was the squirrel really talking or was Todd just hearing her voice?"

"What do *you* think?"

"Ah, one of *those* creators, huh? Leave it all up to the reader to fill in the gaps?" She stared down at her cup as she rolled the bottom in a little circle across the tablecloth. "Fine. I'm going to believe she could talk for real because I like to believe that magic exists, even if only in the realm of fiction." She flicked her head slightly to move that billowing hair out of her face.

"Magic is real... in fiction?" He smirked. She was somehow both sexy and cute all at the same time.

"Oh, shush. You know what I mean." She took one last swig from her cup, although there barely seemed to be more than a drop left. "So how did you get into the comic industry?"

"Passion, interest, a bit of talent, and a lot of luck," he answered honestly. "And the safety net of my parents, I suppose."

"Just a bit of talent?" She raised an eyebrow. "So most of that I get... It must be so freaking hard to break into the industry."

"A lot of talent goes overlooked." He ran a hand through his hair. "I was just lucky with *Wheels*... I self-published it and it got just the right amount of attention and that led to the job on *The Mystified*."

"Thus the safety net," added Brielle. "But about the passion... How come you have like *no* comic books at your house? No fun little trinkets? No posters?"

Wincing, Archer poured himself some more tea and took a drink. "The books are in the video cabinet."

"The perfect place for books, sure."

He grinned. "The rest of the stuff, I don't know. I guess I'm not that type of fan."

"So you're a fake geek boy," said Brielle, staring down at him but with an amused look on her face.

"Mother always found those kinds of purchases useless." He couldn't believe he was bringing her up again or reminding Brielle just how much of a momma's boy he might be, special circumstances or not.

"And is your mother still your interior decorator?"

"I... didn't really care."

"That's right, you said the art was hers." She crumpled the cup in her hand entirely.

He couldn't stop staring at her face, which seemed set with grim determination. "Pretty landscapes make for better wall art than caped men jumping out of buildings, right?"

"Says you." Studying him a moment, she stood up. "Or maybe not. Maybe says *Mom*?"

He lifted both hands in the air up and down as if weighing options. "I guess...? I don't exactly care what my surroundings look like, and I don't want an overly cluttered space."

Grabbing the candle, she flipped it over to switch it off. "Luckily for you, you have an expert on cleanliness and clutter to help you out." She dropped the candle and bottle of tea into his tote bag and flung herself forward, clutching at the tablecloth, pulling it toward her as if her life depended on it. Under a light sweater, she had a fluffy white top that didn't even cover her midriff, and the movement made it ride even higher, revealing a perfectly planed abdomen that dipped only at the navel before disappearing under her jeans. "Thanks for the lunch," she said. "This whole thing has been adorable, but I think I *really* need to study your condo right now. For some design ideas." She shook out the tablecloth and folded it hastily, watching Archer with half-lidded eyes the entire time.

He hadn't been mistaken. She could make any mundane cleaning task seem incredibly sexy.

"I need your design ideas like *yesterday*," he said, taking the tote bag from her. He didn't even care that neither of them remembered to take the blanket along as they started back down the sidewalk.

CHAPTER FIFTEEN

Brielle felt like she could benefit from a little liquid courage just about now. But that was the thing—she usually didn't need it. When in the orbit of Lilac, it was hard to come across as sexy or domineering or anything but a blip in the background. But when she wanted someone, she could be quite bold, if she did say so herself. She may not want to jump every guy who flirted with her at a party, but once she found the guy she *would* like to jump...

So what was different this time? Was it because of his disability? She couldn't even bring herself to ask him *what* his disability was. As if that mattered. But the thought of jumping him made her stomach roar, in both a good and bad way. She'd never felt this way with Daniel or any of her shorter-term boyfriends before him. With Daniel especially, she'd just wanted him to shut up so she could close her eyes and forget it was him she was under the sheets with.

This time she didn't want to keep her eyes closed the whole time. She didn't want to turn off the lights—not that that would even matter since she was about to have, at minimum, a make-out session in the middle of the day.

She let him hold the door open for her—which made her hesitate for half a step because she felt like she should be holding the door open for him—and stepped inside his condo, looking around for a place to drop her purse that wouldn't take her out of his orbit and settling for letting it fall to the floor beside where she kicked off her shoes. She immediately felt her face flush as she remembered the tight space and that he'd have to wheel past, so she bent over, picking up her shoes and purse again and squishing them against the wall.

Despite the close quarters, Archer spun around to shut the door and dropped his tote behind it. He bent to take his braces off, then stopped, one Velcro unfastened. Brielle wondered if she should offer to help—wondered if he'd had more plans for them where he might have needed to walk, then realized she didn't even know when he needed the braces since she'd seen him walking a bit even without them.

Her heart was hammering. *Stop overthinking everything. This doesn't have to mean anything. He's not even your client anymore. Just go for it!* Her legs felt like lead.

Archer spun around slowly, his one pant leg shifted up, his brace sticking up a little awkwardly where it wasn't fastened. "Do you think—"

But Brielle didn't hear what else he had to say. She launched herself forward, bending over to touch her lips to his. It felt awkward and her back strained, but she held the position anyway, softly taking his top lip between hers and letting go. She pulled back, not even remembering when she'd put her hands behind his head, running her fingers through that hair she'd wanted to fondle days ago. She felt something straining in her from her shoulders to her legs, but she didn't want to move as she stared into his eyes. There was a light in those eyes, a hunger.

"You're shaking," he whispered, and after a minute she realized she literally was. Shaking out of nervousness, out of desire.

But she really was in an awkward position.

He tore his eyes away and put his arms behind her back, pulling her closer, practically inviting her to crawl onto his lap.

So she did. The laughter that escaped her lips was quivering, both because she felt stupid but also because she knew she was trying to be sexy and it was a little hard to be as she kept shifting her legs around, trying to figure out how to sit in the tight quarters without crushing him. She settled for sitting on her calves.

"Here," he said, taking first one calf and then the other and sliding them on either side of his thighs. Her legs were flush against the sides of the seat of the wheelchair, but she really didn't mind. She just kept focusing on the feel of his hands on her legs, and how she wished she'd tossed her jeans off before she'd even launched herself at him.

He looked up at her and this time, he strained upward, pushing his lips against hers. Gently, hesitating at first. Then she slipped her hands back through his hair and leaned forward, pushing into the kiss. Each kiss lasted longer than the one before, each moment until she had to come up for air a precious one she didn't want to let go. She kept kissing him and kissing him, her lips moving to the slight stubble on his cheeks, a jolt of excitement running down her torso to her toes at the rough texture beneath her lips. She was hot, *burning* even.

She took a deep breath and leaned back to remove her sweater, accidentally bumping into him with her elbow as she did.

"Oop," he said, reaching out to try to help her get it off. She managed without him, staring down at his heaving chest, his slightly parted lips, the whole time. She had barely closed her eyes —she could barely keep her eyes off him.

She slammed her hand down on the armrest of his chair as she squirmed out of the second sleeve and tossed it behind her.

He stared at her, his gaze flicking downward toward her bare abdomen. She grabbed his hands and put them once more on the small of her back, a moan escaping her lips at the feel of his rough hands against her bare skin.

She pushed forward and kissed him again, kissing his neck and shifting his T-shirt to allow better access to the skin of his shoulder, the skin at the base of his throat. She felt his hands go up her back, up under her blouse, sliding in hard beneath the strap of her bra. She pulled back, gasping, shoving her fingers downward to get up under his shirt.

"Off," she said, clipped, rolling the shirt upward and forcing him to let go and lift his hands up so she could fling the shirt away. She didn't even feel bad when she tugged it up past his face, knocking his nose just a little in her exuberance. She let her fingers run through the soft, fine down on his pecs. *How is he so, so toned?* She wondered if his possibly-daily physical therapy had something to do with it. Daniel was built like someone had let the air out of a man-shaped-being.

Archer placed his hands on her mid-back, staring up at her as her hair teased the side of his face. "You're really not one for small talk, are you?"

She leaned forward and pressed her nose to his, her breath hot. "Do you need more help to get in the mood?"

Almost as if on cue, she felt him harden, his jeans and hers between them. Her thighs and calves tingled and she was overwhelmed with the urge to rip everything right off him, but then she realized her legs had fallen *asleep*, that despite her overpowering desire, she was starting to lose feeling. She laughed and scooched backward, fumbling to bring out her shaking legs to let her feet touch the floor.

He swallowed, watching her, his arms falling down limply. "Sorry," he said.

"Don't be..." She stumbled and he leaned forward, his hand shooting out to provide her some support as she tried to stand up and get some more feeling back in her legs. She laughed. "I just think... We need more space."

"Bedroom," he breathed.

She turned, practically running down the hall, then thought better of it and reached for her purse before she went. "Just in case..." she said, rummaging through and pulling the condom she kept in a buried pocket of her bag for "just in case" types of situations.

He stared at her. She unbuttoned her pants and took them off, shaking her butt as she did, knowing she was imitating virtually every male director's gaze when it came to the simple task of women undressing.

That little shimmy had its uses.

Archer reached out toward her, but she took a step back, grinning. "I'll be waiting." She power-walked down the hallway to the bedroom, giving him time to appreciate the contoured black panties covering her ass.

———

Running over his own T-shirt with a wheelchair only registered with Archer when his wheel got a little stuck and he had to back up to maneuver around it and the pair of jeans Brielle had left beside it.

He couldn't stop staring at Brielle as she walked away, couldn't stop gaping after her even as she turned into the bedroom, leaned over the side of the frame, and smiled before vanishing out of sight.

But once she'd been out of his line of vision for half a minute, the panic set in. He'd left his braces on—half on, for one of them, he noticed, seeing that the one he'd partially unfastened had shifted even more after—and he really didn't know what to do. He'd pictured himself standing to kiss her, but he wouldn't be able to stand up for long, couldn't hold her as he did.

And then there was the fact that his braces made it hard to remove his pants.

Even though he knew she was waiting for him, he decided to remove them right then and there. The wrinkly slip of paper still on his kitchen table—the paper with her name and number on it— caught his eye. "So," he called loudly down the hallway, "you want to work in a museum?"

Stupid. That was stupid. But he didn't want her to think he'd forgotten about her. Good god, he could never forget the way she'd sashayed down the hallway.

"Maybe," she called, and Archer realized that with the mood his mother was in and the fact that he had that piece of paper right there on the table, his mother was never going to get her that referral. As he put his first brace down, he grabbed the paper and crumpled it into his fist, tossing it on the chair so it'd be out of sight. He couldn't risk her disappointment ruining what was shaping up to be one of the best days of his life. He'd tell her tomorrow. Or depending on what she wanted to do tomorrow, maybe the next day.

You do *have a deadline this week, too.* But he couldn't imagine ever wanting to do anything else again, as stupid as that thought was.

"Does it matter what kind of museum?" he asked, getting to work on the second brace. "Or like, are you considering places other than Chicago?"

"*Archer*," she called out loudly down the hallway. "Less talking. More kissing."

He didn't have to be told twice.

Free of his braces, he considered shimmying out of his pants, but he just couldn't picture himself wheeling in there in his boxers, or god forbid, without anything on, and it somehow being sexy.

He knew his top was pretty toned, but he really wasn't ready for her to be staring at his legs. He shifted his pants legs down and headed down the hallway.

Brielle was lying on his bed, her dark hair popping out against his white sheets, framing her face like brush strokes. She got up a little, leaning on her forearms and shifting her hair to one side. She drove him crazy every time she touched her hair like that.

"How should we...?" she asked, studying him.

He wheeled to the grab bars at the side of his bed, self-conscious of how her eyes followed every move he made. "I just need to shift up there," he said, trying not to think about how mood-killing it would all be.

She got up and swung her legs over the side of the bed, watching him. "Need help?"

He cleared his throat. "No," he said, fully aware he'd never done this before with an audience. Even Pauline usually had her eyes diverted on the rare instances she needed to watch him get in or out of bed.

Heart thumping, he slid himself into position and grabbed hold of his rails, pulling... Then slipping as the chair went sailing backward. He'd forgotten to lock it. *Again.* She was such a distraction. His hands grabbed hold of the bars tightly despite the strain in his muscles and though he sank downward, his legs, unprepared for the weight, collapsing beneath him, he at least didn't fall back swiftly.

"Oh my god!" said Brielle, jumping up and crouching beside him.

Panting, he made sure his rear was close enough to be let down gently and he allowed himself to fall all the way down, lowering himself slowly. He would catch his breath and try to pull himself up by the grab bars once in a better position. He knew Pauline would have been able to help—she had the arm strength necessary to help her patients after a fall—but he couldn't imagine Brielle's thin arms doing the job.

"I'm fine," he said, falling back onto his elbows in imitation of how she'd greeted him from his bed. He laughed between jagged breaths, almost too mortified to even care anymore. He'd always known something like this would happen during his first bedroom encounter. That was partly why he'd been so afraid of it.

Brielle examined his front and his back, her brows scrunched together. "Did you hurt anything, though?"

He waved a hand at her. "I fell too slowly for that."

"Good," she said, sitting on her calves and placing her palms on her thighs. Her naked, smooth, amazing thighs.

"Mood killer?" panted Archer, afraid of the answer.

She startled. "No! I just... want to make sure you're okay."

"I'm okay," he said.

"Okay."

They stared at one another, his breath quieting, but his heartbeat growing louder and louder.

"Fuck the bed," she said, and she crawled onto his lap. She cradled his face with one hand, leaning in for another kiss. He let his hand dance up and down her thigh and he felt himself about to explode. It didn't even matter that he hadn't seen her completely in the nude (yet). It didn't matter that he'd screwed up so bad she was now straddling him on the hardwood floor of his bedroom instead of on that soft, comfortable bed.

He melted at her touch.

CHAPTER SIXTEEN

Liquid courage was overrated. Brielle was so glad she'd had full control of her senses, so happy to be fully in the moment with Archer and not have to think about everything that was bothering her. Once she started riding him on the floor of his condo, not once did thoughts of her stalled job hunt or her putrid ex Daniel flash through her mind. She didn't worry about what had happened with Pembroke or wonder if Lilac and Gavin weren't telling her everything she ought to know about what was bothering them. She didn't think about screaming sisters, mothers with misdirected anger, or raised voices and slammed doors. She was so over worrying about the brusque, difficult client with whom she'd gotten off on the wrong foot. She realized it'd been days since she'd even thought about Mrs. Tanaka and her surly cats.

"You doing all right?" she asked, not sure if all the *activity* was bad for him. He hadn't cried out in pain or anything, but he'd just taken a fall before she'd gotten carried away and she'd kind of forgotten the newness of the situation when they'd gotten into the thick of things. She laughed. There she went overthinking everything again.

"I'm fine. Better than fine." He winced a little as he shifted, as if to contradict his own words. "What's so funny?" He rolled over by reaching up to grab on to the bed's handlebar, his legs falling into place after. The way his gaze roved over her naked body, she had no doubt he'd been satisfied.

Her neck ached as she lay on the white shirt she'd turned into a pillow—only after she'd climaxed and slowly, ever so slowly, rolled off of him to lie down. She realized it was unlikely he could ever do missionary, but she wasn't so sure that was a bad thing. She chewed her lip, considering the possibilities of enjoying her new client-turned-friend-turned-sex-buddy.

Because she *so* wasn't in the right frame of mind for him to be anything else.

He poked her. "Earth to Elle," he said.

"Please," she said, "call me 'Bri.' *He* called me 'Elle.'" She regretted the words almost as soon as she'd said them. Like she needed a reminder of Daniel after a lay like *that*.

"Bri," he said, clearing his throat. He traced the line between two pieces of the hardwood floor, averting his eyes. "That guy at the comic store... He was your ex?"

Daniel was the *last* thing she wanted to think about right now. But she kind of had herself to blame. "Yeah," she said, hoping that might be the end of it.

His fingers stopped moving. "So your friend dated your ex without telling you."

"It wasn't so much that as me knowing *what a huge dick* he is and that *still* not being enough to keep her away from him." She rolled onto her side to face Archer. "And he literally sprung the news of some fiancée on me last week, only to show up in my life with a new girlfriend a week later." She rolled her eyes. "And I thought I could finally get away from him."

"Maybe he made up the fiancée to make you jealous."

"Maybe." She shrugged, letting her hair fall down over her shoulder. "I don't even care."

Archer met her gaze at that. "That bad?"

"That bad." She'd have thought the debacle at the store would have made that clear enough. "What about you? Any crazy ex-girl-friends I should know about?"

"No. Remember? No kiss before last week…"

Brielle licked her lips. "I stole your first kiss." She laughed. "You *would* have no crazy ex stories. You having your pick of the litter and all."

He leaned forward more, shifting some of his weight to the palm of his hand. "I can't even tell when you're joking," he said.

"Oh," said Brielle, wondering now that she thought about it if he thought she was saying *she* was the pick of the litter, too. She knew she was no Lilac, not that she thought she was unworthy, but she didn't exactly have to bat them off with a stick most of the time. "Sorry."

"No, I mean… I've had *no* exes. No girlfriends. Remember? Which means…"

The hard floor was starting to make her arm ache, but Brielle couldn't tear her eyes to look away. "You were a *virgin*?!" She didn't know why she hadn't thought of that. D'uh.

He rolled onto his back, the loss of tension in his arm muscles obvious. She leaned over to get a better look at this face; his expression crinkled and his gaze flicked downward. "Do you regret what just happened?"

"Hell no," said Brielle, kissing him on the cheek. "I find that rather hot," she whispered, even if she knew that complicated things.

Because she knew from experience that former virgins tended to get a *little too* attached to their cherry-poppers. If hers hadn't dumped her in high school, she probably would have gone mad following him around with puppy-dog eyes forever, laughing shrilly at his stupid, immature jokes, forever stifling her own feelings of apprehension and regret whenever he acted like an idiot and she felt she was supposed to support him.

But then again, she'd never known a twenty-five-year-old virgin. (Pembroke was close, but she was twenty-two. And who knew with her now…) Perhaps he'd be mature enough to handle it.

Because she didn't want this to end anytime soon, but it couldn't last forever, either.

They fell into a silence only broken by the sound of a phone from somewhere beneath them.

"Mine," said Archer, shifting himself away. He reached for the grab bars above him again to pull himself into a sitting position, then tried reaching toward the pocket of his pants, which were somewhere down around his ankles.

Brielle shot up and grabbed his phone for him, gently pulling his boxers and pants higher up his legs once he took it from her. He watched her without even looking at his phone screen.

"Should I?" she asked, his boxers halfway up his legs. She realized despite what they'd just shared, this moment felt more clinical, more intrusive somehow.

His gaze fell down to his legs and Brielle's did, too, finally looking at his bare legs for the first time. They were skinny—skinnier than she imagined even through his pants—at odds with his torso. There were some bruises along one shin and the other thigh, and Brielle worried that she'd hurt him.

His eyes flittered away from her and she wondered if he could read her face. She hadn't meant to be surprised, hadn't meant to think anything negative, but there was no explaining that, not when she hadn't said anything anyway. "I can manage," he said, clearing his throat. He finally looked at his screen. "I should probably..."

She jumped up, grabbing her panties, bra, and shirt from off the floor. "I'll give you some privacy," she said and instead of heading to the master bathroom, she went for the guest one to put more distance between them.

It took Brielle a second after she stepped out of the bathroom, freshened up best she could without a shower, to remember where her pants and sweater were.

Somehow, in their haste, they'd left a bit of a trail from the front door to the bedroom. She stepped over Archer's braces to snatch up her jeans, sliding them on while searching for her sweater. Archer's voice carried down the hallway, although he was speaking in hushed tones and she couldn't make out what he said clearly.

She was pretty sure he mentioned his mother, which was reason enough to not strain to hear more, after what she'd just done with the woman's son.

After a moment, she heard her own phone buzzing and retrieved it from where she'd left it in her purse. Her sweater was nearby and she slid it on awkwardly one arm at a time, shifting the phone from one hand to the other. She saw a message from Pembroke first and she took in the words "I'm sorry," but her notifications disappeared when she saw her mom calling.

Oh. Lovely. Nothing like a couple of young adults chatting with their moms right after they've had sex.

The incessant buzzing of the phone in her hand made it tempting to ignore the call. But when it went to voice mail and her mom called back seconds later, she figured she'd have to answer and just pretend she'd spent the day in the library scouring the classifieds for job listings in a different environment to reenergize her job search. It was sort of how she'd originally seen this day going, which is why she'd felt okay about putting off doing much during the week. She was hopeful about Archer's mom's contact at the museum but practical enough to know it promised little more than nothing. *Maybe this is about Archer's mom firing us. Mom probably wants to know if I know any reason why.* "Hey, Mom."

"Finally!" exclaimed her mom, even though there were no signs Brielle had missed more calls from her. "Is Nora with you?"

"No," said Brielle, almost sucker-punched by how different a turn this conversation was taking than she'd expected. "What's wrong?"

The sound of her mom taking a deep breath almost said it all. "She left. She was gone before I got up this morning. She isn't answering her phone, either. I just thought... Maybe she went somewhere with you? Or told you where she was going? I didn't want to panic when I got back at lunch, but some of her things are missing."

"No." Brielle felt her palm holding the phone getting clammy. "I haven't even talked to her in days."

"She was here last night..." She never had asked Brielle where she'd been, but Brielle supposed it was a good thing she hadn't been too nosy.

Brielle felt her blood run cold. "Does this have something to do with that language camp?"

A moment of silence hung over the line. "Do you think she went to see your grandmother?"

"With what?" asked Brielle. "Lita doesn't have a ton of money to spare, whatever Nora thinks."

There was audible rifling going on on the other side of the call. "I can't find my debit card."

"She knows the pin?"

"I don't know. Maybe. Yes, probably. She's seen me use it."

Nora, are you freaking serious? "Let me see if there are any flights to Puerto Rico out of O'Hare today." She brought up the browser.

"What if she already left?" It was the first time in a long time Brielle had heard that twinge of hurt in her mom's voice without it being drowned in anger.

"Can you call the police?" asked Brielle. There were two flights to Puerto Rico from Chicago today. One left at 5 in the morning. But the other wasn't going to fly out until 7 P.M.

"It hasn't been twenty-four hours since she left." Always practical, even when her teenage daughter was off doing something stupid. "And she's almost eighteen, I don't know what they'd say..."

"They'd say she's not an adult yet, and you have every right to deny letting her leave the continental U.S. without permission." Brielle took a deep breath. "She could have left at 5 this morning..."

"I don't think so. I don't sleep well these days and she was still here at 6 when I got up. I'm sure of it."

That was a relief. Leave it to Nora's laziness to make sure she didn't catch an early morning flight. "Then there's a chance she's aiming for a 7 P.M. one. I'll send you the details. Can you call the airline and see if they'll release information on whether or not she bought a ticket?" Naturally, she wouldn't have stolen her mom's credit cards. Then they could have checked a statement to see if it matched the airline. As it was, the best evidence they would find was a withdrawal of no doubt hundreds of dollars in cash.

"If they can find her, I'll make them take her aside," her mom said. "Then head there to get her."

"No," said Brielle, having a moment of clarity. "Just ask if they'll subtly deny her boarding? Don't let her know you know what's up. She might bolt or resent everyone making a scene."

"If you think I *care* about her being resentful—"

"It's not about caring. Or what she deserves." Brielle brought up her messaging app, dinging Gavin to see if he was still free today. Too bad O'Hare was still some distance away from the heart of the city. "She just might... respond better to this if we approach it differently. If we let her vent without you there to hear it."

"Brielle, Nora is *my* daughter..."

I'm free, texted Gavin. *What's up?* "I know. You can meet us in the parking lot of the airport—if that's even where she is."

"It has to be."

"Well, I'll hop in the car and head there first myself. My friend Gavin is closer; Nora always thought he was funny... I'll ask him to try to head her off first. Unless she's already past security, but maybe if we explain the situation..."

"I can't ask your friend to get involved with this—"

"Mom, trust me." Brielle's fingers flew over her screen as she explained the situation to Gavin. "This is the way to do this."

"Okay," said her mom, her voice unsteady. "I'll call you back shortly after I hear what the airline has to say." She hung up without even saying goodbye.

"What was that about?"

A small gasp escaped Brielle's lips as she spun around to find Archer behind her, his now-wrinkly clothes back on, but his hair still in disarray.

"Family emergency." Brielle quickly looked back at her screen to finish the conversation with Gavin. He was halfway out the door already, he said, about to head toward O'Hare, but without a car, he was stuck relying on the L trains, and he had to walk a few blocks and make a switch to get to the one that would take him to the airport. Still, she felt better knowing they both would be headed there at once with her mom shortly behind.

"Can I help?" He sounded so sincere, his soothing tone sent a shock down Brielle's body. *Daniel would have just covered his head with a pillow and asked me to bring him some pizza whenever I got back.*

"I..." She signed off the messaging with Gavin. She *wanted* Archer to help. She really didn't want to part from him at all. But she was suddenly struck that she had no idea *how* he could help. It was almost 4:30. She didn't have time to help him get into her car —if he even could get in—or to help him out of it when they got there. She didn't have room for his wheelchair or the arm strength she was sure she'd need to lift it into her backseat—assuming it'd even fit.

She felt terrible for even thinking those things.

"It's my sister," she said. "She's only seventeen and we think she might have stolen Mom's debit card and is at O'Hare waiting for a flight to Puerto Rico."

His eyebrows arched. "That's a... Wow. Can you pull her off the plane?"

"Mom's calling right now to even confirm she made a reservation. I told her to play it cool, have them refuse to board her, and Gavin and I will try to meet her and smooth things over between her and Mom."

"Oh," said Archer, his voice growing softer. He tapped his wheels with both hands. "I could..." He stopped, as if he suddenly realized there wasn't a whole lot he could do.

Brielle pulled her purse over her body. "I have to go," she said. "The flight I suspect she wants to get on takes off at 7, and they usually board those things a half hour early, and it'll take me over an hour to get there if the traffic is good..." She stopped, suddenly realizing the words were tumbling out of her without rhyme or reason. She closed the distance between them and kissed him on the cheek. "This was fun," she said, but her heart wasn't in it. Not with this crisis in the making. "Give me a call soon?"

"Uh, yeah," he said, rolling after her toward the door. "Good luck with your sister... I hope... I hope it all works out okay."

You and me both, thought Brielle as she sprinted outside, not even bothering to close the door behind her.

CHAPTER SEVENTEEN

Useless. It was as if the world had to do this every time he experienced a little happiness—send an undeniable reminder that he was utterly useless.

Not that he was certain Brielle considered him someone close enough to rely on in a situation like this—despite the fact that she'd considered him trustworthy enough to let him touch her beautiful, soft skin, to let him inside her. But he had a feeling if he could walk at more than a snail's pace without needing to rest every half a minute, she wouldn't have minded him tagging along.

Visions of what could have been flashed through his mind. Running down the cavernous walkways of O'Hare, scouring for a mini-Brielle, resting a hand on Brielle's shoulder while she talked some sense into a teenage runaway. Depositing the girl into the arms of Brielle's mother—an older Brielle with gray hair, he pictured—and swooping Brielle into his arms as they walked away. Her kissing him not just because she wanted to be touched, not because she was used to doing this with guys anyway, but because she wanted to feel *his* lips on hers, to thank him for being there when she needed him most.

Instead, some guy named Gavin was going to have the honor. He wondered if this was another of Brielle's ex-boyfriends—at the very least, a guy she trusted enough with something like this. Surely, she trusted him enough to sleep with him, too, if she gave Archer, someone she only barely knew and who'd almost messed things up when they'd met, the same level of intimacy.

And he'd thought *his* phone call had been disheartening. Brielle's was so much worse—and he immediately felt guilty for even thinking that, considering it wasn't *his* emergency to panic over, it wasn't his loved one who was about to make a reckless mistake.

He hadn't even known she'd had a sister. He didn't know if she had more siblings. But he knew the vanilla-like scent of her hair, the touch of her smooth, small fingers.

He wheeled over to his drafting desk, reminding himself that he had a deadline this week and for once, his Sunday (his one physical therapy-free day) wasn't devoted to keeping his mother busy. Not that he hadn't had a bit of that when his dad had called, demanding that he and his mother get back on speaking terms and then handing the phone back to his wailing mother, who'd spent the better part of twenty minutes listing off all she'd done and sacrificed for her son. Only because his dad was somewhat sensible did he eventually take the phone back from her, demand a promise from Archer to talk to her when she called later that week, and leave Archer to bask in silence.

His place was a mess and he knew Brielle wasn't coming tomorrow to fix it, but he didn't really care.

He took his phone out of his pocket and placed it on the table next to a clean sheet of drafting paper, which he pulled out from underneath his desk. He picked up a pencil, but nothing appeared on the paper in front of him. His gaze kept flicking to the phone, as if Brielle would even think of him in all of this. He hadn't even asked her to let him know what happened, and frankly, he doubted he would be on her mind at all, despite the fact that he couldn't get her off his.

She'd been worried, true, but she'd really looked disinterested when she left. So much for getting her help redecorating.

He put pencil to paper. He tried to move it. He really did. His muscles ached everywhere and he was pretty sure he had some new bruises thanks to the slight fall and everything else that had happened back in his room, but for once, he barely even cared.

He picked up his phone and brought up his messages. There were no texts between him and the last number that had called him. There was barely much of a call history. But he didn't want to hear any voices right now. Didn't have the courage to voice his wish out loud.

Dad, he texted, *will you help me get my license and a van so I can drive myself?*

He put the phone down, certain it would be silent. His dad had probably moved on to the zillion other things he did to entertain himself on a Sunday, satisfied he'd done as much as he could to quiet his wailing wife for the day. He wasn't even sure his dad knew *how* to text. His mother certainly didn't.

It was another minute before his phone buzzed.

Finally, the text said. *Of course.*

The message blinked an extra minute before new text appeared.

Is there somewhere you want me to take you in your mother's van before then?

Archer almost couldn't believe it. Surely someone had taken his father's phone and was responding on behalf of him as part of the big cosmic joke against him.

If you're free right now... he typed, not even hoping.

His dad didn't even ask *why* he wanted to go to the airport. Maybe he could assume by the fact that he had no luggage that he at least wasn't going to take off on a trip without letting everyone know. Then again, he probably knew he couldn't really go on a trip alone, not without someone to help him pack and unpack his wheelchair whenever he got to a place that wasn't accessible or even when boarding the plane. (Although he supposed the flight attendants might have helped with that. Perhaps it was possible after all.)

Which made him think again about the car he'd need. His parents had gotten this van with a lift so his mother wouldn't have to lift Archer's chair herself. But he'd need a lift to get the chair up into the driver's seat as well as hand-based controls. (Although he supposed he could load his chair in the back with a lift and climb into a bucket seat if there were stairs that lowered.) Not for the first time, he realized how fortunate he was to have parents who could afford these things.

And that, despite it all, he was sort of on okay terms with the one writing the checks.

It was forty minutes into the drive before his dad even said anything more than the few words they'd shared when they were getting in the car to explain where they were going.

"Is this going to be one of those mad dashes through the airport you see in movies to stop a girl from getting on a plane?"

Archer's jaw dropped and he stared at his dad. He seemed so serious, but there was something—a little twinkle in his eye—that made him question whether or not his dad found this whole venture an annoyance after all.

"I've seen you with a clear path in front of you," continued his dad. "I know how fast you can blaze down an aisle. You're going to get stopped at security unless you buy a ticket, though. Hollywood always seems to forget that."

"Not to mention it takes them an additional ten to twenty minutes to scan my chair to make sure I'm not smuggling anything," added Archer, grinning. "No... Well... A girl I know is trying to stop her sister from flying, and I thought... I don't even know what I thought. I just wanted to be there."

The more he thought about it, the stupider he felt. Just because they'd had sex didn't mean he was her boyfriend. He knew it was a bad idea to be her boyfriend, considering her plans to leave the area (probably). He'd known her... less than a week. This was all wrong, but for some reason it felt so right.

And if it screwed things up between him and Brielle—as much as that hurt him to think about—fine. They needed to end at some point anyway.

"So what you're saying is we're sort of on a fool's errand." His dad's voice got clipped, and Archer winced. He knew it was a Sunday, but his dad always had a dozen things to do.

The landscape zipped by outside the window and Archer shrugged.

His dad cleared his throat. "I was joking, son. I said I'd drive you wherever you wanted to go."

Archer knew that the longer he let the silence sit between them, the more awkward it would be, so he blurted out the first thing that came to mind. "Was Mother... Is she terribly upset?"

"I'm sorry I even had her call you today," spat his dad. "You need to stop worrying so much about your mother's moods. The only one who can fix those is her, and she's had decades of practice in letting her anxiety get the best of her." His dad tore his eyes off the road for a second to reach a hand over to Archer to pat his shoulder. "It's not for you to fix, okay?"

"I know that... But I..."

"It's understandable you don't like to know she's suffering," said Mr. Ward. "But you can't let it make you feel bad. I was glad to hear you put your foot down about her showing up last night. I asked her if you'd wanted her to come and she was so dodgy about the question, I had this gut feeling something was up."

"It's not that I didn't *want* her to come; I just wanted something to myself. To enjoy something without worrying about her."

"I understand." As the sign leading off the highway to O'Hare came into view, his dad checked his blind spot before changing lanes. "And even if she never acts like it, I think your mother does too. She just... doesn't want to accept it."

"Dad, I..." Archer didn't even know what else to say.

Luckily, his dad filled the silence for him as they made their way to the O'Hare parking lot. It was crowded, but he supposed it might have been worse during the week with all the business travel. "So what's the plan?" he asked, probably deciding it best to leave the rest of the words unspoken between them. They weren't going to fix their relationship overnight, but Archer already felt better knowing his dad cared enough to spend just tonight with him. He'd thought he was as good as dead to his dad practically. "Call this girl, get you a ticket to wherever the sister is going so you can get past security?"

If not for the speed bump they went over, Archer would have laughed more audibly. Only his dad could think nothing of wasting money on a plane ticket no one intended to use. And that was assuming there even were any tickets left at this late hour. "I don't have a passport. She's headed to Puerto Rico."

"No passport necessary. Puerto Rico's part of the U.S."

Archer winced. So much for his dad thinking well of him. He was too dumb to know basic facts, let alone run a company.

His dad laughed. "No need to look so serious. You wouldn't be the first one to make that mistake. I honestly thought D.C. was in Washington state until I was eighteen."

They pulled into a handicapped parking spot and Archer scrambled to get the placard out of the glove compartment. "Yeah, but I'm way older than that..."

"And you focus on things that are more important to you. I get that." He turned off the ignition.

Archer still felt he ought to be better informed, but he let the compliment stick unchallenged. This entire day felt surreal. He never would have imagined he'd get the guts to ask out a pretty girl in the morning, lose his virginity in the afternoon, and then have a moment with his dad at the airport of all places that same evening. "I'm sorry I couldn't... take over the business," he blurted out.

His dad froze, his hand on the button that would automatically open the trunk to get the chair out. "I never expected you to."

It was like a punch to the gut. Archer swallowed.

His dad cleared his throat. "That... sounded bad. I just meant. If you wanted to, that would be one thing. But I didn't want to force my child to follow my footsteps, like my dad did."

"Still... I'm the first in four generations not to take over..."

His dad's face darkened a little, and Archer wished he could tell if it was from embarrassment or something more. "Look, I... All I ever wanted was to provide for my family and to have enough to provide my child with the future he wants. I... may not understand your art books, but I'm glad you found something that makes you happy. I'm glad other people who understand these things recognize your talents." He smiled.

Archer almost felt like he was going to cry.

"So we'll talk about the license and the car," continued his dad. "But first I'll help you get your chair out and then... Wait here while you take care of business."

"Thank you," choked out Archer. "Thank you..." It was all he could say.

CHAPTER EIGHTEEN

Gavin descended on Brielle almost as soon as she walked through the check-in doors. "I looked for her everywhere before security. She's almost definitely gone through. I didn't know if I should buy a ticket and hope I could return it or talk to a security officer to have her pulled aside, but then I figured I was no relation to her, so I wasn't sure if they'd allow—"

"It's all right," Brielle said, embracing Gavin and giving him a quick peck on the cheek. "Thank you." She grabbed his hand and pulled him toward the front of the airline's line.

"*Excuse me*," said a man in line.

"It's an emergency," explained Gavin, wincing.

Brielle just ignored him. "I need to speak with a manager," she explained to the woman behind the counter, who was halfway through probably telling her she'd need to get to the back of the line. "It's about a minor flying without permission."

Although the woman sighed and hardly seemed concerned, she at least sent a message over a walkie-talkie before curtly asking them to step aside to an unused counter.

Gavin and Brielle exchanged an awkward glance as they waited, Brielle's phone clutched tightly in one hand, drumming her fingers on the counter. She'd given calling Nora a shot, thinking maybe she might have felt more up to talking to her than their mom, but it'd gone unanswered. Big surprise.

"So... life, huh?" said Gavin. "Not exactly what we expected post-college?"

Brielle cradled her head in her palm and let out a light laugh. "I *cannot* believe we graduated a week ago. I feel ten years older."

"This stuff with Nora been that bad?"

"No," she said. "I mean, maybe... That's the thing. I was barely tuned into her issues. I... was just so wrapped up in my own."

"Understandable," said Gavin. "I've barely spoken to my grandma since graduation, let alone my sister."

"Yeah, but you're not still *living* with them." She winced. She didn't mean to bring up memories of how he hadn't lived with his sister for years thanks to his bigoted parents. Was there no one without this kind of family drama? "Sorry," she said.

He shrugged and stuffed his hands in his pockets, staring at his feet. Brielle wondered if he wanted to say more, but he seemed to be stopping himself. Whatever his issues—or Lilac's for that matter—perhaps he thought it inappropriate at the moment.

"Hey," said Brielle, gently putting a hand on his shoulder. "Thanks again. I... I don't even know why I called you." She chuckled lamely. "What did I think you could do that I couldn't, just because you could get here first?"

"It often helps to have someone else present for family drama," said Gavin. "People tend to hold their tongues a little. Well, *some* people." He shrugged. "I don't mind. You don't have to feel bad about relying on your friends, Brielle."

"Yeah, but... You have your own stuff to worry about."

He grimaced. "I'd rather not think about all of that right now anyway. And this is more important."

Brielle raised an eyebrow, unsure if she'd consider her sister acting like a bratty teenager that important, really. Especially since they'd likely catch her before she got anywhere, and if she really was about to visit Lita, she didn't think she'd be in any danger anyway. "Is Lilac okay...?" she asked, remembering Gavin's anxieties from that morning. That morning. It felt like weeks ago.

A muscle on Gavin's cheek twitched. "She needs some space right now." He swallowed, and Brielle felt a bit of a sinking feeling in her stomach. What if Gavin had been right about Lilac's boss? "What about you? What happened on your date?"

Brielle felt the heat rush to her face—and at the thought of Archer and what she'd done, the heat wasn't content to just stay confined to the upper portion of her body. "It may have... gone a little better... than expected."

His eyes widened and he looked around the room for an approaching employee. "I... want to know more, but I'm afraid you'll just be getting to the good part when someone walks up. Where *is* the manager, anyway?"

Brielle's brow furrowed as she scanned her phone for any new messages, but her mom hadn't texted since confirming Brielle's detective work and saying she was on her way. How would this evening have played out if her sister hadn't gone all drama queen to the extreme? She supposed it was too late to go "dinner and a movie" on Archer now that she'd slept with him. She wondered if it had been a good idea to basically define their relationship in terms of a hookup—even if she'd told herself it wasn't exactly like she was in a good place in her life to commit.

And then there was the fact that he was—had been—a virgin. Would *he* take their fling to mean more than it did?

Was she so certain it didn't mean more than she told herself it did?

"Miss Reyes?" A stern-looking woman in an airline uniform approached Brielle and Gavin from behind.

"Yes," said Brielle, snapping to attention.

"We have your daughter in security; if you'll follow me." She turned on her heel.

"*Sister*," muttered Brielle, exchanging a look with Gavin. She couldn't possibly look old enough to have a teenager, could she?

Could she?

Stepping onto the escalator, Gavin studied her face and laughed. "You don't look forty-five, if that's what you're wondering."

Brielle winced and finished her text to her mom as she stepped in line behind him. The thought was quickly pushed to the back of her mind a few minutes later as she got to the security office and came face-to-face with her sister, a gym bag stuffed under her seat and her arms crossed so tight it looked like she was trying to squeeze the breath out of herself.

At least she's safe, thought Brielle.

"What are *you* doing here?" Nora stared up at Brielle and then Gavin, trying to send daggers at them with her eyes. She looked like an angry toddler painted up to slightly resemble a mature college-aged woman. If the situation weren't such a hassle, Brielle might have laughed.

"I really shouldn't have bothered you with all this," said Brielle, gesturing around her at the airport as they exited the security room. Her mom was still back there with Nora, trying to get all the paperwork sorted out to get a partial refund on the ticket. Brielle clapped her hands together and cringed. "I'm sorry."

"Are you kidding? That was... interesting." Gavin chuckled, shoving his hands back into his pockets.

His presence had kept things a little less heated than they might have otherwise been once her mom had shown up. Maybe the security guards alone would have been good for that, but like Brielle had guessed, Gavin had taken charge immediately, sitting next to Nora and letting her vent without judgment. Brielle had had to bite her tongue and feign interest in her phone to keep from commenting more than once, but Gavin had taken it like a champ and tried to slowly, but surely, get Nora to acknowledge that she was going about everything the wrong way.

That she was almost eighteen and she could travel on her own at that point, but until then, it was best to save. And there would be a language program next summer—a goal to work toward this year.

And that if she wanted to keep on good terms with her mom and sister, she couldn't go behind their backs like this.

Basically, Gavin had been the subtle educational YouTube video she hoped he would be. But she still felt bad for making him come.

"It's been a *long* day," said Brielle, cradling her head at the onset of a headache. "I feel like we should catch up, but also that we haven't even been separated that long..."

He gave her a hug, holding her tight against his chest and squeezing her. "One of these days, I need to give you a tour of the whole city."

"I've been to Chicago before." Brielle laughed as she pulled away, her hands still on Gavin's back.

"It's different when you do more than just go to a museum and back," said Gavin. "I don't even know if I'll ever have time to get to a museum..."

"I'm looking into museum jobs." Her phone buzzed in her purse and she let go of Gavin to fish it out. "Well, sort of. Not many openings, but I may know someone who can get me in front of people at the Natural History..." She stopped.

Gavin peered down at her, but he likely couldn't see the screen. "What is it?"

"I got a text from..." Brielle looked up, toward the elevator. Sure enough, Archer was wheeling over toward her, his phone in his lap. Their eyes met and he waved. She waved back.

"*Oh. My. God.*" Gavin stared at him, slack-jawed. "Is that seriously the hot young comic artist you're banging?"

"We're not... Well, we..." She swallowed and shoved the phone into her pocket, staring at Archer as he wheeled toward her. Too late, she realized she should probably move toward him. But shock made her lose control of her limbs for just a little bit.

Archer slowed down, his face falling slightly, but she waved at him and remembered to smile, and he started wheeling over faster.

"*He is so gorgeous*," whispered Gavin into her ear.

She pinched his forearm as Archer drew closer, embarrassed and unable to stop picturing him mostly naked on the floor beneath her.

Archer cleared his throat as he pulled up in front of them. "I'm sorry I... I probably shouldn't have come, right?"

His faltering smile seemed to keep switching between ashamed and smarmy and Brielle didn't know if he was trying to be charming or was genuinely embarrassed. Or probably both.

"No," said Brielle. It was like she'd slapped Archer. Her eyes widened as she flapped her hands. "No, I mean... No, I don't mind, really! Um, but what are you doing here?"

"I..." Even as he spoke to Brielle, Archer stared at Gavin. "How's your sister?"

"Her sister." Gavin nodded at Brielle.

Archer shook his head. "Uh, yeah, of course... I meant... Oh, it's kind of hot in here, isn't it?" He fanned himself with his hand.

Brielle bent down to get a closer look at his face. He'd lost some color. "Are you okay? Did Pauline drive you here...?" She looked back and forth to find the woman.

"My dad did," he said, wincing. "And he's waiting in the car. He had some business to conduct."

"In the car?" asked Gavin.

"On the phone." Archer drummed his fingers atop one of his armrests. "I'm fine." He swallowed.

"Oh, well... Thanks to the airline's help, we got my sister before she boarded." She gestured over her shoulder. "My mom's still with her, but she told me to head on home first."

"You don't need a ride because you drove yourself..." Archer's phone screen lit up as it buzzed from his lap, but he ignored it. "I, uh... You know, I don't know why I came..."

"So..." said Gavin after a moment's silence. Brielle could feel his eyes boring into her the whole while. Extending his hand, he bent forward a little to reach toward Archer. "I'm Gavin, Brielle's friend from college."

Seemingly glad for the distraction, Archer took the man's hand firmly and shook it. "Archer. Archer Ward."

"Oh, I know." He bumped against Brielle. "This one won't stop talking about you every time I check in with her."

"Shut up," said Brielle, but she was laughing. "*He's* the one who said you were hot, by the way."

"Are you two talking about me behind my back before he even got to meet me? I'm flattered." Resting his fingertips atop his chest, Gavin chuckled.

"Oh," said Archer, and strangely, his face lit up as he studied Gavin. "You're *that* friend."

"The one and only." He turned to Brielle. "Well, I should get going. Fewer late night trains."

"Right," said Brielle. She wrung her hands as Gavin kissed her on the cheek. She didn't know how she felt about being left alone with Archer just then, in just about the last place she'd expected to see him. "Thanks so much for everything. See you online?"

"And in person soon, too, I hope," he said, tapping her nose lightly. "Nice to meet you, handsome," he said to Archer, and then he left before Archer could even do more than say, "You too..."

Brielle and Archer stared at each other. Running a hand over the back of his head, Archer looked almost sheepish. "Would you believe I happened to be in the neighborhood?"

A joke. He was, despite stern appearances, surprisingly prone to them. She couldn't believe how much he'd changed in her eyes in less than a week—in so many different ways.

But this didn't seem like a good sign. He was clearly following her around like a puppy because she'd been his first. And she felt so bad about it. Just because it'd been a few months since she'd last been with Daniel. But Archer had been so hot and willing...

I don't need a relationship right now. She should have just kept her pants on, especially after he'd confessed he'd never been kissed.

"You wanted to help me," she said, a smile skirting her lips. "That's sweet of you."

Relief seemed to wash over Archer's face. "I don't know what I thought I could accomplish," he said. "I just thought maybe... You'd need some support."

Brielle reached forward to grab hold of his hand and squeezed it. "Thank you," she said.

"But then I should have thought how you'd already asked your friend—"

"No, *thank you*. I mean it. I... I would have asked you to come along if I thought you could. I know that's dumb and that we hardly knew each other, but I didn't like feeling like I was just walking out on you after—"

"Bri?" said a voice. Both Brielle and Archer turned, their hands still clenched together. Brielle's mom readjusted the strap on her purse and looked from Brielle's face to her hand and back. "I thought you were headed home."

From behind her, Nora snorted.

Brielle dropped Archer's hand like it was a hot potato.

CHAPTER NINETEEN

Brielle's mother looked tired, haggard—absolutely on her last straw. Considering the sullen teen behind her—the one with both hands clutching a gym bag, staring at them like she was seconds from popping invisible popcorn into her mouth—was probably the sister who'd started this whole mess, it made sense.

But Archer couldn't help but feel that this slightly plump, attractive older woman was studying him like he was to blame for everything.

"I was," said Brielle, and Archer suddenly remembered her mother had said something about her heading home. "I ran into Archer on the way out." She gestured to him and then clasped her hands together. "Mom, Nora, this is Archer. Archer, my mom—Leah Clark—and my sister, Nora."

Archer rolled his shoulders and extended his hand. It took Ms. Clark an extra minute to move forward to take it. "Archer Ward?" she asked. She really did look like she'd just finished running a marathon.

For a second, Archer thought Brielle's mother was a fan of his. He laughed when he realized the truth. *She owns the cleaning company.* "Yes. Nice to meet you. Brielle's been... great. She's been a great job. I mean, she did a great job." His throat went dry. Where was he going with this? Was he trying to compliment her as a worker, despite the fact that he'd just slept with her? But he didn't want her to think she was being let go because of anything she'd done. Not that he was even sure his mother had canceled the service yet.

"I just got a call to cancel the account," said Brielle's mom, frowning. Nora's eyes lit up, though she tried to mask her sudden spike in interest with a forced look of boredom.

Brielle stared at him, her lips slightly parted.

"Right, well, it wasn't that she wasn't good at it. Because she was." Archer felt like an idiot. He could speak in front of a crowd of fans, but put him in front of someone he didn't know well and expect him to speak one-on-one and he grew a second tongue he didn't know how to handle. "My mother is just concerned I was relying on her too much."

"She said something about my '*maid*' fraternizing with you too much." There was no missing the look that passed between her and Brielle. Her mom shook her head, cradling her forehead. "I can't deal with this today. I'll see you at home, Bri." She smiled awkwardly. "Nice to meet you, Mr. Ward. Thank you for your business. I'm sorry it wasn't satisfactory."

"No, it *was*—" started Archer, but Brielle's mom had already moved around him toward the exit to the parking garage.

Nora lingered a beat, staring Archer up and down. He winced under her gaze. Sometimes he could tell when someone was biting their tongue. Maybe the girl knew she'd already bitten off more than she could chew with her antics for the evening.

"Nora!"

The girl stared at Brielle and nodded, heading off without a word.

"Sorry about that," said Brielle after a beat. "So, um... That was why, huh? It wasn't about you cleaning up after yourself—it really was about me 'fraternizing' with you?"

He imagined his mother's face from the night before, hurt but haughty, the perfect recipe for swearing revenge. "My mother can be unreasonable…"

"I thought she liked me after last night," said Brielle. "Sort of. Enough to refer me to someone at the museum anyway."

Archer had almost forgotten all about the museum. And how the fact that he'd been able to text Brielle—that this whole unforgettable, amazing day had happened—was because his mother had forgotten entirely about her promise to make a few calls to aid with Brielle's job prospects. "She did," lied Archer, but he had a feeling she'd dislike any woman she thought he might be remotely interested in, despite all her talk about setting him up. She probably only said those things because she hoped he never would take her up on them. "I mean, it was more about her and me. It's true that she didn't like that I was relying on you too much."

Chewing her lip, Brielle broke into a faltering smile. "Well, you *are* pretty tidy. I don't think you need a daily house cleaning." She tapped her fingers on her thigh, again drawing Archer's attention to those form-fitting jeans. "But you never even told her last night that we were…" She stopped, maybe trying to think of how to define them.

He wanted her to define them. But she wouldn't finish her sentence.

"She blamed the 'fraternizing' for canceling when calling your mother no doubt, but really, it was about me. Her and me." Archer swallowed. He wondered if she could smell the mommy issues that stank all over him. "We've had… problems when it comes to her ignoring my privacy."

"You didn't expect her to show last night, did you?"

"No," he admitted. "And things kind of went south from there, once you left." Eager to change the subject, he started scrolling through his phone screen for nothing in particular. "Is… your friend from last night okay?"

"I don't even know." She shook her head and looked off behind him. "So much has happened, I can't even believe it's only been twenty-four hours."

"But your sister was stopped," he said. "That's good." He really had no skills when it came to this communication thing, did he?

"Yeah," said Brielle. She paused. "Did you really come here just to... offer me moral support?"

He tried to smile, but he was pretty sure the best he offered was a lopsided grin. "Stupid, wasn't it?"

She laughed. At least he had that going for him. "No, I... I appreciate it." She squeezed her fingers together. "I guess I won't be seeing you tomorrow, huh?"

"I still need some help redecorating. We didn't exactly get around to that."

More laughter. *God, seeing her laugh has got to be the best form of foreplay.* "I'd be totally fine with stopping by later this week."

His heart sank. *Not tomorrow?* He'd pushed too hard, come on too strong. "I'd like that," he said, his voice faltering.

At least she wasn't done with him entirely.

CHAPTER TWENTY

A part of Brielle pictured Archer at the airport like one of those star-crossed lovers in a movie. Rushing through security in a comical way that would get someone arrested in real life. Pledging eternal love and a desire to make things work, even though there was a reason why the lovers were being parted at the airport in the first place—probably something to do with their plans for life leading to such different places. And those differences weren't going to vanish just because the credits rolled and the music swept in, portending a happily ever after.

But she wasn't the one getting on a plane, leaving him behind— at least not yet. And they hadn't discussed their future plans. They'd just met—what future was there to speak of?

Curse you and your gorgeously handsome self. She knew better than to jump in bed with someone too quickly. That hadn't gone well with Daniel either of the times she'd let her sex drive take over her brain.

It'd been five days since she'd seen Archer. Her mom hadn't even pressed her about why Mrs. Ward had considered her to be "fraternizing" with him. She didn't even ask why he had been at the airport. Perhaps she really did believe it was a coincidence.

Brielle herself wasn't sure what him showing up at the airport had meant. It meant he liked her—like *really* liked her maybe. Or perhaps he just thought it was the nice thing to do. But to go out of his way to that extent—to get a ride from his dad? Did he have it bad for her?

Did that make her feel good—or bad?

Her confusion on that matter was why she'd eventually promised to see him this weekend, feigning being busy during the week. Slow it down. Make it more casual. She *did* have other clients to clean for and jobs to apply for, but mostly she'd been spending her evenings in sweatpants munching on chips while watching YouTube videos. The most activity her brain had had after her grueling five-a-day-minimum jobs she sent resumes out for was getting into a debate with some stupid user about whether or not *The Walking Dead* TV fans could even call themselves fans without reading the comics. The asshole had even questioned whether or not she knew what a comic was.

Archer's *Wheels* comic sat tantalizingly staring at her every time she was in her room from the top of a pile of boxes next to her desk. She'd read it twice more that week, tracing her fingers over the wheelchair-using Todd she imagined to be Archer's stand-in. She'd forgotten to get it signed. At a signing.

"Meh meh." One of Mrs. Tanaka's cats—Tigger—rubbed up against Brielle's thigh as he made cute little chirping noises. She took off her rubber glove and pet the top of his head with one finger. For some reason, this cat really liked her this year.

"No, Tigger, it's not lunch yet." Mrs. Tanaka swooped in to her bathroom to scoop her cat up. She kissed his cheek and Brielle laughed at the cat's panicked expression. "And Miss Brielle isn't the one who gives you food."

She smiled up at her client—a woman she found far less irritating this summer, along with her cats—as she went back to scrubbing the tiles. She didn't think the tiles needed it three times a week, but who was she to argue with a client?

"So," said Mrs. Tanaka, still holding the cat, "your mother tells me you intend to quit being my house cleaner."

The brush in Brielle's hand stopped mid-scrub as she stared back up at the slightly elderly woman. "That's not true," she said.

"She said you're looking for a 'better' job."

"Oh," said Brielle, moving her hand in a circular motion again. "That's true, but there's nothing promising yet."

Tigger squeaked and started pushing against Mrs. Tanaka's shoulder, so she bent over to let him scurry off behind her. "What kind of work are you looking for?"

She crossed her arms and stared down at Brielle, strangely interested in Brielle's life instead of her own for once. "I'm not sure," admitted Brielle, cringing. "I studied history and philosophy, so I thought maybe a museum. Or research. Or something."

"You don't sound like you have much of a plan."

Dipping the brush in a bucket of water, Brielle shrugged. "I never knew what I wanted to be. I just knew what I liked studying. I figured the rest would fall into place later."

Snorting, Mrs. Tanaka fluffed at her hair in the bathroom mirror. "To be young and hopeful," she said. "And what about a boyfriend or fiancé, hmm? How does he play into this?"

"I don't have one." The words came out so quickly, she almost regretted it. No, she just had a guy she couldn't stop thinking about, a guy she practically had to force herself to wait and see. Part of her wasn't sure why she'd feigned being busy until the weekend, but she was afraid of giving him too much hope. Only one more day. Archer had said he'd blocked off the entire day for her, had asked her to a movie and said Pauline was giving him a ride so he could meet her there. Maybe he thought it too awkward for them both to ride with her like school kids.

Her blurting didn't go unnoticed. "You sound defensive," said Mrs. Tanaka. "Recent breakup?"

"Yes," said Brielle, knowing she wasn't lying since she had just been dating Daniel a few months ago. The thought made her want to hurl just a little. "But that was definitely for the best. Believe me, I'm *not* having second thoughts there."

"You should get back into the dating scene." Mrs. Tanaka

grabbed her hair brush off the sink—Brielle hoped she wouldn't expect her to wipe the stray hairs away again. "A rich husband could solve all your problems."

Brielle had to laugh at that. Somehow, she couldn't picture herself wining and dining the days away, arm-in-arm with a rich guy in a suit who would trade her in for a newer model in a decade or two. *Archer's rich, apparently. Sort of. Or his parents are.* She wasn't sure why she'd thought about that. Even if she married him, she wouldn't be hobnobbing about town arm-in-arm. Where did rich people hobnob in a small town anyway? The country club? That tiny downtown art gallery? But that was all beside the point. She was in no position to consider marriage.

"I'm not opposed to dating again," said Brielle. "I'm sort of seeing someone," she added before Mrs. Tanaka could offer up some nephew or cousin's son. "But I don't want to get settled in a relationship when I don't even know where I'm going to be in a few months."

"Be here," said Mrs. Tanaka, looking over her shoulder, where several drawn-out meows were echoing throughout the hallway. She patted Brielle. "You're a good cleaner."

"Thanks," said Brielle, spraying some more cleaner around the base of the toilet.

For some reason, being told she was good at this job instead of just being talked her ear off about how she needed to do better made her feel even worse about the prospect of being stuck with it.

The breeze was that deceptively tepid kind that made you feel like if you closed your eyes, you just might be on a tropical island instead of in the Midwest (before the occasional blast of cold air snapped you out of it), so Brielle waited for Archer outside of the cinema. She couldn't remember the last time she'd seen a movie in the afternoon instead of the evening—or the last time she'd seen a movie in a theater, period.

Her eyelids were still closed when she jumped at the sound of a van door opening and a familiar voice. "Did we keep you waiting so long you fell asleep?" asked Pauline. "You'll have to excuse him. My grandpa drives faster." She stepped aside and gestured behind her through the open passenger door toward the driver seat. Archer sat there in his wheelchair in front of the steering wheel.

Brielle covered her mouth in surprise. "You can drive!" It sounded stupid when she said it.

She could have sworn she saw his cheeks color. "Driving's one thing. Parking is another."

"Oh, you can park just fine. It'll just take some more getting used to." Pauline turned around to grab her purse from the van floor. "In fact, I'm going to let you handle this one solo."

"I'm not supposed to drive without supervision yet," said Archer, the panic clearly coloring his face. He winced as his gaze brushed past Brielle's. "Learner's permit."

"Dear me, I think you already technically put the car in park just now." Whipping a pair of sunglasses out of her purse, Pauline slid them over her nose and shut the van door. "Guess I'll be on my way." She slid her glasses down to wink as she passed Brielle. "Seriously, though, come get me if he crashes into anything. I'm going shopping while you're at the movies."

Archer visibly took a deep breath and then shifted gears on the wheel, pressing some buttons that didn't exist on a typical car to get the car moving. His eyes widened as the car pulled away from the corner a little too fast, but he pushed some buttons again and seemed to get a handle on it. Brielle lost sight of him as his van found an open handicapped spot a few rows over from where she stood. She walked down the sidewalk and watched as his door opened and a ramp extended to get his chair down. It was actually pretty cool. She didn't know cars could be made that accessible for disabled drivers.

He started heading toward her, then turned in the completely opposite direction. Brielle stood puzzled for a minute and then felt dumb when she realized there was only one ramp up to the sidewalk and she was standing nowhere near it. She walked toward him.

He paused in front of the theater door, rifling through his pocket to pull out his wallet. Brielle realized the door wasn't one of those automatic ones, so she pulled it open for him.

"Thanks," he said, pulling out his credit card and going through.

"Oh, I'll get it," said Brielle. "You made the lunch we had the other day."

"Already bought," said Archer, heading for one of the automatic ticket kiosks. Brielle clutched her handbag as she stood behind him, wondering if this was okay. He may have more money than her—and her school loan was about to come due before she knew it—but him treating her more than once made this feel more real.

Like the start of an actual, real relationship.

The thought filled her with more panic than the thought of finally getting a positive response from one of her job applications.

She took a deep breath. This wasn't Daniel. This wasn't a mistake. But it wasn't in her plans, and that's why it felt like it was.

"That's so cool that you're driving," she said, for want of something else to focus on. She needed her heart to stop beating quite so quickly every time she looked down at him.

"I just started this week," said Archer, and he surprised her by wheeling ahead of her and getting the next door. He pulled it open with such finesse, she felt stupid for scrambling to get the door for him before. "Long overdue, I know."

"Thanks," she said, referring to the door. "No, I understand. I was scared enough learning to drive as a teen. I couldn't imagine learning how to handle all those buttons and levers."

He laughed as he handed the tickets over to the greeter. "Now I feel like I'm piloting a spaceship or something." He pointed to the concession stand. "Want anything?"

"No thanks. A bit overpriced." *And I don't think I should*

encourage you to offer to pay again. "But I'll get you something if you want it. To pay back for the ticket."

"Don't worry about it. So," he said, swallowing, "you've had a busy week?"

"Yeah." Brielle tucked her hair behind her ear as she walked into the theater. "Cleaning. Applying for jobs. Applying for more jobs."

"You're really determined to leave this place, aren't you?" He winced as he headed toward their seats—or more accurately, her seat next to an empty spot in the front row. "Sorry, he said, as she sat down. "I'm not saying I blame you."

There was a bar practically at her chin level in front of her, and she shifted uncomfortably, gripping both armrests and trying to slouch slightly so her neck didn't strain as much looking up at the screen. She'd never sat so close before. "I'm not trying to leave," she said, shrugging. "Although I guess I figured I would. But if I found a good job here that could help me afford to live on my own..." She left the sentence unfinished. "But I don't think this place is ripe with jobs for history and philosophy majors."

"We have a few museums downtown," said Archer, examining his hands. He'd pulled his chair close. *Really* close. Like practically slamming into her armrest.

"I guess I could get some experience there and leave later," said Brielle, thinking it over. "But I haven't seen a single job posting for any of them." She watched Archer for a minute and wondered what he was thinking. "What about you—have you ever thought about leaving the area?"

"I can do my job anywhere." He pulled his phone out of his pocket and checked the screen before switching it off, reminding Brielle to do the same. She saw a message from Pembroke waiting for her and felt a jolt in her stomach. To be fair, she'd been ignoring her for far too long after that comic shop fiasco. But she didn't feel like dealing with it all just then.

"Then why not go elsewhere?" She switched off her phone. Then she felt obtuse again—he had concerns she couldn't even dream of, probably needed to be closer to his family than she did. His family certainly *cared* about him staying closer than hers did. She didn't even have grandparents or aunts or uncles to speak of, not if you didn't count her dad's family, which she didn't. It was just her, her mom, and Nora, and they seemed to be functioning (or disfunctioning) as their own little two-person unit, letting her stop back in as a guest, eager to get her back out the door.

"Why not?" he pondered, and he genuinely seemed curious. "I couldn't tell you, really. Just that... I'm too scared to. I'm not sure my parents would support it. Well, maybe my dad would..."

"Do you even want to go somewhere else?"

He shrugged. "I don't know. I've never had a reason to. It seemed too much work to bother."

Brielle wasn't sure if he really wanted to and his situation was holding him back or if he actually didn't care. She opened her mouth to say something more, but the theater darkened and the commercials before the previews before the movie began. She slid back into her seat and did her best to get comfortable.

But it was hard to focus when, a few minutes into the movie, Archer slid his hand over hers.

"I could see this on your wall," said Brielle, pulling a canvas print of an old cover of *The Uncanny X-Men* out from behind a display of city scenes, flowers, and inspirational sayings. "Although it's too bad there's none of your art in here."

Shimmying his wheelchair backward into the cramped aisle to try to get a closer look, Archer laughed. "*The Mystified* is popular, but not 'generic wall art' popular. I don't think anyone outside of comic circles really knows it. And I haven't been doing the art long enough to be the one whose work would be a print."

"I was thinking more of *Wheels*." The fake-faded design on the canvas appealed to her. She wasn't even sure where she ranked the

X-Men in terms of favorite superheroes, but they looked more colorful here than they did in the movies.

"That would *never* happen." His chuckle and that smile—the slight, sensuous curve of his lips—made her knees buckle. This was why she'd waited to see him again. This was why this was all a bad idea. Because part of her really, really wanted this to make sense.

"Oo, I bet you could get some canvas of your art printed from a place online." She started putting the *X-Men* canvas back, but he grabbed it out of her hands. She smiled and shifted other canvases around until she found a faded *Captain America* printing. "Like Cap?" she asked, holding it up.

"Give or take. Not really until the movies." He studied the *X-Men* canvas a moment and settled it on his lap. "You know, when you said I should add some comic book décor to my condo, I didn't actually expect us to go looking at a general discount store." He nodded toward the fluffy, bright pink pillows stuffing a shelf to capacity a few feet away. "I didn't think we'd find anything crammed among general décor like that."

"That's probably because you haven't ever shopped at this type of place before."

His resigned nod told her she was on the right track. She put the *Captain America* one aside and kept sorting through until she found one of *Dick Tracy*. Flipping it around, she said, "How about this one? Stylish—but in a pop kind of way."

"Nobody still reads *Dick Tracy* in the twenty-first century," he said, laughing. His head tilted. "But I do kind of like it."

She placed it atop the canvas already in his lap. "Now for something to liven up those plain white dishes in your kitchen." She squeezed past an overly large display to get over to the mugs and dinnerware. It wasn't until she'd spotted and grabbed the sort-of matching Wonder Woman and Batman mugs that she realized Archer was nowhere to be found.

A display of tote bags hanging at the end of the aisle wobbled, almost toppling over, but two hands shot forward to steady it.

"Sorry," said Archer, wincing. "Not a lot of space to move around in here."

Brielle felt stupid for not considering that. For not realizing all of the simple things she took for granted.

"You want me to buy those cups?" he said, not even seeming that bothered by the claustrophobic displays.

"Oh? Yeah." She examined the cups in her hands, her joy at picking out these cute touches of flavor for his condo slightly diminished when she started thinking about how hard things must be for him. Then she felt guilty for even thinking about him differently.

She really wasn't sure how she was supposed to think.

"Get them both," he said, smiling and patting the canvas wall art on his lap. She put the mugs down just as his phone buzzed.

"Damn," he said, trying to shift the pile on his lap to reach his pocket.

"Oh, I can..." She stopped herself and pointed toward his pocket. "Should I get that for you?"

Something like delight danced across his face. "Please."

She knew why a second later when her fingers brushed over his thigh to pull it out. She felt her face—her whole body—growing hot.

He grinned as he shifted the pile back into place and took it from her. His smirk quickly turned into a frown as he clicked the screen.

"What is it?" asked Brielle, wondering if it was his mom again and feeling a bit turned off by the thought. What was it about her that made her determined to think of all the bad possibilities of this relationship? Why was it when she told herself it didn't matter because she just wanted to keep it casual, she knew, deep down, that was a lie? She had to turn around and stare at a display of plates because she couldn't even look at him without wanting to bend over and kiss him.

"Work." He started texting a reply, but he looked up a moment, the corner of his lips curling up. "I need to redo a splash page. The writer changed his mind after my deadline." He raised his eyebrows as he set the phone down. "As the man is wont to do. Hope you don't mind if we cut the shopping short." He patted the pile on his lap. "Although I still hope you'll come back to the condo with me. To help decorate. And for coffee."

"There are all of four things there to decorate with."

"Ah, but I need your help hanging these," he said. "Pauline is going to make herself scarce afterward. If she won't stop talking, I'll tell her I have work." He picked up the phone and started typing again, maybe to text Pauline to meet him back by the car. They'd walked—or walked and wheeled—over to the store together after the movie.

She laughed as she picked at a fraying piece of leather tied around one of her zippers on her purse. "I don't know what a splash page is, but it sounds important."

"It sort of is," he said, leading the way toward the cashiers. "It's a full-page single illustration, and this time it's even the first page of an issue."

"What was wrong with it?"

"I don't know if anything was *wrong* with it," said Archer, rolling his eyes. "Topher just had a different idea for it."

There wasn't much of a line, so Brielle stepped past the cashiers to wait for him to finish paying. Remembering her own message she'd ignored, she dug her phone out of her purse.

There was a new message on top of Pembroke's from Gavin.

She read Pembroke's first: *I just wanted to say I'm really sorry, and I really appreciate what you and your boyfriend or crush or whatever he is and his mom did for me that night.* Brielle winced at the word "boyfriend." *I was an idiot for ever falling for Daniel's lines. He and his ex-fiancée broke up after graduation and he saw me sitting alone and I just needed something then to hold on to. I needed something to look forward to. I knew things ended badly between you, but I thought... I don't know what I thought. That it might be different. That it might just be a little fun.*

Brielle felt bad. Wasn't that what she kept telling herself she was doing with Archer? Just having a bit of fun? Not entering into anything serious?

I still don't have a job, Pembroke's message continued. *I've been applying for practically anything. I didn't want to become a nurse, but I didn't want to wind up working retail or something. But now I'm getting desperate and am strangely finding the retail jobs don't want me, either. That having a degree makes me "overqualified."*

This sounds like I'm complaining, she admitted. *And I guess I am. I didn't want to bother you—any of you—but I figured I owed you at least an apology.*

Brielle guessed Pembroke didn't have a job lined up, but neither did she, not really, so it hadn't seemed entirely odd. But she didn't realize she'd resorted to looking for grunt work—and that she wasn't having luck with that, either. Now that she thought about it, Brielle didn't even really care about the Daniel thing anymore. He and Pembroke hadn't even been dating a full week. It was just like Daniel to get handsy and possessive after such a short amount of time. She'd email Pembroke back later.

Lilac wants to come home, read Gavin's message. *I've been trying to get her to stop and think things through, to consider the things she likes about being there, but I was right. She was nearly assaulted. And I can't get her to report her boss.*

"Ready?" Archer rolled up in front of her, a gigantic bag on his lap. "You okay?" he asked after a minute of Brielle just staring at the screen.

"Yeah." She swallowed and tried to smile. "I'll walk you back to the parking lot, then meet you there."

CHAPTER TWENTY-ONE

"What are you doing?" Archer asked. Brielle moved a rag up and down his wall above the cabinet where he stored his books. There was no avoiding noticing the way her jeans flattered her from behind, especially when she stood on her toes.

"It says to clean the wall first." She rolled back onto her heels and stared down at the cloth, folding it before standing back up again. "And to dry it."

"You are the only person who actually follows instructions like that when it comes to Command strips."

"I *am* a cleaning expert." Tossing her hair back over her shoulder, she placed the cloth on the edge of his kitchen table. It was covered in dirt, even though his walls hadn't even looked that grimy. She caught him looking at the cloth. "Okay, so I didn't exactly scrub your walls when I was your house cleaner."

He laughed. "Nor would I have expected you to."

She peeled both sides of the strip and fixed it to the hook, squishing it hard in her palms with a comical look on her face like it took quite a bit of effort.

"I can do that much," he said, grabbing the package to get the second hook ready.

She watched him. "You've got to press really hard," she said.

"*Really* hard. To make sure it sticks to the wall when the art is hanging on it."

He flexed one of his arms. "I can handle it."

Biting her bottom lip, Brielle danced her fingertips across his bicep. "How do you get arms this ripped?"

"Not easily, considering my muscles aren't exactly the strongest throughout my body." He dropped the hook on the table and wrapped an arm around her waist, causing her to cry out—happily, he thought, or hoped, at least—as he spun her to sit on his lap. "But I have to get physical therapy in every day anyway." He lifted his chin to nudge his nose into her shoulder. Her hair smelled of flowers.

Brielle shifted on his lap and turned her head slightly to look at him. "Is Pauline your trainer then?"

"Pauline and a basketball," he said, inhaling her, wrapping his arms around her torso completely.

"What do you do when it's too cold to play?"

"We play indoors. At the YMCA." He pulled back. "Although I don't get there as often as I'd like, especially when the weather is bad."

Brielle went quiet. "I never even thought about that. Using a wheelchair in the snow."

He laughed. "I take 'snowed in' more literally than some might. But I don't know a lot of people who relish going out there before the snow plows have even gone through if they don't have to."

She fidgeted, turning around somewhat, and Archer loosened his grip. "Yeah, but even after it stops snowing and the main roads are clean... I mean, *I've* slipped on store sidewalks not very well salted."

"Believe me, you're not telling me anything new." He watched as her face fell and he scrambled to make the situation lighter. "Are you saying I should move to Florida?"

That was a mistake. She looked downright grim now.

"What is it?" he asked. "I wasn't serious..."

She shook her head. "No, it wasn't you. I just... have a lot on my mind."

"Like what?"

She didn't say anything. Instead, she slipped off his lap and went back to standing on her toes, affixing the hook he hadn't realized she'd still had in her hand the entire time she'd sat on his lap.

"You can talk to me, Elle."

She visibly winced and Archer remembered how she'd asked him not to call her that because her ex had. "Brielle," he said, tripping over the name in his rush to correct his mistake.

"I barely know you." She looked irritated as she hung the *Dick Tracy* canvas on the hook. Archer couldn't even focus on the way her back arched as she tried to line it up just right because her face had soured.

It was like she'd slapped him. "On the contrary, I think you know me better than anyone ever has before."

She twirled around, crossing her arms tightly across her chest. "Can you stop doing that?"

"What?"

She gestured toward him vaguely. "*That.* All that. Speaking like someone out of an English lit essay—"

"I didn't realize my vocabulary was a *problem.*"

"—acting like last weekend was a bigger deal than it was." The way her eyes widened as she stared down at him, he couldn't help but feel like she'd pulled back the veil on something he'd known all along. That she didn't feel the way he felt about her, that he'd messed up every step of the way thus far, that he seemed like a love-stricken, idiotic fool.

He didn't say anything. He couldn't. If that was how she felt, he couldn't change her mind. He'd tried to give her some space, even though being apart from her for a week had *killed* him, had almost made him call up Scrubbing Cherubs to request her and pay for her services out of his own pocket. But part of him had known. She couldn't have been *that* busy, especially since a slot in her afternoons had suddenly opened up unexpectedly.

"Look, I'm sorry." She threw her hands in the air before leaning back against the wall space beside the cabinet, her head brushing against the canvas she'd hung up. "I shouldn't have pushed you—"

"You didn't push me."

"I should have figured out you were a virgin because you said you'd never been kissed before. I should have backed off."

Archer felt acid run over his tongue. "I wasn't *saving myself*, Brielle." He gestured to his lap. "I had additional concerns most people don't when it comes to making that decision. Was I supposed to remain a virgin forever?"

"No. No, that's not even what I mean." She tousled her hair, and he would have found it alluring if they weren't arguing. "It just shouldn't have been with *me*."

"Because you didn't want to have to deal with me afterward? Because you couldn't picture yourself dealing with someone in a wheelchair forever—because you could see the burden that lay before you after you'd just taken one step through that doorway?"

"You're putting words in my mouth." Her eyes narrowed. "This isn't about you being in a wheelchair. Or about you at all."

"Don't give me the old, 'it's not you, it's me' thing." He gripped his wheel rims tightly, although he didn't even know where he planned to go.

She raised an eyebrow. "Because you've heard that so many times?"

"How would you even know? You never ask me about anything."

"You're proving my point. We barely know each other."

He slammed his fist against his armrest. "I *want* to know you. I *want* to support you through whatever's bothering you. But you act like I'm this pest, like you just wanted to jump me once and then walk out of my life entirely."

"I'm here, aren't I?" She gestured around her.

"So why are you?"

"I don't know. I... I might not even be here in a few months. In a few weeks. We just met at a really bad ti—" She bent down to pick up a piece of paper that had fallen beneath one of the kitchen chairs. "Your mom forgot my information? Did she put it into her phone or...?"

"No," said Archer, swallowing. "She forgot all about it. We fought that night—"

"Over what? Over me?"

I thought she didn't want to know anything about me. "Over a lot of things."

She held the paper up between her middle and index finger. "But I was one of them. She has no intention of getting in touch with the museum people for me."

"No, I suppose not."

"And you knew? Last Sunday you knew even, and you didn't think to mention that to me?"

"I didn't really think it bore *mentioning*. It's not like she guaranteed you a position. I hope you weren't *counting* on that."

"No, I wasn't *counting* on anything. Just hoping. And, after all the rejections and silences and frustration I've dealt with during this job hunt, it would have been nice if you'd have torn down that hope as soon as possible so I didn't spend all this week thinking just *maybe*..."

"Really? You're blaming me for my mother making a stupid, casual offer and then not telling you not to rely on it? If it's that important to you, I can press my dad—"

"That's not the point!"

"Then what *is* the point? Brielle, I'm sorry I keep doing everything wrong—"

"I never said that."

"Then I'm sorry. Okay? I'm just sorry." He ground his teeth. "I'm sorry for caring too much about you, for coming on too strong or whatever it is you think of me." His brows lifted. "I've never had the luxury of knowing how to act after a girl jumps into bed with you on a whim. Stupid me, I always thought that was the sign of intimacy, but no, I guess it's all the stuff one does when *clothed* that's too much for you right now—"

She pushed past him, standing on her toes to squeeze between his chair and the kitchen table.

"Where are you going?"

"Home," she said, snatching up her purse.

The full realization of what he'd said hit him. Sleeping with him on a whim? That seemed to imply such a thing was a habit with her. Not that there was anything wrong with girls who did that in general, but in the heat of the moment, he'd known what he was saying—*how* he was saying it—was hurtful and he'd kind of meant it to be. Because her recoiling just now had hurt him. He ran a hand over his face, then followed her down the hall. "I'm sorry, Brielle."

"You said that already." She lifted a foot up and unceremoniously slapped a shoe against it.

"No, I mean, I'm sorry for what I said just now."

"Noted." She squeezed her foot into the other shoe.

"I don't want this to be the end," he said, more quietly. "I'm not saying you have to marry me, be trapped here, or whatever, but I just feel... I'd hate to have us end like this."

"There is no 'us.'" Her lips trembled. "There's nothing to end."

"If you really feel that way—"

"I do," she said, turning on her heel.

Archer watched her go, feeling as if she'd sucked out all the air in his home along with her.

CHAPTER TWENTY-TWO

Nora was out of school. And surprisingly, more than a few of her friends had summer jobs—or, as Nora so sullenly remarked, summer camps—to go to, so she had no one to really hang out with. And she kind of owed their mom a quiet summer of working for Scrubbing Cherubs after the stunt she'd pulled several weeks before.

"If I have to be exposed to a lot of chemicals, my polish is going to wear off." Nora picked at a chip on one of her pinky fingers as she approached Mrs. Tanaka's door with her sister. She'd agreed to carry a bucket over her arm full of clean sponges and brushes, but she'd balked when Brielle had told her Mrs. Tanaka bought her own cleaning sprays and scrubs and they wouldn't need the soap Brielle kept in her trunk for clients who didn't care so much about what products were used to clean their homes.

Brielle nodded at the yellow elbow-length gloves peeking out from the top of the bucket. "That's what the rubber gloves are for."

Running her fingers over the rubber, Nora's nose wrinkled. "They feel gross."

"Not as gross as pulling clogs out of sinks and bathtubs will be without it."

Nora made a gagging sound and reached into her pocket to pull out her phone.

Brielle put a hand on her arm. "No phones while on a job."

Nora rolled her eyes and shoved it back into her pocket. "Well, we're not technically *on the job* yet."

Before she could even knock, Mrs. Tanaka opened the door, a smile plastered on her face. "Welcome, ladies! Your mother told me she would be sending the new girl to do training. You must be very excited."

"Yes. Ecstatic," muttered Nora. "It's not like I've ever cleaned before." Her gaze roved over the open doorway. "Kitties!" she squealed.

Before she could run out to pet them—not a good idea, since the cats were already twisted sideways with arched backs in an effort to seem scary instead of cute (they failed)—Brielle whacked an arm in front of her chest. "What do we say?"

"Oh my god," said Nora, crossing her arms tightly and looking away.

"No..." said Brielle. She stared at Nora until the girl finally opened her mouth.

"Scrubbing Cherubs, here to shoot your home with the arrow of cleaning power!" She put her fingers over her brow in a V-shape like a magical heroine.

Mrs. Tanaka laughed and clapped. "Very good. Now come on in before one of these two rascals slips out."

Brielle considered what a good client Mrs. Tanaka made for one of Nora's training sessions. (True, she had worked last summer, but barely, considering all of her social commitments and summer school, and not particularly well. Their mom had insisted she start from scratch this time, working as a trainee first)

"Mrs. Tanaka likes us to start in the kitchen," said Brielle, feeling like an instructor. Maybe she should look into teaching after all. A few more days of fruitless job searching and she would probably burst. Part of her felt like going back to school for some expensive and probably useless graduate degree just so she could spend a few more years cowering beneath her blankets, and another part of her didn't think working as a cleaner for the rest of her life would be so bad. It had been comforting, the routine, in the two weeks since she'd last seen Archer. If only her mom would let her stay on without sitting her down for another lecture at least once a week.

Nora stopped cold in the kitchen entryway. "It's spotless in here."

"Thank you," said Mrs. Tanaka, sliding past to get to the cupboard where she kept cans of her cats' food. "I cleaned it this morning before you girls came."

Staring after Mrs. Tanaka, Nora raised an eyebrow. "Then should we move on—"

Brielle shook her head vigorously and shot her a look. "You make our jobs easier, Mrs. Tanaka."

"Best to be extra thorough." She popped one can open and plopped its contents into a cute paw-print-adorned porcelain bowl and scraped it out thoroughly before disappearing down the hallway toward her recycling bin with the empty can in tow.

"Why are we cleaning if it's already been cleaned?" hissed Nora.

Brielle made a throat-slashing movement, trying to end the conversation. "Later," she said, taking the bucket from her and removing a folded cloth from it. "Since Mrs. Tanaka has quartz counters, we need to make sure we never use abrasive materials or cleaners to wipe them."

Nora opened her mouth, but Brielle lifted a finger and she snapped it shut again. Grabbing the cloth, she turned on her heel.

"Brielle?" called Mrs. Tanaka from the hallway. "Might I have a moment?"

Brielle rattled off some instructions to her sister, who simply widened her eyes and nodded, and headed off toward their client, wiping her hands on her apron. Mrs. Tanaka was sorting through her mail. "How's your job hunt going?"

A twitch tugged on the corner of Brielle's lips. "It's... Well, it's not really... going anywhere. I got a few more rejections from jobs I applied to weeks ago, but..." She lowered her voice so Nora couldn't overhear and use it to deflect an argument with their mom. "I haven't applied for much for the past two weeks."

Mrs. Tanaka raised her eyebrows, even though she kept staring at a catalog. "Two weeks? Leah surely wouldn't like that."

Mrs. Tanaka and her mom were on a first-name basis. "She doesn't know."

Clicking her tongue, Mrs. Tanaka put the stack of mail on a table in the hallway and grabbed for her letter opener. "If I had children and I was really so determined they not work for my own business, I'd be checking to make sure they were applying every day."

Brielle decided not to comment on the fact that children applying for jobs would hardly be at the age where peering over their shoulder at the computer would be appropriate. "I should get back to applying more often." She ran a hand over the inside of her arm. "I will. I just... got distracted."

"Got *lazy*, my mother would have said."

After a few weeks of them falling into a sort of alliance when she'd gotten back into the work this summer, Brielle had almost forgotten how she used to find Mrs. Tanaka distasteful. But she had a point. And maybe the old her, the pre-graduation her, would have bristled like Nora would have in her position, but she had to admit she was right. "I guess I just got overwhelmed. And comfortable in my day-to-day routine."

Tossing aside an empty envelope, Mrs. Tanaka pulled her reading glasses from their resting place atop her head. "I take it you didn't take my advice to jump into the dating scene."

Brielle grimaced. "I think I might have briefly, but that didn't turn out well."

"Why not?" Mrs. Tanaka's eyes never left her letter.

"Well, I shouldn't have dated him to begin with, right? Not until I knew where I was headed."

"And what if you wind up staying right here for months or even years to come? What then? Would you regret not having dated him longer?"

"I don't think my mom would be happy about that." Brielle felt like she was being mined for details for the woman's next session of town gossip. "And besides, I think I already kind of messed up."

"Nonsense. Nothing an apology won't fix." She shifted her glasses back to the top of her head and handed Brielle the letter.

Brielle stared at her a moment, taking the mail from her cautiously, figuring she was just being asked to add it to the pile of mail and straighten it.

"Read it!" Mrs. Tanaka sighed, exasperated. "You know, I got a job right out of high school. I never went to college. Then I married Tomokazu and quit to stay home and he got transferred to America after a few years of marriage..."

Brielle wasn't sure if she was supposed to read the letter or pay attention to the woman's story just then. The way Mrs. Tanaka's voice got choked up toward the end, Brielle felt compelled to listen.

"Tomokazu was a good provider." She nodded, as if approving of the house around them. "I really didn't even need to work. Especially since we had no children. But I loved staying busy. Being with people. I didn't care if it was not a *good* job."

Unsure where she was going with this, Brielle nodded and forced a smile on her face. Perhaps she was about to be told to stay a cleaner forever again—not that she would even care about that as much as her mom might. Even so, with the clock ticking on her first payment due for her student loans... She glanced over the letter. It was from the historical museum downtown.

"I worked at the museum downtown for years," said Mrs. Tanaka. "Decades really. Just as a cashier and a greeter. It might not have exactly been the type of job one could bank on for retirement, but I was lucky—I snagged that rich husband." She winked at me.

The letter, addressed to "Emiko," said it was wonderful to hear from her and that the letter-writer was glad to know she had met a young woman interested in museum work. He couldn't promise a position at the moment, but he had an opening for a Museum Assistant in Collections. If the "young woman" was interested, he'd be willing to interview her first before he advertised. Brielle gasped.

"I know it's not a fancy city," said Mrs. Tanaka, "but whether you use it for more experience and connections or you wind up loving the work so much, you stay here for decades to come, what's important is that *you* decide. And that you don't let that mother of yours devalue her own career by insisting you get a 'better' one."

"Thank you!" shouted Brielle, screaming and jumping in place. "Yes! Yes, I'd definitely be interested in an interview."

"Good," said Mrs. Tanaka. She sniffed. "Because I got a little impatient about waiting for the postman to bring my response, so I went ahead and called Jim and I already said you'd be interested..." She laughed. "I was going to feign you got another job offer if you refused me."

"No, I wouldn't..." She stared down at the letter, shaking her head. "This is the closest I've gotten to a job offer in a field I'm interested in. Or a job offer at all, really."

"I'd say it's more than an offer. I acted as your reference, and so long as you show up wearing clothes and smiling, I'm pretty sure you got the job."

Brielle screamed again and hugged Mrs. Tanaka once more as a thunderous sound echoed in the hallway and both of her cats ran past and up the stairs.

Clomping her feet into the hallway, Nora folded her arms, the cleaning cloth still in her hands. "Okay, seriously? You have to tell me why you keep screaming. You scared the kitties."

"I think I got your sister a museum job."

Brielle grinned and grabbed the woman by the shoulders. She didn't even care that Nora scoffed as she did. "Thank you!"

"Awesome," said Nora. "So you're moving out and I get to take over all your shifts. Is that hot disabled guy still your client?"

"No, remember?" said Brielle, stepping back and smoothing her apron. "And his name is Archer. Besides, it's the museum downtown. I don't know if I need to move out."

"Oh, Mom will *love* that." Nora examined her nails. "She thinks as long as you still live with us, she can't downsize."

Brielle frowned. How did Nora know their mom intended to sell the house, but not Brielle? Maybe her mom didn't want to put added pressure on her. But is that why she cared so much about her finding a job?

"About that," said Mrs. Tanaka, grabbing for her purse on the hallway table. "I may have told you about my cousin's daughter, who moved here last year? She got a job at the same company Tomokazu worked at."

Brielle didn't remember this cousin or her daughter at all, or even know why Mrs. Tanaka would expect her to catalog her obscure relations, but she supposed she'd probably told her about it last summer, when Brielle's mind had wandered whenever she'd had to deal with her. She was on such a high from the maybe-probably job offer, though, that she just grinned and nodded.

"Well, she had a roommate until last month, when the woman just up and left without much notice." She flicked at her phone screen. "She was charging her roommate dirt cheap rent, so I don't know how the girl could be so ungrateful if you ask me. It was about a boy, I'm sure." She shook her head. "It's a two-bedroom, second-floor condo my cousin and her husband outright bought for her. She just wants three hundred dollars a month from a roommate to help with taxes and utilities."

Nora glowered. "Her parents *bought* her a condo? And she still wants a roommate?"

Mrs. Tanaka nodded. "Her mother doesn't feel comfortable with her living halfway across the world alone. I offered a room in my house, but the girl refused. Something about my cats."

Nora chortled. "Three hundred? I'll move in with her if Brielle won't."

"No you won't," said Brielle, gripping the letter tighter in her hands. She had no idea what this job would pay yet and how many hours she'd work, but she'd be crazy to pass up rent for only three hundred dollars. It probably wouldn't be much longer before her mom expected her to chip in just as much—or even more. And she was tired of walking on eggshells around her about the whole thing. She wanted this. Unless it was in a bad neighborhood or something. "Where is the condo?"

Mrs. Tanaka turned her phone around so Brielle could read the screen. It was a Google map showing an address. "It's not that far."

Brielle laughed. She stared at it and laughed again.

"What's so funny?" asked Nora, stuffing the cloth into her apron pocket and peering over her shoulder.

"Mrs. Tanaka might just be my guardian angel," said Brielle.

Nora looked confused but shrugged and tapped the Scrubbing Cherub art on the back of Brielle's T-shirt. "I think you mean 'guardian cherub.'"

CHAPTER TWENTY-THREE

"Did you draw this?" Mrs. Ward stood back to gaze up at the canvas Brielle had hung about a month before. The other one stood stuffed between two of his cabinets, out of sight but rarely out of mind.

This was actually the first time his mother had been to his condo in weeks, so he couldn't have asked her to hang the other canvas if he'd wanted to. But Pauline came on an almost daily basis, and his dad had stopped by for lessons. He just couldn't bear anyone else hanging it.

"No, Mother, I did not draw *Dick Tracy*."

"Is that was this is?" All Mrs. Ward was missing was the monocle. She squinted and finally tore her eyes away. "I don't know why you'd hang something so garish if it wasn't one of your comic drawings."

"Thanks, Mother." Archer rapped his knuckles on his armrest. Silence lingered conspicuously in the air, but it was interrupted by the occasional thump from his upstairs neighbor's condo.

"Why don't you have any of your art in here? I bet you could have it printed and hung on canvas."

The suggestion brought to mind Brielle, and it stung. Archer's reply was more biting than even his mother deserved. "Because *you* decorated it, so of course you only hung your art."

She looked as if he'd slapped her. "I thought you liked these pieces," she said, her lip quivering. "You said you got your love of art from me." She slipped past him to grab for her painting of a vase of flowers and fruit. "I can take them back. Or just throw them out..." She choked on her words.

Archer cradled his forehead. "Mother, no, don't. Please. I'm sorry." He looked up at her. "I'm sorry, I mean it. I do like your art."

"Could have fooled me." She crossed her arms and stared upward.

"Thank you... For giving me space these past few weeks."

"Well, your father *insisted*." She dug into her purse for a tissue and dabbed at her eyes. "All of a sudden, teaching you to drive was worth skipping all of our dinners for weeks. But heaven forbid *I* visit you even once a week."

The hallway toilet flushed at just the right moment, giving Archer time to think over his response. "You could have come once a week," he said. "I just didn't like... that we made an appointment of it. Besides, Dad and I haven't spent much time together in years."

"What about your old man?" said Mr. Ward as he joined them from the hallway. "He's getting on in years?" He wrapped an arm around Mrs. Ward and pecked her on the cheek.

She blushed, the hurt and anxiety that so often colored her face around Archer dissolving. "And handsomer with each passing one."

Archer almost missed seeing them together. He saw another side of his mother she so rarely showed him. It was like just thinking about her son turned her into a ball of nerves, and his dad was the only known antidote.

"Okay now," said his dad, "none of this arguing you two always wind up doing."

"We don't *argue*—" started Mrs. Ward.

"Sure," said his dad, sticking his hand into his pocket. "But today is about celebration. Today we celebrate Archer earning his driver's license!" He tilted his head down at his son, beaming.

A little more than a month ago, Archer hadn't been certain his dad could ever be proud of him for anything. But it seemed like all that had been holding him back was a way to relate.

"I need a drink just thinking about it," said Mrs. Ward, pulling away.

Mr. Ward grabbed her by the arm. "Uh-uh. This is a *good* thing, and we'll limit our drinking to when we toast him tonight." He winked. "Though none for you, son. You're the designated driver."

The doorbell rang. "That must be Pauline," said Archer, still grinning from his dad's dumb joke, even if he was wincing at the idea that maybe, yes, his mother drank too much. "I'll get it." He wheeled down the hallway and opened up the door.

"Hi," said Brielle, her fingers threaded together.

Too late Archer realized the obvious: Pauline had a key. A few days after he'd last seen Brielle, she'd had her mother drop her pair of keys off when she'd closed out the contract. Pauline had dealt with her. Archer had cowered in his bedroom.

That, and only Brielle was polite enough to ring the doorbell. Despite him practically chewing her head off the first time she'd done it.

He realized he hadn't responded and his jaw was practically on the floor. "Hi."

They stared into each other's eyes for what ought to have been a very uncomfortable amount of time if either were cognizant of it.

"Archer, ask Pauline to come in before we go—" Archer's mother appeared behind him in the hallway and stopped midsentence. She played with a bracelet on one of her wrists, adjusting it farther up her forearm. "Oh. Brianna? You didn't tell me you invited her."

"Brielle," said Archer and Brielle at the same time. Brielle looked as if she were hiding a grin when their eyes met again.

Clearing her throat, Brielle seemed to take in their attire. "Oh. Sorry. Is this a bad time? Are you going somewhere?" They were dressed admittedly on the fancy end of things. His mother didn't like to celebrate at the Olive Garden when they could indulge in a local high-end bistro. Suddenly feeling choked and embarrassed, Archer tugged at the bottom of his navy tie, folding it over his lap time and again.

Mrs. Ward pulled her phone out of her little clutch purse and glanced at the screen. "Yes, we have reservations."

His dad stepped into the hallway. "And they won't kill us if we're late, Geneva." He put both hands on her shoulders.

"No, but they might give away our table. They're very hot in demand these days, you know."

"On a Tuesday night? And considering what I spend there? I don't think so." He guided her forward and they squeezed against the wall to get past Archer. He extended a hand to Brielle. "Baldwin."

Brielle stared at him before realizing she was meant to shake his hand. "Oh! Brielle. Hi. Nice to meet you."

"I've seen you before," he said. "At the airport. From afar." He grinned and smirked down at his son, and there was so much that look conveyed but left unsaid. Archer could feel his face flushing.

"Right. Of course." Brielle tucked a piece of hair behind her ear.

Archer willed his lower half to calm down, especially considering he was sitting like a foot away from his mother.

"Why don't you join us?" asked his dad.

"I made the reservation for *four*," interrupted his mother.

Brielle looked down at her clothes—yoga pants and a skin-tight T-shirt, both a little stained with sweat—and grimaced. "Thanks, but I can't right now anyway."

Archer's dad nodded and looked over her shoulder. A van was pulling in and had to maneuver around a moving truck parked in the middle of the lot to get a good spot. "There's Pauline now. We'll go greet her." He reached into his pocket and tossed a pair of keys at Archer, who caught them despite the lack of warning. Archer felt almost smug about the fact that Brielle had watched him catching them, like he'd just caught a tricky pass in a neck-and-neck basketball game. "Congrats again, son."

"Baldwin, I really think we should get going..."

"We are, we are." He patted his wife's shoulder and guided her past Brielle to the cars behind her. Mrs. Ward looked over her shoulder back at the condo, frowning, but said nothing more.

"What's the occasion?" asked Brielle, perhaps oblivious to the daggers Archer's mother was shooting at her. "Congrats...?"

"Oh." Archer snapped back into the moment and jingled his car keys. "I got my license since... since we saw each other last." He tried to smile, tried to seem friendly, but the fact was, it still hurt to think of how they'd parted ways. Even if she'd never guaranteed anything more than a single lay.

"That *is* congrats!" Brielle shook her head and waved a hand at her face. "That is, I mean, *congrats...*"

"Thanks." He really smiled this time. He wasn't sure why, but she seemed so nervous. He still wasn't sure why she was even there. Peering around her torso, he backed his wheelchair up. "Want to come in?"

"Don't you have to go?" She gestured over her shoulder. Pauline and his parents stood gathered around the side of Pauline's van, talking. His mother's head kept turning toward the condo while Pauline's kept glancing at one of the chiseled moving men whenever he passed by.

"Please," he insisted.

"Okay," said Brielle. "Just for a minute, though. I..." She glanced over her shoulder and bit her lip. Did she know that drove Archer crazy? He had to look away as she stepped in and shut the door behind her.

"I'm sorry."

That made Archer look up. "What?"

"I'm sorry." The pale pink of her nail polish—a new addition, he noticed—distracted him as she clutched her hands together tightly in front of her thighs. It made her fingers look so long and elegant. "I'm sorry I got so defensive. I'm sorry I got freaked out about *us*. I'm sorry I jumped into bed without spending more time just as friends and getting to know you—"

"I never complained about you jumping into bed with me," said Archer, sure he ought to make that clear. "Although to be perfectly honest, we never quite got to the *bed*, did we?"

That actually made Brielle snicker. Archer took that as a good sign. But an uncomfortable thought flitted to the forefront of his mind. "I haven't heard from you in weeks." He grimaced. "A month."

"I'd say I didn't hear from *you*, either, but I think I know why." She ran a hand over her forearm. Even slightly shiny with sweat, her skin was so irresistible. Maybe *because* she was slicked in sweat. Had she been working out at the park? "I wasn't in a good place a few weeks ago, and I had no business starting something—anything, a friendship even—with you and then just... walking out on it."

Friendship. It took every fiber of Archer's being not to deny that word. It would probably push her away again. Besides, he knew they weren't *more* than friends. He just knew he wanted them to be. "I'm sorry for coming on too strong," he said. "I'm sorry for anything I said that disappointed you... I'm sorry I didn't tell you about my mother forgetting all about her promise—"

"No, it's okay," she said. "I mean it." She took a deep breath but didn't say anything more, choosing instead to stare at Archer's knees.

He felt a bit self-conscious about how thin they looked in his dress pants. "But now you're in a good place?" he said, remembering what she'd said before "friendship." He tried to smile again. He *wanted* her to be happy, no doubt about that, but a small, jealous part of him—an irrational part, he knew, like a woman's happiness was solely defined by such a thing—was worried it was partially due to a new boyfriend.

God forbid it was *that* ex-boyfriend.

"Yeah." Her dark red lips went wide as she smiled. "I got a museum job."

"That's great!" said Archer, and he meant it. Even if the news hit him as if the floor had been ripped out from underneath him. *Stupid. It's not like you had any hope at this point.* He wondered if she came then to make peace, to start her new life without the awkwardness of how they'd parted ways hanging over her. He swallowed. "What city?"

She cocked her head. "Oh!" Her eyes widened in acknowledgement. "Here! I mean, I got a job at the museum here—downtown. The history museum."

The museum so dinky Mother can hardly bear to support it? He laughed at himself. Like *he* cared about such things. His mother might like to pretend she was really from Chicago, banished to this shadow in Chicago's presence only by necessity since his dad's business was here, but he couldn't care less about the "prestige" of the museum. Especially since that meant Brielle wasn't going far.

"What's so funny?" asked Brielle, but she looked like she hoped he would let her in on the joke.

"Nothing," he said, quickly. "I'm just... glad you'll be here. I mean, I guess that makes me horrible—"

"Why does that make you horrible?"

"Because I *wanted* you here." He ran a hand through his hair, gripping the short strands as if trying to assuage some of his guilt. "I wanted to get to know you better. I wanted to be more than just a one-night stand. I wanted to be... more than friends. But I knew you had plans to leave this place, and I didn't think it would be appropriate for me to go with you—if I could even figure out how to manage that with my mother and Pauline and everything my parents do for me—so I wanted you to stay. Which makes me horrible."

Closing the already-cramped distance between them, Brielle laid a hand on his shoulder. "That makes you really sweet." She leaned in, her lips brushing his ear. "Especially since you weren't *going* to try to stop me if I did wind up leaving." She kissed his temple and laughed. "Sorry, I kind of stink right now."

"You don't stink." He reached an arm out and grabbed her from behind, intending to aim for the small of her back but getting her butt instead and not even feeling sorry about it. "You smell great," he whispered to the space beneath her breasts. "I missed you."

She leaned into him, resting her soft breasts atop his head. "I'm glad," she said. "I thought I totally messed things up with you."

"We barely had anything to mess up yet," he said. "Besides... If you could forgive me after I treated you like *the help* during that first meeting, I can forgive you anything."

The sound of her laughter was like the first warm day of spring. "The help? Okay, rich boy."

"Sorry," said Archer into her shirt. He didn't even care that it was damp. Her wetness was intoxicating. "I wasn't even rude to you because I actually thought that. I just..."

"Didn't like being around people?" she offered.

"Didn't know how to act around someone so gorgeous." He squeezed again, taking more of her ample buttock into his grip. Firm but gentle, trying to take hold of as much of her as he could without hurting her. Trying to hold on to her before he opened his eyes and discovered it was all a dream.

"I don't stink *and* I'm gorgeous? You're such a flatterer."

A loud clonk from the condo above made them both jump and despite what he actually wanted to do with her just then, Archer pulled away. She was staring up at the ceiling. "I should get back," she said, peering back down at him. "And you should get to your dinner."

He felt like she'd taken the wind out of him as she pulled away, dancing her long, elegant fingers over his shoulder and grinning as she headed closer to the door.

Then she stood stock-still. She chuckled and shook her head. "But I should *tell you* why I even came down here just now." She pointed above her. "I know you were worried that *you* were being the creepy one by wanting to keep dating me despite thinking I might move away. But I, uh, moved upstairs without consulting you and... I understand if you don't want to see me, but I hope we can start over again. I'm... That is, I've grown a touch fond of you."

That was the last thing he'd pictured her revealing just now. Upstairs. *Upstairs.* He didn't even care that there was no way he was ever safely climbing up those stairs to see her place, she was going to be mere feet above his head, a thirty-second-post-text away, a part of his life for the foreseeable future.

He grabbed for her hand and squeezed it. "Welcome to the neighborhood, new neighbor," he said. He lowered his voice. "I think I'm more than a little fond of you, too."

He was a little late joining his parents at his new car. And he didn't even notice his tie was crooked and his top few buttons had come undone until he fastened his seatbelt.

EPILOGUE

Brielle pulled into the guest parking lot—Naomi took the detached garage space for her car, which was only fair considering it was her place and she had a much nicer vehicle to protect from the elements anyway—right next to where the handicapped spaces ended and felt a warmth in her abdomen at just the sight of Archer's van.

She knew he'd be home. He was pretty much always home. And despite the progress he'd made in the many months since she'd known him, he was still a bit scared to drive alone. And his mother was no help, naturally. She still insisted on driving them whenever they went out—even if his dad had suggested they replace their van with something sleeker since Archer had his own vehicle. She wouldn't hear of it, insisting that there could come a day when she had to drive him to the doctor because he wouldn't feel up to it. So if Brielle hadn't made him drive them out on dates half the time and Pauline hadn't made him drive on errands, he might not have gotten much use out of his newfound skill at all.

Considering his girlfriend lived a *very* short walk away.

Brielle jumped out of the car and clicked her car remote to lock it, took a step toward the sidewalk, then remembered her phone and the books Jim had given her to read up on for the upcoming exhibit. *Oh my god.* She'd been distracted enough to leave her phone on the seat. And her purse. And everything. Luckily she'd had brains enough to grab her keys before she locked the door.

Her phone buzzed as she shoved the books into her tote bag— there were more books than there was space—and tossed the purse strap over her head in a hurry. It practically choked her as she bent over to grab the phone.

She'd been exchanging some mushy sentiments with Archer the last time she'd used it. The picture he'd sent her had made her want to rush home—or more accurately, rush to *his* home. Screw the bathroom and freshening up trip she often made to her place first. She didn't want to wait even one more minute.

CALL ME read the text. It was her mom.

She didn't cringe every time her mom wanted to talk to her anymore since even though her mom hadn't been thrilled with the sort-of-low-end salary she'd been offered at the museum, she wasn't living at home, either, so her mom had little room to criticize. Plus, she *was* doing something with her degree. Not that her mom had revealed any concrete plans to downsize since, but maybe that was because Nora was still living with her.

Nora. Grimacing, Brielle decided she had to call and make sure her little sister hadn't run off once again. She'd thought she was making progress and it was too late for that language camp she'd wanted to go to (she said she was saving her earnings from the summer to go to the camp next year—promised she'd even keep working one day every weekend during the school year), but you really could never tell with Nora.

"Hi, Mom," said Brielle, adjusting the phone between her shoulder and her cheek so she could shuffle all the crap she was juggling in her hands. "Everything okay?"

"Yeah," replied her mom. "What do you mean?"

Brielle rolled her eyes, even though—or more likely because— there was no one there to see it. "I just got a jolt of panic when I saw your text is all."

"Oh, sorry, no. I just wanted to check in with you. How's work?"

"Great," said Brielle. And she meant it. "Jim is giving me more and more responsibility every day. I might have a big part in the presentation of the next traveling exhibit."

"Wonderful!" The phone went silent for a moment. "I wanted to ask you... and Archer... over for dinner. Maybe this weekend?"

"That's nice of you to ask," said Brielle, straightening up and switching the phone to her other ear. When it buzzed with a notice of a text, she pulled the phone away from her ear to see that it was from Gavin. Leave it to everyone she knew to be contacting her when all she wanted to do was run inside and jump Archer's bones after she saw what he'd teased her with when he'd sent her that picture. She snapped back to the point at hand. "I don't know how easily he can get up the couple steps to the porch," she said. She'd gotten used to that—thinking about accessibility. Something she never thought she'd have to think about until maybe her mom was so old she required more help from Brielle than Brielle did from her.

"Right," said her mom. "I didn't think about that. We can go out or... Maybe I can ask someone to install one of those ramps?"

Brielle almost dropped the pile of papers in her hands. Wow. Her mom really *was* being supportive. "Another railing would do," she said, placing her large pile atop Archer's van's hood and hoping it didn't cause a dent. "He can get up a couple of stairs if he has the right support, just really carefully."

"Hmm," said her mom. "That would work. It might help with the value of the house too."

Brielle had gotten used to her mom dropping little hints like that. That she wanted to downsize, that even their small three-bedroom ranch was getting to be too much for her to clean, that she was tired after spending all day cleaning and just didn't have the effort to put into its upkeep. "Just let me know when you want me to finish clearing out my stuff," said Brielle.

Her mom laughed. "Don't worry about it. I think Nora would kill me if I made her move before the end of her senior year."

Brielle started shuffling her pile again, feeling her heart jump as one of the papers started fluttering and almost went flying in a gust of wind. She snatched it only a few inches into the air and clonked her elbow down on the hood, wincing at the loud sound.

"What was that?" asked her mom.

"Wind," said Brielle. She wasn't entirely lying.

"So how about Saturday? 6:00?"

"Sounds great," said Brielle. "I'll check with Archer to make sure he doesn't have a deadline he can't miss, but I'm sure he's free."

"Okay," said her mom. At the sound of more rustling paper and more clomping on the car hood, she laughed. "Bri...?"

"Yeah?" Both hands spread out on the hood, the phone cradled on her shoulder again, Brielle spit out a piece of hair.

"I'm proud of you," said her mom.

That so stunned Brielle, she almost loosened her grip and lost a pile of papers. She was going to propose they focus more on digital handouts in the future. Bring the museum out of the mid-twentieth century already. "Thanks..." she said after a bit.

"I'm sorry for how I acted this summer," her mom added. "I'd just been thinking and well... There was the stuff with your sister to deal with and I'd read so many stories about kids moving back home after college and I was afraid. I was afraid things would never change for any of us, afraid you'd be just as stuck in a rut as I was, afraid you'd make mistakes you couldn't take back."

"Mom, is this about me or about you and Dad?"

"No, not about him. Not even about you really. Just about me and not knowing what I was going to do when I was your age. If I hadn't had you girls, if I hadn't separated from your father, I don't know if I'd ever have found direction. I only started this business so I could provide for you girls."

"I know," said Brielle. "Thank you."

"You don't need to thank me," she said. "You've got a good

head on your shoulders. You're a smart woman and a good person. Thank *you*, Bri." She went silent as Brielle stood back up, shuffling the papers now that the gust of wind had died down. "See you this weekend."

Brielle's phone buzzed again. Gavin was practically screaming at her in text form to answer already. She chuckled. "See you, Mom," she said. "Thanks for the invite." She hung up and sighed. She was mere feet from Archer's door, but she really wasn't going to get there at this rate.

What? Sorry. Busy. Papers flying everywhere. Mom having epiphany.

Off work and about to shag hot comic guy? replied Lilac.

Oh, thought Brielle. It was a group text.

Basically, she typed back. *Why, your dorky mascot still in his costume and you're trying to fill the time while he gets his handler to get him unstuck?*

Shut up, answered Lilac, but she added a smiling emoji. *No one gets him out of his costume but me.* Brielle was glad things were better with her after what she'd been through earlier that summer. Glad things were settling down for her. While she never would have thought Lilac would find him a pleasing prospect from what she'd heard about him, this guy she'd hooked up with down in Florida... He seemed to give Lilac something she'd been missing. Something she needed.

Okay, dirty ladies, typed Gavin. *Can we move on, please? I gathered you here today for a very important announcement.*

How are we 'gathered' anywhere exactly? asked Lilac, but Gavin ignored her.

First... Pembroke has something to say.

Pembroke was lurking in the conversation, as quiet in the chat as she would have been had they been gathered in real life.

A bar appeared to indicate she was typing, but she sure took her time.

I think I'm in love, she wrote.

No one responded for a bit. Then the screen exploded with questioning emoji.

How? asked Lilac. *I thought you said you weren't into romance.*

She isn't into sex, said Gavin. *Big difference.*

Maybe for you, typed Lilac. She paused. *Told you you just hadn't found the one, Pem.*

That's not how it works, responded Gavin. *Lilac, open your mind already.*

Brielle shook her head and readjusted her butt against the hood of the van so she was sitting on the pile and it couldn't escape her. *Guys*, she typed, *can we let Pembroke talk please?*

She took a little while to respond. *I still don't want sex*, she wrote. *But I don't know... I kind of like kissing. Maybe someday.*

Archer chose that moment to continue his own text conversation with her. *Where are you?* he asked. *I'm getting worried.*

In the parking lot, Brielle typed back quickly. *Be right there.*

Pembroke texted more. *I'm romantic ace, I guess. I don't have the rest defined.*

The rest? asked Brielle, genuinely curious.

Questioning, typed both Gavin and Pembroke at once. Brielle figured they'd know better than she would, so she decided to let it go and wait until Pembroke felt like explaining more.

In any case... Glad to hear! Happy for you. Brielle cracked her neck. It was getting sore from all the weird gymnastics she was doing to pay attention to her phone and the mountain of paperwork currently beneath her buttocks.

Yeah. Good for you. Lilac seemed to be biting her tongue, which was probably the best one could hope for from her. She probably thought she'd hold the "told you so" until Pembroke revealed whatever it was she was holding back.

ANYWAY, typed Gavin. *I'm super happy for Pem, but I wanted all three of you here at once to ask you one thing: Will you be my groomsmaids? Boyfriends, partners, and dorky mascots welcome to come as guests.*

The screen practically went blank for a minute.

SHUT UP, said Lilac. *How could you not tell me you were getting married?*

Holy cow, wrote Pembroke. *You just started dating!*

Um, yes! typed Brielle. She noticed no one else was actually answering his question. Not that she wasn't shocked, but Gavin deserved happiness more than any of them.

...So only Brielle is going to stand beside me? Gavin added a frowny face.

UM, I'M THE MAID OF HONOR, RIGHT? typed Lilac. Of course she'd be the one to ask that.

I'd love to! wrote Pembroke.

Congrats, added Brielle. A door opened and she lifted her head up on instinct. *Send more details soon*, she added. *Sorry, got to go!*

She finally shoved her phone into her purse and that was going to be the end of it for the next few hours at least.

"I didn't think my van qualified as one of those hot cars sexy models pose on," said Archer as he wheeled closer. "But I think the right hood ornament can make any car sexy."

"Oh, be quiet, you," said Brielle, wrapping one arm around his shoulders and bending down to kiss his forehead. She struggled to keep her papers under her other arm. "Putting on a clown routine trying to keep all these papers from blowing away hardly qualifies as 'sexy.'"

"Says you." Archer grabbed her around the waist and brought her closer. Her folder almost dropped again and he reached forward to catch it, laying it flat on his lap so he could grab her with both arms. "Have a nice day?" he asked, leaning up for a quick kiss.

"Yeah," she said. "And it's even better now." She was practically toppling over, but leaning in for that second, longer kiss was worth it.

"Flatterer," said Archer, but that didn't stop him from squeezing her tightly.

Since she was about to topple over or fall onto his lap—which might have been his goal, now that she thought about it, even if they were in the middle of the parking lot and the chilly weather wasn't exactly inviting—she pulled back. "You've got to show me."

Wincing, Archer cocked his head. "You sure you don't want more kisses first?"

"I'll get those later," said Brielle, arching an eyebrow. "And maybe more than that if you're up for it today."

"You can't seriously not know the answer to that..."

She ignored him. "But you can't just tease me like that and not show me."

He sighed, gripping his wheels and turning around to head back to his condo. "All right, all right. If you'd rather look at some drawings than my naked torso, then I guess that's what we'll do."

"Har har," she said. "I'm not even going to stroke your ego and tell you what you already know I think about said torso."

"Okay," he said, pushing the door open. "I'll settle for you stroking something else after we've had a bite to eat."

"You dirty little charmer," said Brielle, kicking her shoes off and dropping her purse behind the door. The fact was, she loved it. When Daniel had "talked dirty" to her, it was just gross—*he* was just gross. But any time Archer opened his mouth, she felt a warm flush throughout her body from head to toe, so she didn't care how dirty those words were. In fact, she really liked the boost of confidence it seemed to give him. More confidence equaled less rudeness. She still caught him snapping at anyone he didn't know who dared to disturb his little work sanctuary, like the plumber he'd had to hire when his sink had overflowed. Luckily, she'd been there to knock some sense into him.

"Act like they're all your fans," she'd said. It seemed good enough advice, since he put on a million-dollar-smile for them. *"And stop acting like everyone who walks through your front door is an invader."*

He could still be grumpy sometimes. When his muscles ached, when he didn't feel well, when the physical therapy was too much or he'd pushed his limits and walked too far. But she knew how to put a smile on his face. And he was starting to become *her* surly guy. So long as she reminded him that the people he was taking it out on had nothing to do with how he was feeling and hardly deserved it, he'd lighten up. All it took was reminding him how terrified she'd been of him the first time they'd met.

"Let me see, let me see!" She bounced as she followed him to his drafting table and computer desk, where he tossed her papers. He'd been working on the sequel to *Wheels* for months—said he didn't even care if his *The Mystified* publisher didn't want it (they did, it turned out, and they also wanted to rerelease the first volume), that he'd wanted to draw it for her—and he hadn't let her even *peek* at it until it'd gotten to this stage. His publisher had sent over a draft complete with inks, colors, and text, and there it was, waiting on his computer screen, open to the first page.

Brielle grabbed a chair from the kitchen table and rushed over to the screen.

"There are still some editorial notes to go through," said Archer. "I mean, I thought we had it finalized, but someone higher up got a look at it—I mean, the changes are minor—"

"Uh-uh." Brielle held her hand up and squeezed her fingers together like she was puppeteering her hand so he would shut his trap. "You're finally letting me read this. Give me silence."

He guffawed and wheeled a short distance away to the drafting table. She heard him pick up a pencil and start sketching, but she could tell just from the sound alone that he wasn't being serious about his work. He seemed to be dragging his pencil in a circle over and over again.

She read *Wheels* volume two. She laughed and she squealed and she was actually crying by the end.

Covering her mouth, she turned around to face Archer with tears in her eyes. "You adorable little talented... Thank you!" She scooched her own chair closer so she could throw her arms around his shoulders and kiss him on the cheek.

"Are you my girlfriend or my mother?" he asked, smirking, staring down at his pencil sketches of circles.

"Ew, mood-ruiner," said Brielle, laughing.

In *Wheels 2* (subtitle to be determined, as Archer kept telling her), Todd had fallen in love. With a house cleaner. His little squirrel approved, but Todd kept trying to tell himself not to follow his heart. Because he wasn't worthy of her. Because he was a burden. Because she had dreams that would take her out of his orbit.

And he let himself fall in love with her anyway.

Brielle had known Archer loved her, but she hadn't quite known how much. Hadn't known what he'd been feeling while she'd been worried about the direction her life was going in.

Hadn't known how much she'd really have missed out on had she left and gone somewhere else.

"Then how about you kiss me like my girlfriend would?"

That smile of his. *Oh my god, that smile.*

Brielle jumped up so she could climb onto his lap, forcing him to back up from the table so she could squeeze between them. Her arms were wrapped around his shoulders and neck, her legs kicking off the other side of his wheelchair, her thigh squished tight against the drafting table. She could feel him get hard almost as soon as she sat down, and he turned red as she shimmied and shifted into a more comfortable position. To tell the truth, she kept shimmying a bit more than she had to once she saw the effect it had on him. "This is how you drew Todd and Angie," she said, referring to her counterpart in the comic.

"I almost asked you if you'd model it for me," he said. "But then I couldn't see it from this vantage point anyway."

"We could have set up a camera on a timer," said Brielle, huskily, softly, peppering his neck with kisses.

"But then that would have given away the ending," he said, nuzzling his stubble against her cheek.

"Well, you could have asked me to do it without the picture and counted it as a little empirical study," she said, beaming.

Even though it was unlikely he'd ever need to draw characters kissing in that position again, she made sure he got *a lot* of empirical study.

that life doesn't always turn out the way you expected.

Just weeks before graduating, Lilac Townsend throws away her elementary school teacher job offer in Minnesota to work in Florida at the official resort of her favorite vacation spot, Tildy World. Pushing down all second thoughts, she fills her mind with visions of sunny beaches and Tildy Tapir, the cartoon character who always promised to make her childhood dreams come true. Unfortunately, between a sleazy boss and a community college student in a character suit who manages to fray her last nerve, Lilac soon learns that working behind the scenes at the park is hardly "happily ever after."

Nolan Gregosky had plans after graduating high school a few years back: go to college, join a fraternity, and make some memories before earning a degree. Instead, tragedy sidelined those dreams, but his job posing for pictures with drooling, snot-nosed kids as Silly Sandgrouse gives him a chance to unload some pent-up energy. When the stunning but uptight new assistant manager at the resort proves a distraction in more ways than one, Nolan realizes it's up to him to show her what it means to eat, live, and breathe life at the park.

A relationship at this unsteady stage of their lives might not be the brightest idea for either of them, but it's hard to ignore that tingling sensation whenever the paths of this plush-suit beast and naïve beauty collide.

Watch for the release of Stay in Touch Book 3 (*Touch of Comfort*, Gavin's story) and Stay in Touch Book 4 (*Touch of Romance*, Pembroke's story)!

Also by Joy Penny

Kiss. Marry. Kill. Nineteen-year-old June Eyermann has always known exactly which of her favorite Byronic heroes goes where. She'd kiss moody and possessive Rochester from *Jane Eyre* and marry prideful but repentant Darcy from *Pride and Prejudice*, leaving obsessive and spiteful Heathcliff from *Wuthering Heights* to be chucked off a cliff—but no. She couldn't leave any of her heroes behind. She lives for her favorite fictional worlds.

But June is about to get a serious wake up call when she returns home for the summer after her college freshman year. Stuck somewhere between feeling like a kid again under her parents' roof and being forced to start acting like an adult with worries about her future career, June looks at the library volunteer position offered to her as a way to keep her sanity for the next few months before she can go back to school.

What June doesn't expect to find at the library is her favorite romantic heroes brought to life—all in the same man. Obstinate, prideful and even a bit rude, Everett Rockford shouldn't exactly be "dating material," even if June's heart rate accelerates whenever she's near him. But after discovering his enigmatic past and witnessing a few fiery moments of tenderness, June can't help but see Rochester, Darcy and even Heathcliff in Everett. If she's going to make it through the summer without becoming a tragic heroine in her own story, she has to separate the man from the ideals of fiction in her head. Because if there's one thing she knows about Byronic love stories, it's that they don't always end happily ever after.

ABOUT THE AUTHOR

Joy Penny writes books, devours stories, and geeks out about everything from classic romance books to manga. When she's not working as a freelance writer and book editor, she's probably immersed in her favorite TV shows, period dramas, and anime series. She also writes YA speculative fiction as Amy McNulty, and one of her books, *Nobody's Goddess*, won The Romance Reviews' Summer 2016 Readers' Choice Award for Young Adult Romance.

Visit my website and sign up for my newsletter!

bookbub.com/authors/joy-penny

facebook.com/JoyPennyWriter

twitter.com/JoyPennyWriter

instagram.com/authorjoypenny

Lose yourself in the magical forests and charming towns of the Pacific Northwest, where picturesque Victorian homes hide mysteries spanning decades, faeries watch from the

trees, and romance awaits... for those bold enough to seek it.

Cass is a drifter. When she inherits an old Queen Anne Victorian in rural Oregon from her great-aunt Alexandra, all she wants is to quickly offload the house and move on to bigger and better things. But the residents of the small town have other plans in mind. Her neighbors are anxious for her to help them thwart the plans of a land developer eager to raze Alexandra's property, while a mysterious girl in the woods needs Cass's help understanding her own confusing, possibly supernatural abilities.

And though little surprises Cass (thanks to her own magical powers of prediction), she never could have anticipated her newfound feelings for the handsome fourth-grade teacher at the local elementary school—feelings that she thought she'd buried long ago. Cass has sworn off love, but Matthew McCarthy is unlike anyone Cass has ever met. If she isn't careful, he could learn her secret. Or worse—he just might thaw her frozen heart.

But falling in love could spell danger for both of them. Because it's not just the human residents of Riddle that have snared Cass in their web. Cass's presence has caught the attention of the fae that dwell in the woods. They know she has the Sight, and they don't want to let her go...

With its unique blend of small-town romance, cozy mystery, and light fantasy, the Northwest Magic series is sure to delight anyone who believes in faery gifts and happily-ever-afters.

Christmas. A charming small town and a Scrooge that might have potential.

Cassie Paige threw herself into her business — Cassie's Confectionary & Cafe — after her husband left her a year ago, but she's decided to make this a great Christmas on her own. Then her childhood crush arrives in Mount Honey Grove for the holidays, stirring up emotions she hasn't felt in years.

There are two things Trent Ellis dislikes — his hometown and anything related to Christmas. While home for a visit, a family crisis has him helping out at the local bakery. The owner, even with her love of Christmas, is making Mount Honey Grove a bit more appealing.

Can Cassie help Trent find joy in the holidays again? Will that be enough to heal her heart and bring them love under the mistletoe?

If you love sweet romances in a small town filled with Christmas joy, you'll love A Mistletoe So Sweet.